The Whisper in the Gloom

NICHOLAS BLAKE

A Nigel Strangeways Mystery

"*The Whisper in the Gloom* is rather a Christmas cake of a tale, richly mixed with a double portion of murders, kidnapping, adventurous, intelligent little boys, and assassins, one of the last being a drug-addict; there are also a tycoon, his ex-principal-boy wife, an ex-Commando, a charming sculptress and a shady club proprietor. To these must be added an old house with a secret chamber.... Mr. Blake makes it continuously interesting and maintains the highest spirits throughout."
—*The* [London] *Times Literary Supplement*

"Wonderful book ... one that kept me completely enthralled from the first word to the last. It is one of the best thrillers I've ever read."
—Cornelia Otis Skinner

Other titles by Nicholas Blake available in Perennial Library:

The Whisper in the Gloom

Nicholas Blake

PERENNIAL LIBRARY
Harper & Row, Publishers
New York, Hagerstown, San Francisco, London

Designed by Stephanie Krasnow

First PERENNIAL LIBRARY edition published 1977

I SBN: 0-06-080418-1

79 80 10 9 8 7 6 5 4 3

Contents

Part
One

1

The Round Pond Killing

Bert Hale, the world-famous inventor, walked into Kensington Gardens with his latest invention under his arm. It was the afternoon of Sunday, August 1st. High overhead, in a fitful easterly wind, kites were dancing, like spots before liverish eyes. From the bandstand, as if a door were being intermittently opened and closed on the music, the strains of a Gilbert and Sullivan medley blared out, then receded to a pianissimo, rose and were shut off: the scarlet and brass of the bandsmen twinkled between the low trees, as the leaves stirred nervously. A newspaper sheet wrapped itself round Bert's leg. He rubbed his eyes, into which the wind had puffed some dust, and stamping the newspaper flat, read the headlines:

SOVIET DELEGATION HERE TOMORROW

IS IT PEACE?

Bert's mind registered the headline as part of something that was in the air, something talked about all round him, tuning with the gay, vague, yet exasperated atmosphere of the summer afternoon, the high-flying kites, the strolling crowds, the children and dogs weaving among them—an atmosphere of suspense. But he was not concerned with it: his own private suspense was concentrated upon a single point—would the invention work?

He paused, just inside the gate, to glance at the regulations set up by the L.C.C. on a board there. It was not that Bert, known to his associates as "The Brain," was a specially law-abiding citizen; simply that he was a great reader, an addict of print. His eye lit upon one of the regulations:

*No person shall operate a power-driven craft . . . without reasonable
consideration for other craft or waterfowl.*

Sucking in his lower lip, Bert moved on toward the Round
Pond, lost in calculation. He had learned early the discipline
of detachment. Just as, during his first year at school, he had
mastered the art of totally withdrawing his attention from any
teacher who, he judged, did not deserve it, so now he drove
away, by an involved bout of mental arithmetic, his anxiety
over his new invention. The problem he set himself was
academic perhaps, but none the less absorbing: suppose that
every time I go to the hairdresser I lose three ounces of hair,
and suppose that I go twice a month, and suppose that a
mattress contains fourteen pounds of hair, how many mattresses could I have stuffed by the time I am seventy-two? . . .

Dai Williams entered the Gardens by another gate. Never
in his life, not even in the old, unregenerate days when it
was, so to speak, a *sine qua non* of his professional activities,
had he so urgently felt the need for a crowd of people around
him. He knew in his bones that he was being followed—had
been followed since last night. And he knew that he had lost
his nerve. All he had to do was to ring up a certain number at
New Scotland Yard. There was no telephone in his lodging
house, of course: but there were telephone booths in the
streets. Yet he had passed them by, afraid of what might
happen if he so much as made to enter one. He could go up to
a policeman. He'd always got on well with the cops, and he
was on their side now. Indeed, that had been his intention—
until, in Church Street, only a few hundred yards from the
Kensington Police Station, he saw, crossing the road in front
of him, toward him, two men; and one of these was the man
he had noticed leaning against a lamppost outside, when he
got out of bed this morning. So he had abruptly turned left,
up the side street, attaching himself to a convoy of prams
bound for the Gardens.

What had finally frayed through his nerve was their inactivity. The sort of mob he had to deal with made it short and sharp—the chiv, the boot, hospital. Normally, they'd think nothing of pushing their way into his lodging house and doing him up. It was a vocational risk he ran, as a Finger who'd turned Snout. What were they waiting for?

In his close escort of prams, nurses, mothers, cavorting children, Dai Williams moved toward the Round Pond, a small, respectably dressed man, with the prison pallor on his face still, and sharp, frightened eyes. He glanced up at the kites, hanging or swerving in the washed-out, nondescript sky. Why had they put a tail on him? What were they waiting for? He began to sweat. A flurry of dust made his eyes water. Suppose someone had said, "Spot Dai Williams"? Perhaps they were just jollying him along till the operator turned up. The sweat in the small of his back went cold. But Jesus Christ!—they didn't put the cross on you for—He'd done nothing yet; only kept his ear open, as the Super had asked; and, last night, heard a few words that didn't make bleeding sense anyway.

Skirting the Round Pond, Dai Williams began to walk toward the bandstand, where the crowds were thickest. He'd always liked music, sung in Chapel choir once, played cornet in the Colliery Silver Band. Those were the days. He took a green chair, well out in the open where he could see all round him, drew a wad of newspaper from his pocket, spread out the paper, and stared at the headlines unseeingly, his heart thumping hard as the big drum in the bandstand.

One of the two men who had followed him made the lightest movement of his head toward a third man, strolling on the grass at a little distance, then said to his companion, "Leave it to the Quack now."

The pair sat down on the grass, behind Dai Williams' back, forty yards away. They looked as if they were enjoying the sun and the music. . . .

The shore of the pond made a Brueghel-like scene, all movement, shifting groups, gossip, vigorous colors, figures in violent activity or relaxed—watching everything and nothing—an everchanging frame and fringe round the oval of water. Babies in prams gazed stolidly at the maniacal antics of the seagulls, to which their nurses were throwing bread. Urchins, with jam jars and shrill cries, waded out after minnows. Lovers, hand in hand, walked round and round and round, like donkeys in a treadmill, oblivious to place or time. Middle-aged men loped after their model yachts, ignoring everything but the set of a sail and the slant of the wind. Carrying a tiny, perfectly constructed brigantine, an ancient and red-nosed mariner, who appeared to have braved a thousand years the bottle and the breeze, tottered toward the waterside.

On the pond, too, all was brisk and glittering. The surface rippled, the big yachts thrashed their way, racing from west to east. Two ducks, rendered neurotic by the persecution of the model speedboats, were picking on a small, defenseless sailing vessel, swimming beside it and pecking glumly at its stern and mainsheet. A yacht, sailing too close to the wind, stood suddenly upright, stammered with its sails, then paid off on the other tack. A power boat buzzed out in a crazy semicircle, scattering a covey of waterfowl and causing an adjacent swan to remove its head from among its tail feathers and glide huffily away. A radio-controlled trawler, its owner and his apparatus surrounded by a little crowd, performed its private evolutions among the other occupants of the pond, like a self-conscious only child in the hurly-burly of a children's party. . . .

As he approached the pond, the intrepid interplanetary navigator, Bert Hale, glanced up at the kites. Kid stuff, he thought: silly wobbling things. He had worked out the problem of the hair mattresses, and was engaged in calculating the number of days it would take his space ship, traveling at x miles per hour, to do the round trip of half a dozen selected planets. He was twelve now. In eight years he could reckon to start building it. Allow three for the building and another two for exhaustive tests. So he'd be twenty-five by the time he started. Pretty old; but not too old to enjoy the triumph.

The First Man on Mars. Commodore Hale Plants the Union Jack on Saturn. Hale Commandeers Moon. Air Marshal Hale, the Columbus of the Solar System.

He was brought down to earth by a man bumping into him and nearly knocking the new invention from under his arm. The man lurched ahead, with a prancing, pigeon-toed gait, leaving a wake of some queer smell behind him. What Bert's mother called "a rancid odor." Bert walked slower. He was beginning to feel really frightened. He was glad he hadn't brought the other members of the Martian Society with him. Suppose the invention didn't work? It'd be bad enough to have all the Round Pond kids jeering him. But, if the jet-propelled craft he had built failed to jet-propel itself on this maiden voyage—if it blew up, or sank, or just wouldn't start at all—he could imagine what Foxy and Copper would say. Results were what they expected from the President of the Martian Society, not formulae.

Bert laid his jet-propelled craft on the grass, and prepared to tune it up. A small, white-faced man on a chair nearby peered at him over the top of a newspaper which shook violently in his hands. Other men were lying about on the grass, in shirt-sleeves, asleep. They might well have been dead; nobody would notice the difference; least of all Bert, intent on his model. . . .

Drops of sweat, trickling into Dai Williams' eyes, blurred the headlines. This Russki lark, he thought: will it come to anything? Peace in our time. The cold war. He made a move to take off his coat, but desisted: it was as if the cheap, respectable jacket gave him protection; in his shirt-sleeves he would feel so much the more vulnerable. His mind was dragged back, for the hundredth time, to those few words he had heard last night, whispered in the gloom of the alley just outside the back door, the secret door of the night club.

The toff he was following had turned down into the alley. Dai had to approach cautiously; he knew of this night club by hearsay, and he knew it was not healthy to know about the position of its escape hatch. So it took him a couple of min-

utes to creep up within earshot of the voices, and by the time
he'd got there, they'd nearly finished talking. All he heard
were those few whispered words. Then the door unexpectedly
opened, a shaft of light struck Dai full in the face, and he did
a Nurmi. But he must have been recognized—by the toff? the
man whom the toff had been talking to and Dai hadn't got a
glimpse of? Anyway, they'd picked him up, and they'd not
let him drop since then; and now their educational committee
was tailing him around, awaiting a suitable moment to educate him.

What worried him most, because it didn't fit in with the
general set-up, was that he didn't recognize these men. He
thought he knew all Sam Borch's mob, and the night club
was certainly one of Sam's interests: but the two blokes following him were none of the old familiar faces. Looking over
his shoulder he could see them, reclining on the grass, peace-
ably smoking, among the playing children and the dogs; and
he did not know them. Well, they couldn't start anything
here.

There must be something big in the words he had heard,
though, or why should they go to all this trouble? Dai took
out a pencil and jotted down a memo of them on the margin
of his newspaper, as if to see them written would reveal their
meaning. It did not. But they led his eye to something printed
beside them, at the bottom of the column—at the end of the
story which lay beneath those glaring headlines. And at once,
two minutes before he died, Dai Williams was granted an
inkling of the truth, of the reason why he had to be removed
from the board. Glancing involuntarily over his shoulder, he
saw that the two men had risen from the grass and were
strolling, slowly, at their leisure, toward him.

He turned his chair to face them. Which was just what they
wanted. A third man—a man with a prancing, pigeon-toed
gait, the pupils of his eyes abnormally diminished—moved
upon Dai Williams from behind. . . .

Bert had screwed down the engine of his boat so that it
ticked over nicely, and was carrying it to the water's edge.

Once again it was nearly knocked out of his grasp—this time by a kid running fast to get his kite into the air. Yelling an unseemly word at the kid, Bert moved on.

In the bandstand, a baton was raised and the band of the Welsh Guards, sweating in their scarlet uniforms, went at it with a crash and a blare. Everyone, except the devotees by the pondside—even the lovers lying on the grass—turned their eyes eyes toward the band for a moment when that glorious tune struck up.

The Quack had chosen his moment well. This was the sort of job he enjoyed, particularly when they let him coke himself up for the occasion. He felt beautifully exhilarated, free as the wind, treading on air. In his hospital days, before he was struck off the Register, he had been considered a most promising surgeon. The present operation would not be bungled. They were paying him enough for his professional services to keep him in cocaine, and other luxuries, for quite a time. He knew the precise spot at which to make the incision, kept his pinpoint eyes fastened upon it as he pranced gaily up behind Dai Williams' back.

He arrived there just after the band struck up, drowning the slight sound of his footsteps on the grass. He withdrew the instrument from his pocket. It flashed across his mind that it was not sterilized, and he chuckled inside himself. His hand started the instrument on its way toward the vital spot. But at that instant he felt a tap on his shoulder.

The kid who had fallen foul of Bert had not quite succeeded in getting his kite into the air. It swung wildly, dipped abruptly, hit a man on the shoulder, bounced upward again, and soared well away.

It was a light tap, but enough to divert the Quack's instrument by a quarter of an inch. The instrument punctured the skin, drove home, was withdrawn—almost faster than an eye could follow; and if anyone had been watching, he would have thought he'd seen a man clapping a friend on the back, then moving briskly away. But the point just missed its mark: though Dai Williams had a mortal wound, death was not, as the Quack had aimed for, instantaneous.

The two men who had occupied Dai's attention now stood in front of him, twenty yards away, lighting cigarettes. They watched the Quack move off. It was quite unnecessary to cover his retreat, for nobody around them had noticed anything amiss. Even Dai himself hadn't given a squeak; he just sat there looking surprised. Surprised, but not—regrettably— dead. After what might have been thirty seconds, he rose and began to walk, rather drunkenly, toward the Round Pond. The two men, keeping their distance, saw that his mouth was opening and shutting. They could not hear, through the noise of the band, that in fact Dai Williams was singing.

Dai had felt a blow, a smarting. As often happens with a mortal wound, he felt at first more surprised than hurt. But then he was aware of a pervading weakness—his vitality draining out of him like water from a bath. He knew he was finished, and at the same instant he heard what the band was playing: "Land of Our Fathers." He was at Cardiff Arms Park, years ago, on his feet, singing, while the red-jerseyed heroes trotted out onto the field. Dai Williams had never been any sort of a hero; but now, for the first and last time, the divine spark in him blazed up, and he was consumed with one single aim—to pass on his information before he died.

To his clouding mind, all men were the enemy, not to be trusted. He did not know how many of Them there were around him, mixing with the crowds, reading to intercept his message. He remembered a boy with a boat, near him on the grass—a boat whose deck came off like the lid of a box. He could see the boy, by the water now, about to launch it. Dai Williams began the long, long journey to the waterside, thirty paces away.

The two men saw him blunder through the crowd strolling round the pond, and go down oddly on his knees beside a boy in gray shorts and shirt. They started moving fast toward the group which stood behind the boy. . . .

The Quack, pausing in his brisk walk, bent down to do up a shoelace, and took his opportunity to remove the skewer-like instrument from inside his sleeve and push it deep into the earth with the sole of his shoe. Talk about a needle in a haystack, he muttered, gleefully chuckling inside himself. He had not looked back once at his patient; the operation, though slightly interfered with, could not have been anything but successful. He walked on, out of the Gardens.

Bert, offering up a prayer, placed his invention carefully in the water, and adjusted the rudder. This was it. Success, or shameful failure. There were people behind him, watching. Then it happened, all in a few seconds. A funny little man, gray-faced, with imploring eyes, was on his knees beside Bert, tearing a piece off a newspaper.

"Here, sonny," he said, in a queer, wheezing whisper, "put this in your boat. For luck, see?"

Luck was what Bert wanted. He took the tiny ball of paper, put it in the boat, replaced the deck, drew a deep breath, and set the engine at full revs. The little man was down on hands and knees now beside him. Just as Bert released the throbbing boat, the man thrust out a hand, pushing its rudder straight. The boat tore off, not in a semicircle, but heading straight across the pond. Bert ran wildly round, cursing the man; either the boat's power would fail before it reached the other side, or it would dash itself to bits on the far shore before he could get there.

At the spot where the boat had begun its maiden voyage, Dai Williams remained, lying full length now, his wrists trailing in the water, his arms stretched out as if in longing toward the farther shore.

"Must be blotto."

"A touch of the sun, I reckon."

"Better carry him onto the grass."

"Get a park-keeper."

"Looks like it's a doctor he needs."

"Gave the nipper a bit of paper. Put it in the boat. For luck, he said."

While the group of bystanders were discovering that they had a dead body among them, the two men moved round the pond after Bert. They dared not run fast, for fear of calling attention to themselves; but they went at a loping trot, like the owners of model yachts.

Bert's speedboat did only too well on its first trial. It crossed the pond in a huff of foam, its engine crackling sweetly, and ran itself right up onto the far bank half a minute before Bert got there. He saw that it needed repairs before it could take the water again; so, annoyed but not disconsolate, he put it under his arm and set off toward the Bayswater Road.

He had not gone far when two men came up on either side of him, and fell into conversation.

"Smashed it up, son? That's a shame."

"Went a treat, it did. We seen it."

"Oh, it's not damaged much," said Bert.

"You make it yourself?"

"Yes."

"Bloody marvel these kids are nowadays, Fred. Tell you what, son. I've got a nipper, about your age, always on at me to buy him a motorboat. What'll you take for this one?"

"But I don't want to sell it."

"Look, I've taken a fancy to it. I'll make it worth your while." The man drew a roll of notes from his pocket, winking at his companion. "Strictly cash transaction. No income tax to pay."

"Thanks awfully, but—"

"Couple of quid do you? Make it five, if you like; among friends."

Bert found himself hot with embarrassment. He walked faster. "I'm sorry. I don't want to sell it."

But the man—a jovial, red-faced man—kept on at him; kept on at him a shade too long. Bert was quite old enough to sense something abnormal in this persistence. Though he was beginning to feel frightened, his brain still worked all right. The boat wasn't worth quarter of the money now being offered. Therefore it couldn't be the boat they wanted. Therefore they must want the bit of paper that gray-faced man had given him. Bert's mouth set obstinately; his eyes flickered round on the strolling people, none of them quite near enough, and the children's playground ahead.

"Ever seen one of these, chum?" said the man called Fred, withdrawing his right hand, with a brass contraption on the knuckles, from his side pocket, and quickly replacing it.

Bert, as a matter of fact, had seen one. His friend Copper's father was a policeman, and possessed such a souvenir.

"Beauty treatment," pursued the man called Fred. "A bit of face-lifting might improve your looks."

Bert ducked and ran for it. The sauntering couples, the fond parents and larking children beheld a familiar sight—a red-faced man chasing, with jolly cries, a small boy among the trees. Nobody paid any special attention to the cheerful little family scene; nobody remarked how white was the boy's face. Like Dai Williams only five minutes before, Bert felt the fugitive's universal mistrust; there might be more of them than just those two men; he dodged and swerved past innocent strollers, then raced into the children's playground, just ahead of the two men.

It took him a very short time to realize that what had seemed sanctuary was in fact a trap. The playground, with its horde of children swinging, see-sawing, giant-striding, yelling their heads off, protected him temporarily, no doubt; but it had only two exits, and Bert saw that on the grass, opposite each, one of his pursuers was now sitting.

His first impulse was to open the boat and look at the paper inside. But this he rejected at once. The men might see him doing it, and he must not give them any inkling that he guessed what they were really after. He looked round desperately for an attendant or a park-keeper, but there was none in sight. Sitting down in the sand pit, he forced himself to think coolly about his predicament. Sooner or later, a keeper would be bound to turn up. Well then, he need only wait. But would any grownup believe his story? Would the hard-faced, skeptical genus of park-keeper believe him? Suppose he threw himself on the mercies of such a one, and then the two men

waiting outside swore that he had stolen the boat, or that he
was the son of one of them? He couldn't imagine any keeper
believing his story, then.

So what? Wouldn't the best plan be to get himself arrested?
to do something so blatantly criminal that the two men,
however much they protested, couldn't "rescue" him from
it? Bert's mind ran rapidly over the offenses listed upon the
notice board which he had so often studied on entering the
Gardens. He recollected, for example, a clause to the effect
that:

*No person on horseback shall take into or have in the Gardens any
dog.*

This was typical of the general far-fetchedness of the regulations, and of their utter irrelevance to his own dilemma.
Indeed, there seemed nothing for it but to await the arrival of
Authority, and then commit an all-out assault upon one of the
repulsive infants who were mucking about beside him in the
sandpit.

Bert's meditations were abruptly ended, however, by a
new development of the situation. The enemy had decided to
break the stalemate. Sauntering amid a group of children,
with whom he was affably chatting, the red-faced man entered the playground. Bert found himself being edged away
toward its other exit, where Fred and his knuckle-duster were
stationed. At this moment, his terror increasing at every step,
he all but chucked in his hand. But, as he approached the
exit, holding out the boat to Fred in a gesture of surrender, a
brain wave came upon him. If the red-faced man could use an
escort of children to get in, *he* could jolly well—

"Uncle Tom! Hello, Uncle Tom!" Bert yelled to a total
stranger who was walking along the path outside the playground. The advancing Fred halted. Bert shot through the gate,
ran past him, and hurled himself enthusiastically upon the
stranger.

"I thought you were never coming," said Bert.

A pair of very pale blue eyes scrutinized Bert. They

seemed to take in, at one glance, himself, his deadly terror and his desperate maneuver.

"Couldn't think where you'd got to," remarked the stranger equably, putting his hand on the boy's shoulder and steering him off down the path. "What's up?" he said. "Someone frightened you? And—" he lowered his voice— "what is all this about, anyway?"

"Two men tried to take my boat," was all Bert could get out at first, his lip trembling. "Are they following us? A red-faced, big man, and a beastly chap with—"

The stranger stopped dead, turned round.

"Those two?" he asked, pointing at the men, who had also halted, thirty yards behind.

"Yes." Bert gave a small whimper. "Please don't let's stop. The other one's got a knuckle-duster."

"Has he indeed?" said the stranger as they moved on. His voice was mild, interested; it gave Bert quite immense confidence that the stranger should so readily accept his story.

"I know it sounds batty, I didn't think you'd believe me," came out with a rush from Bert.

"They tried to take your boat?"

"Yes. Well, actually they offered me money for it first. Five pounds."

"It's a nice boat," the stranger commented seriously, "but hardly worth that much I suppose."

"Oh no. Nothing like. I made it myself, you see. From parts, of course."

"Why did they want it so much, I wonder."

It was on the tip of Bert's tongue to tell his new friend about the boat's cargo, the little ball of paper. But he'd had a bad fright, he wasn't sure that he could trust any stranger. The hand upon his shoulder seemed to tighten, and panic flooded him again. They were at the north gate of the Gardens. A bus, which had stopped at the pedestrian crossing, began to move on. Bert wriggled suddenly from his companion's grasp, dashed across the pavement, and swung himself into the bus.

The stranger shrugged his shoulders, then side-stepped as a red-faced man rushed past him through the gate and went pelting after the bus.

"Well, what *is* all this about?" thought Nigel Strangeways. It took him only a short time to discover that, whatever the game was, he was involved in it; for he himself was now being trailed by the other man whom the boy had pointed out to him. He shook off this individual with no great difficulty; but he could not shake off the impression made upon him by the white, terrified boy.

Bert, meanwhile, had spotted the red-faced man pursuing the bus. Luckily there weren't many taxis in the Bayswater Road on a Sunday afternoon. But Bert was not going to risk the man's getting one and following the bus. He jumped off at the next traffic lights, took a bus which was going up Church Street, alighted again at Kensington High Street station, and returned to Notting Hill Gate by Inner Circle. When he came to the surface, the coast seemed to be clear.

He walked home, took the boat into his workshop, locked the door, and opened the boat.

Nothing that had happened on this eventful afternoon had prepared him for, or could equal, the shock he now got. Smoothing out the crumpled ball of paper, he saw written on it—the indelible pencil marks blurred a bit by the water in the boat's engine room, but still perfectly legible—his own name, and in figures after it, his age.

2

The Martians—and Others—Confer

"I've got it," said Foxy, snapping his fingers. "It's a warning. They're going to kidnap you."

"The snatch racket," said Copper.

"But why should anyone want to kidnap me?" Bert asked.

"For your bulging brains, of course. They're always kidnaping inventors."

"Snatch 'em young," said Copper.

"The head of the gang," said Foxy hoarsely, warming to his theme, "is a mad scientist, see? He's doing a series of experiments. Human vivisection. He's heard about the Brain. All right. He wants to graft the Brain's brains onto a monkey, and vice versa, and see what happens."

"I could tell him," put in Copper. "The monkey'd become more of a silly ape than ever."

Bert hurled himself upon his friend and brought him to the floor, where Foxy presently joined them in indiscriminate combat. It was the morning after Bert's experience in the Gardens, and he had summoned an extraordinary meeting of the Martian Society to discuss it. Copper, as the son of a Detective-Sergeant, had expressed considerable skepticism at first about the whole affair; people were always making up stories that they'd been threatened or attacked, he weightily announced, just to get into the Press. He even hinted that Bert himself had done the writing on the piece of newspaper. However, a severe grilling of Bert on the details of his story convinced Copper there was something in it.

Bert clinched it by borrowing a morning paper from one of

his mother's lodgers. Under the headline, MAN STABBED BY ROUND POND, appeared a brief description which tallied with that of the gray-faced little man he had received the message from. Before his friends arrived, Bert had tested the piece of paper for invisible ink, holding it to the gas fire, breathing on it and rubbing it with dust, treating it with dilute ink, but all to no effect. The Martians were still faced by the total mystery of a dying man's having written Bert's name and age on the paper.

The Martian Society rose from the floor and resumed its conference. Bert maintained the view that the writing was in code; but he had spent much of the previous evening trying to break it down, by every possible application of the figure 12 to the letters of his name, without result.

"I bet the clue's in some book. On page twelve. The chap who got stabbed was a Secret Service agent. His organization has arranged for a certain book to look up; they just turn to page twelve, or it may be line one of page two—"

"What book?" asked Copper dishearteningly. "You going right through the Public Library?"

"Oh shut up!" said Bert, pushing away the sheets of squared paper on which he had tried to break the code. "Do you want to co-operate, or not?"

"Playing at spies! Gah!"

"If you'd been threatened by a thug with a knuckle-duster, you wouldn't talk about playing."

"Copper couldn't look worse if he did get his face bashed," said Foxy.

"Order, order!" cried Bert, beating on the table with a hammer. "I put it to you, gentlemen—when a chap passes a secret message and gets murdered, and when two thugs try to get hold of the message by hook or by crook, it's not a game. Are we agreed on that, gentlemen?"

"Yes, my lord."

"O.K., chummie."

"Are we agreed, furthermore, that this Society is empowered to take suitable action in respect of the aforesaid situation?"

"Blow me down! The answer is in the affirmative."

"What action?"

"That is now open to discussion by this meeting." Bert glanced round authoritatively at his associates. A deepening silence confronted him. "Well, shall we take our information to the police?"

Foxy spat. Copper pointedly ignored the gesture, and said, "Describe the two men who molested you. Height, weight, color of eyes, how dressed, any distinguishing marks."

"Well, one had a red face, he was a big man, and—er—the other was thin, sort of slimy looking, in a drape suit," Bert uncertainly began, then petered out. He had been far too frightened to take in much of the men's appearance, nor was physical description ever his forte.

"You see? Can't expect the Force to apprehend every suspicious person with a drape suit or a red face. Stands to reason."

There was another glum silence. Then Foxy snapped his fingers again. "I've got it. Advertise for them."

"Don't be so soft."

Foxy's sharp face, surmounted by a mop of carroty hair, was alight. Foxy knew his way about. His father was a barrow boy in a big way, with a family of red-haired children so numerous that he had lost count of them.

"No, wait a minute. These two wide boys. They want Bert's boat, see? For the message inside it. So they want Bert. O.K. They're looking for him now, shouldn't wonder. We put adverts in a few stationers' windows round here. 'If the gentlemen who wished to purchase a boy's speedboat in Kensington Gardens on August 1st, ult., will come to—' "

"Hi, Foxy, I don't want them coming here."

"Quee down!—'will be outside the Notting Hill Gate G.P.O.—' "

"Why the G.P.O.?"

"Because it's public, you silly goon. We can keep a better watch for them there without being seen ourselves:—'outside the G.P.O. between seven and seven-thirty any evening, they will hear something to their advantage.' How's that?"

"Out!" said Copper. "It's crazy. If those chaps are on the crook, they'll suspect it's a trap. They'd never come."

"Look, they want the message enough to offer Bert here a flim for his boat and then flash a mike at him. They still want it, don't they? O.K. They'll send another mob, if they're windy about coming themselves."

"So what do *we* do? Arrest them for loitering?"

"We turn up at the rendezvous. Bert keeps out of sight. If he recognizes one of these blokes, he gives us a signal and we follow them home. Find out where they live."

"And if they send another bloke?"

"We'll spot him, hanging about; he'll be keeping one eye open for the dicks and the other for an innocent little cheeild who's thought again about the five nicker."

"So we put a tail on him," said Copper, almost with enthusiasm, "and let him lead us to his confederates?"

"Listen to his mind working!"

"But why should they ever read our advertisements?" objected Bert.

"It'll get around," said Foxy darkly. "They're the wide boys' notice boards, some of those little stationers. *And* I know which. Bert's buddies'll hear about it soon enough."

"It's an idea," Copper conceded. "Then we pass the info to the police, and they raid the joint."

"It'll make a nice change," said Foxy.

"What'll your Dad say? Doesn't he want you on the barrow?"

"Oh, I'll just disappear for a day or two. He won't notice." In which Foxy spoke truer than he knew.

"What about the money for the adverts? How much do you have to pay?" inquired Bert.

"Just mention my name, or my Dad's, and they'll give you a reduction."

"Give *me?*—I say, I can't go round—"

Foxy explained patiently that it must be Bert, as the enemy would very likely ask the stationers who had paid for the adverts, and would suspect a trap if it turned out not to be the boy whose boat they had tried to buy. Bert fancied there was a flaw in this logic, but Foxy could be as persuasive as the Tempter himself when he was in the mood. Half a dozen cards were written out, Bert polishing the English of the advertisement, and the committee got down to finances. Foxy had inherited his Dad's business acumen and made plenty of pocket money during the holidays by more or less dubious transactions in the Portobello Road. Bert was his widowed mother's only child, so he did pretty well too. The poorest of them was Copper.

"I can manage a bob," he said. "But we'll get the money back, won't we?"

"Get it back? No soap."

"Why not? Aren't we going to sell them Bert's boat?"

A gleam came into Foxy's eyes—large, innocent green eyes which could sell a pup to Cerberus. Then it faded.

"They wouldn't buy it if they found the bit of paper was gone."

Copper surpassed himself. "Give 'em a bit of paper. Write out some message, in guarded language, and put it inside the boat."

The three looked at one another, put up their thumbs in unison, and went off into witch-like laughter.

The plan was now altered. If either of Bert's two men turned up at the rendezvous, Bert would emerge from hiding and attempt to sell them the boat with a fake message in it; the man would then be trailed to his lair by the other two.

Bert started off on his round of the shady stationers recommended by Foxy, at the hour when Nigel Strangeways entered New Scotland Yard and was taken to Superintendent Blount's office. He had rung up Blount yesterday evening, and what he had to say obtained him an interview. Blount was looking more worried than Nigel had ever seen him. He greeted Nigel with "I want you to tell your story to Wright here. He's the D.D.I. in whose manor this stabbing was done."

Blount introduced Nigel to the rangy, saturnine Inspector who was leaning against a filing cabinet, and whose eyes never left him till he had ended his account of his meeting with the terrified boy in Kensington Gardens. Inspector Wright then glanced at the Superintendent.

"It adds up, sir."

"Aye, it does." Blount sighed heavily, massaging his bald scalp. "I'd be obliged, Strangeways, if ye'd give us a detailed description of this wee laddie, and the two men. Here you are." He indicated a dictaphone and switched it on. When Nigel had finished, he sighed again. "It's the boy we want, and you make him sound like a hundred thousand other wee boys. Gray shirt and shorts, brown eyes and hair, about twelve years old, spectacles, a protruding forehead, grammar school type but no school tie or blazer to narrow it down. Ah weel. What about the men, Wright? Do you know them?"

"I don't think they're locals, sir. But there's been a lot of moving about lately, especially in the Notting Dale area."

"Don't I know it. And we're stretched thin, vairy thin, just now."

"Poor old C.I.D. Making the way straight for the Russians, eh?" said Nigel.

Inspector Wright's piercing gaze seemed to pin Nigel to the wall, like a butterfly captured for his collection. Blount said, "The Tito visit was a picnic by comparison." He scratched his chin. "You'd best tell him, Wright. Strangeways has ideas, now and then."

"Very good, sir. An eyewitness told our chaps that the murdered man, just before he died, gave a boy a piece of paper to put in the model boat he was just launching."

"I see. That explains it." Tilting back his chair, Nigel studied the ceiling. "Now it's your turn, Blount. Yonder dead man, who was he? where and what his dwelling?"

"He was an ex-pickpocket and ex-lag, name of Dai Williams, last domiciled in Easington Crescent, Notting Dale."

"An enlisted man, I take it."

Blount gave Nigel his blankest stare.

"Oh, come now, you know what I mean. You'd enlisted him in the forces of law and order. He was a nark, nose, snout, grass, squeaker, or whatever coarse word is current for it just now."

"You see, Wright, Strangeways does have ideas."

"Who'd you put him onto? Or was it a roving commission?" persisted Nigel.

Superintendent Blount pushed back his chair, walked over to the window: for a minute he brooded on the great sunlit panorama of London. Half to himself, he presently said, "I suppose a battlefield always does look peaceful, if you're far enough up above it. I was reading *The Dynasts* a month or two ago." His powerful shoulders braced, as if to resume a burden, and he turned to Nigel. "I'll give you the picture; and if you're in the habit of talking in your sleep, you'll just have to do without sleep for a while."

It was a fortnight ago, he said, that Scotland Yard became aware of abnormal activity in the underworld. Just as, through aerial photographs, raids, captured information, a general may discover the large-scale movement of enemy troops and know that a major offensive is impending, so Scotland Yard had got wind of coming trouble. At first it was no more than something in the air—a matter of rumors, whispers, little thrillings of the grapevine. Contacts in the underworld had grown shy, evasive, or had disappeared. The seedy cafés, where you could always hope to pick up a useful tip, had, so to speak, drawn down their blinds. Something, beyond that, was brewing up—something bigger than normal. The delicate instruments by which Scotland Yard gauges the activity of its eternal enemy, the whole complex organization of routine reports, unorthodox feelers, unobtrusive surveillance, was now vibrating to a violent pressure—the precursor, it was judged, of a crime wave which might build up to tidal-wave dimensions.

It took no great intelligence to deduce that this would be timed to coincide with the Russian visit. Although reserves had been drafted in from the provinces, the police were still woefully undermanned for handling the elaborate precautions which the visit entailed, and at the same time coping with an outbreak of ordinary crime. Political malcontents, home-grown or alien, had to be watched; new arrivals at ports and airports screened: every route along which the Russian Minister and his colleagues would drive must be swept clean just beforehand—empty buildings examined, vantage points quietly occupied, an unremitting vigilance maintained over every yard and minute of the delegation's movements.

And it was not only assassination which must be guarded against. As Blount gravely pointed out, a few organized demonstrations, if successful, could do almost as much harm as an attempted assassination, in the present ticklish state of international affairs. The Soviet suspicion and touchiness, overcome to the extent of sending this delegation of V.I.P.'s, would be revived in full force if the patient work of diplomats were ruined by a bad reception. So the police had to be ready to break up any hostile demonstrations along the route.

Even this was not all. The Home Secretary had expressed great anxiety about the effect which a crime wave, breaking out during their visit, would have upon the delegation. Their naïve ideas of the decadence of the West would be confirmed. They would see Britain as a country where gangsters and bandits flourished, and this might influence their attitude to-ward the delicate negotiations for which they had come.

"So there you have it," said Blount, sitting down again at his desk." "And I'd give half my pension to know we'd get through this week without trouble."

He glanced at his wristwatch. "They'll be here in four hours' time." He was like a general whose plans are all made, his troop movements and supply lines organized, and who can only sit back now waiting for zero hour.

"This crime wave," said Nigel. "Don't tell me the Master Criminal of fiction has really turned up at last."

"Och no. I wish he had. I'd sooner have one big hole to

deal with than stopping up dozens of little leaks all over the place."

"I'd hardly call that bank robbery last night a little leak." As Nigel said it, he was aware again of Inspector Wright's eyes upon him; they had a keenness, a sort of frosty, scintillating excitement in them.

"Aye, it was a bold business. Well organized, too," said Blount. "Now, this Dai Williams. We were—e'eh—in touch with him. No a bad wee fellow, but he couldn't keep his fingers out of other people's pockets. He was keeping his ears open for anything he could pick up about a character called Sam Borch. A versatile lad, Borch. He has a string—"

"Prostitutes?"

"Uh-huh. And other interests. We suspect him of receiving, but we've not quite been able to pin anything on him yet. Now, a couple of days ago, one of our chaps—e'eh—happened to come across Dai in a café. Dai said he'd got a new lead on Sam Borch, which he was following up. He was just beginning to say something about a piece of toffee, when they were interrupted."

"A piece of toffee?"

"That's their argot for a toff, sir," said Inspector Wright.

"Dai ducked out of the café. Someone'd come in he didn't want to meet, not in company with a dick no doubt. That was the last contact we've had with him, alive. We've searched his lodgings. Nix."

"Just how was he killed?"

After a glance at Blount, Inspector Wright handed Nigel the police-surgeon's report.

"H'mm. Quite a professional job. Haven't you got a line here?"

"Maybe," said Wright cautiously. Then he expanded. "That sort of a weapon—we haven't one chance in a million of finding it. We've radioed an appeal for eyewitnesses. You wouldn't believe it. It must have happened somewhere between the bandstand and the Round Pond, but with all those crowds nobody saw anything. Whoever did it was a slick operator. It wouldn't be either of the chaps you saw. They'd be there to cover the murderer's retreat, if there was any trouble. The murderer himself wouldn't risk that business with the boy afterward.''

"The boy. Yes—"said Nigel slowly. "Isn't he the one you should be making a radio appeal for? If Dai Williams discovered something so vital that they had to kill him, and presuming he passed it onto this boy—"

"That's just the trouble, sir. If we broadcast an appeal for the boy, these criminals will realize that we set great store by the bit of paper. And that'd be the end of the boy.''

"Unless we found him before they did," said Blount, polishing his pince-nez and rather noticeably avoiding Nigel's eye.

"You are the only person," said Inspector Wright, "in a position to identify him.''

"Ah. The sales talk begins.''

The Inspector's thin mouth twitched at one corner. His sallow hatchet face seemed to be aimed at Nigel like a cutting edge. He said, "There's another point too, sir. The criminals saw you in company with the boy. He called you 'Uncle Tom.' They may have good reasons to suppose that he has showed you the piece of paper, or told you what was written on it.''

"The disagreeable inference being that I had better find the boy before they find me?''

Inspector Wright rose, came to Nigel's side and put his hand a moment on Nigel's shoulder. "The Superintendent has told me about you. I'd like to have you with us, sir." His sudden smile was unexpected, lively, extraordinarily appealing. "And you do live in my parish.''

"All right, vicar, all right. I'll look for your waif and stray. But how the devil do you expect me to find him?''

Blount relaxed in his chair, blowing out a hugh sigh. "I knew he would. You can't keep Strangeways out of mischief. . . .''

Three hours later, the big black Daimlers swept into London from the airport. The route ahead of them had been cleared; the traffic lights were cut off, and point-duty policemen had taken over. A screen of goggled men on motorcycles, looking like the death riders in Cocteau's *Orphée,* headed the convoy. The arterial road was thinly lined with spectators, kept well back on the pavements, or leaning from the windows of suburban villas, decorated here and there with red flags or union jacks. There was a feeling of incredulity, unreality almost, about the whole affair. After so many false alarms and false dawns, the public seemed apathetic, beyond hope or fear. They knew they were witnessing a historic event, but they'd had an overdose of history during the last twenty years.

"Makes 'em feel at home, all this lot," said a bystander, as the para-military convoy swept past.

"Show 'em we can do it better than they can," said his companion.

"And they call it a free country," remarked a third. "Ain't it lovely?"

At Shepherds Bush a smoke bomb was thrown in front of the leading car. The thrower was instantly removed, as if by some sleight-of-hand, and plain-clothes men politely confiscated the camera of a press man who had snapped the incident, handing it back empty. A police official riding in the first car said to his companions,

"Lucky for us that wasn't a real bomb."

The first two cars were, in fact, decoys. "Minesweepers," their occupants called them. At an interval of several hundred yards, three more followed, escorted in front, on the flanks and in the rear by another buzzing cloud of motorcycle police.

Where the way narrowed, at the top of Holland Park Road, the flank escort dropped back; the cars slowed a little, but not much. The crowd was thicker on the pavements here. A small girl felt her doll being snatched from her hand, saw it falling through the air in front of the second group of cars. Ducking under the outstretched arms of the soldiers lining the route, she ran out into the road. Superbly driven, the car avoided her by a hand's breadth, swerving and braking hard to a stop. A polite altercation was seen to take place inside this car. Then a small, white-haired, stocky man got out, and walking back, picked up the doll, handed it to the little girl, who was being led away by two soldiers. He stroked her hair, and spoke a few words to her, his dour face breaking into a charmingly unofficial smile.

The crowd gave its first wholehearted cheer. The Russian Foreign Minister got back into the car, waving his hand to them. The Important Personage accompanying him covertly mopped his brow; it had all turned out for the best; but supposing the first hour of the Soviet delegation's visit had been marked by the killing of a small girl? . . . *Varium et mutabile semper,* said the Important Personage to himself. He was thinking, not of the nature of woman, but of that equally capricious, unpredictable thing known as public opinion.

3

The Cannibal Party

Breathing heavily, his two fellow Martians watched Bert write the message they had concocted. He wrote it, in shaky capitals, with indelible pencil, on the margin of last Sunday's *News of the World*, tore off the bit of paper, squeezed it up, and put it in the hull of his boat. The message—a masterpiece of noncommittal ingenuity, they thought—ran as follows:

Halibut twelve all set. X 520. Pass on

The message ended with an artistic, jagged scrawl, as though the writer's strength had failed him before he could write down the destination to which it should be passed on. "Halibut twelve" had been voted a judicious scrambling of the original message; "all set" made the thing sound both more business-like and more mysterious; "X 520" was, of course, the dead man's code number in the Secret Service. The Martians raised their thumbs, cackling with witch-like laughter, and sallied forth toward the General Post Office.

Notting Hill Gate was busy this Tuesday evening with people returning from their Bank Holiday excursions. Bert and Copper took up their position in the doorway of a shop diagonally facing the Post Office, whose clock said seven P.M. Foxy, wearing a large cloth cap to conceal his red hair, was sitting on his bike by the pavement opposite. The minutes passed. The crowds passed. But neither of Bert's two men was among them.

"Bet they won't come," he said, not without relief. "They're windy."

"Expect they haven't heard about our advert yet. It only went up yesterday."

The clock hands in the Post Office moved to twenty-five past seven. Only five more minutes, Bert thought, and I can go home.

"See that spiv there?" Copper indicated a character with an appallingly elaborate coiffure and a cigarette dangling from the side of his mouth, who was propping up a shop window next to the G.P.O. "He's been there quarter of an hour. Go and give him a dekko of your boat."

"But he's not—"

"*Who* did you say was windy? They may have sent him."

Bert crossed the road and approached the undesirable character leaning against the shop.

"You the kid put in that advert?" said the man out of the corner of his mouth, his eyes flickering over the passers-by to left and right. "Come on then. Kept me waiting long enough." He began to move off toward the tube station.

"Where are we going?"

"See the gentleman who wants to buy your boat, of course."

Bert stopped dead. Panic had flooded back into him, though Copper was reassuringly in the offing.

"Why couldn't he come himself? How do I know—?"

"He's a busy man. You want to sell it, or not?"

"I'll sell it now," stammered Bert. "I haven't time to go with you. My mum's expecting me home."

"Anyone come with you?"

Bert shood his head, looking up at the man with what he hoped was a passable imitation of Foxy's wide-eyed innocent stare.

"Because you'd better not of brought no one," the man went on. "Let's see it, then."

Bert reluctantly held out the boat. The man inspected it briefly, took off the deck, peered inside. Even Bert, who was anticipating it, could hardly follow the swift movement with which two fingers tonged the little ball of paper and palmed it

"All right. How much?" said the man.

"Five quid, they offered me."

"Don't make me laugh. The price's gone down. A quid, take it or leave it."

"No. I want—"

"Tell you what. Give us yer name and address, and the gentleman'll send yer a postal order. Two quid."

"I want the money now."

"Just give us your name and address, and the Boss'll stump up," wheedled the man. "Don't you trust me?"

"No."

"Deal's off, then."

The spiv handed back the boat and slouched off. Bert didn't know whether he felt more relieved or disappointed. They could have done with five quid, or even two.

Foxy, wheeling his bike on the other side of the road now, saw the spiv go up to a gentleman in bowler hat, tight trousers and dark-gray Edwardian-style jacket, who was buying a buttonhole at the flower stall by the tube exit. The spiv asked for a light. Foxy deduced, rather than saw, that he passed something to the young gentleman. He made a sign to Copper, indicating that he would follow the gent. Copper, accordingly, tailed the spiv, who had turned on his tracks and, Copper soon realized, was following Bert.

So they wanted to know where Bert lived. Copper was not a quick thinker, but he could smell danger when it was stuck under his nose. He ran across the road, got well ahead of Bert, then recrossed it and waved to his friend. When Bert came up with him, Copper fell into step, saying, "Don't look round. That bloke is following you. You'd better not go home. I know. Go to my house. That'll put him off the scent. See you later."

Copper sheered off. The spiv presently saw his quarry let into a house; he heard him call out, "Here I am, Mum." He walked past, noting the number, and moved on. He had not been near enough to see the surprise on the face of Copper's mother when Bert gave her this domestic greeting, and slipping past her, firmly shut the front door.

Meanwhile Foxy was pedaling madly after a taxi into which the young gentleman with the buttonhole had stepped. Luckily for him, it did not go far. Foxy saw it pull up outside a tall, narrow house in Radley Gardens. The gentleman got out, carrying bowler hat and tightly rolled umbrella, the evening sun shining upon his round head of heavily pomaded, flaxen hair. Foxy watched him pay off the driver and let himself into the house. All his cockney inquisitiveness had been roused by recent events; he was pretty sure that the spiv had given their faked message to this posh young gent; the bait had hooked a very fine fish indeed.

Leaning his bicycle against the pavement, Foxy took a ball from his pocket and began bounciing it against a wooden fence a few doors away from where the young gent had gone in. Number 34, Radley Gardens. It was a class neighborhood, thought Foxy, surveying the elegant, freshly painted houses, their front gardens full of flowers, expensive perambulators, well-groomed dogs. Number 34 was taller than the rest, newer looking, with one very large window on the second floor. A burst of radio music came out as the third floor window was opened, and a smooth, round, blond head emerged for a moment, looking down the street. When the head was withdrawn, Foxy allowed his ball to bounce toward the doorway of Number 34. As he retrieved it, he read the names on the brass plates beside the door; the occupant of the top flat was one Alec Gray. Foxy looked over his shoulder at the Bentley which stood by the pavement, then on an impulse rang the top bell.

Almost immediately the front door buzzed at him. Foxy leaped back in alarm; he had not come across buzzing doors before, and he half put up his fists at this one. But, since the door did not attack him, or explode in his face, he cautiously tried it and found it was now unlocked. A neat gadget, he thought as he walked up the stairs; might get the Brain to fix

one up for my dad's front door. He rang the bell outside the
top flat. The door opened, emitting a blast of music, and
Foxy found himself looking into the eyes of the young gent of
the buttonhole—slightly protuberant eyes, with a veiled in-
solent stare in them.

"What the hell do you want?"

"Mr. Alec Gray?"

"Yes."

"Clean your car, sir? Bob a job. Kensington Scouts,
Bullfrog Patrol," Foxy reeled off glibly.

"No thanks. Good-by."

"Good cause, sir. Our holiday fund. Any job you want
doing?"

"Just clear off, will you?"

"Tune your radio, sir?"

Foxy was swung round, and a hard kick in the backside
landed him near the head of the stairs. Well, he'd asked for it:
but he'd got the toff's name, anyway; and Mr. Alec Bloody
Gray had better watch out, that's all. But this was not the end
of the first round with Mr. Gray. Foxy heard footsteps coming up the stairs; and the next moment he was seized by the
smart young gentleman and thrust inside a large closet on the
landing. The footsteps mounted and passed. Before Foxy had
sufficiently recovered from this shock treatment to yell out,
Mr. Gray's visitor entered the top flat. With that radio on
full blast, he could not possibly hear Foxy's cries now. Foxy
investigated his prison. It contained some bottle crates and a
bunker of coal. Foxy, picking out the biggest lump of coal
there, hurled it at the door, which instantly flew open, revealing an empty landing.

Thoughtfully he went down the stairs. It was perfectly
clear that the Gray bastard had unlocked the closet door as
soon as his visitor was inside the flat. Therefore he had only
put Foxy in the cupboard to prevent him from seeing the
visitor. From which it followed that the visitor must be on the
crook in a big way. A passionate yearning to set eyes on this
mysterious stranger invaded Foxy's bosom; with a half-

conscious impulse toward concealment of identity, he smeared his coal-blacked hands over his face as he stepped out again into the street.

There, three doors away from Number 34, ensconced in the front gateway of a house which showed a "For Sale" notice board, Foxy settled down to wait. Sooner or later, the mysterious visitor must emerge; he would be immaculately dressed, in full evening rig, with silk-lined cloak, opera hat and long cigarette holder, like a De Reszke advertisement: or he would be a gorilla, a torpedo—padded shoulders, down-curled Fedora, eyes like a basking snake's, a livid scar from temple to jaw. In pleasurable anticipation Foxy waited. The street was empty, the twilight deepened.

At last he heard the front door of Number 34 open. Peering out from his concealment, Foxy saw two men in black hats and long black coats get into the Bentley. A street lamp had just lit up overhead, throwing leaf shadows like a dancing lace on the pavement as a breeze stirred the plane tree outside Number 34. Foxy's mouth pursed in a silent whistle. The men were distinguished not only by black coats and hats; their faces were black too; and one of them moved with the gait and figure of Mr. Alec Gray. The other, the mysterious visitor, had a graceful, self-possessed, catlike walk, which Foxy had seen often enough before, on the flicks—the tread of the trigger man. As the car moved off and Foxy came out of hiding, his senses registered another thing: a faint, sweet odor, as if someone had been sucking violet cachous.

Without any lively hope of getting further with the mystery tonight, Foxy pedaled after the car. He saw it, in the distance, swing left into Church Street. It was held up by the Bayswater Road traffic lights, so that he came close again, and turned right, behind it, when the lights went green, pursuing it for a few hundred yards more until it swept through the gateway of Millionaires' Row. Here it was stopped by a group of policemen; while they were examining a card which the driver handed them, Foxy took the opportunity to abandon his bicycle and slip unnoticed through the side gate. The Bentley moved on slowly, then parked in a row of cars beside a huge, lighted mansion just ahead of Foxy, who saw the two men get out, hurry toward the house, run up a flight of steps, and disappear through the front door, which opened and closed as if by magic.

As far as Foxy was concerned, it was now an open-and-shut case. A daring robbery, the thieves admitted to the house by an inside accomplice, while the family was at home. He gloated over the imminent undoing of the insufferable Mr. Alec Gray. He thought for a moment of fetching the cops from the end of the road, then thought better of it; cops were too slow in the uptake. Foxy ran up the flight of steps, shot through the magically opening door, under the arm of a butler, only to be firmly gripped by a stalwart individual in knee breeches.

"Burglars!" yelled Foxy: at least, he meant to yell, but it came out as a sort of croak.

"Now then, sonny, none of that. Out you go!"

His captor was propelling him toward the door, when a beautiful voice—a voice which reminded him afterward of a Walls choc-bar, so cool, sweet and creamy, said, "Just a minute, Anderson. Who is this boy?"

Foxy beheld a vision advancing upon him down the stairs, a Hollywood dream come true. He had the presence of mind to take off his cap, but not quite the nerve to kiss the dazzling creature's hand as gentlemen do on the flicks.

"I am Lady Durbar," she said, "This is my house. Have you an invitation?"

"No ma'am—lady. I came—I've been following two—" Foxy gave a suspicious look at the pouter-breasted menservants beside him. "Can I speak to you alone, lady? It's private."

The vision gave him a deep, deep look from her blue, blue eyes; then she took him into a little room off the hall, closing the door on a hum of conversation and music.

"I been following two crooks, lady. One of your stuffed shirts out there let them in. They've come to burgle the house. Probably at it already. We got to move fast."

"But how do you know they are criminals?"

"S'easy, miss—lady. They blacked their faces, see?"

"Like yours?" The lady smiled at him captivatingly, and Foxy blushed under his grime.

"They shut me in a coal cellar. That's how I got my face dirty. Look, you must believe me—"

"Oh, but I do believe you. Just come with me, and see if you can identify these two men."

Lady Durbar led the way into a high, long room, sparkling with chandeliers, its walls lined with tables displaying more assorted grub than Foxy had ever seen in his whole puff. She walked through open windows at the far end onto a balcony and silently pointed to the garden which lay just below them. Foxy gazed. His mouth fell open. There was a great mob of people dancing there under the fairy lights, and more than half of them—both the guys and the dolls—were black.

Foxy turned disconsolately to his hostess. Her red lips quivered, and she broke out into a delightful, irresponsible fit of giggling. He smiled at her uncertainly, then gave way to mirth himself.

"Well, blow me down! Sort of fancy-dress do," he said. "Dressing up like niggers?" Another long look at the crowd below suggested to him that "undressing up" might have been the more accurate description; but he had no wish to be rude—especially when confronted by Lady Durbar's neckline, which plunged like the Big Dipper at Battersea Pleasure Gardens, and made him feel far dizzier.

"Do you like it?" she asked. "It's my cannibal party."

"Sounds a bit soft to me."

"I'm not sure you're not right. Well, we can't stop it now. Perhaps they'll all cook and eat one another." She indicated caldrons, with fires burning under them, dotted here and there among the trees; some of the more unbridled guests were already capering round them, shaking spears and emitting bloodthirsty but well-bred cries.

"How boring people are," murmured Foxy's ravishing companion. "I must have been mad. What's your name?"

"My friends call me Foxy."

"Would you like to stay on for a bit?"

"Whizzo! Just ask me. But look, I can't—not in these clothes."

"Fancy dress optional," she said. "Come along, and we'll rig you out."

"Well, what have we here, Hesione?" said a deep voice behind them. Turning, Foxy saw a small, broad-shouldered, baldish man, hook-nosed, with eyeglasses on a thick black ribbon.

"My new boy friend. Foxy, let me introduce you to my husband. Oh, Rudolf, he just isn't true. It's utter heaven. Foxy came to warn us about two black-faced burglars he saw entering the house! I was just about to pass away from boredom, but he's quite made the evening for me."

"You're incorrigible, Hesione. I must have a talk with this observant young man." Foxy fidgeted; he did not like the way his host's black eyes seemed to be weighing into him. Sir Rudolf continued, "He may be right. This damfool party of yours, Hesione—anyone could get in."

"You should have thought of that when you suggested it, my dear."

"Can you describe these two men?" he asked Foxy. "What made you suspicious of them? And what were you doing, in any case, hanging about outside?"

Foxy opened his mouth to tell the whole story. Then an instinct of caution, inherited from a long line of cockney ancestors in their guerrillas with Authority, made him say instead, "Just happened to be passing, sir. Seeing the sights. They had black coats and hats; didn't notice anything else."

"Were they carrying a bag? Burglars need tools."

Foxy decided in a flash against lying. "No sir, I don't think so. Unless they had them under their coats."

"Now please stop cross-examining my Foxy," said Lady Durbar. "He and I will search the premises."

Sir Rudolf gave a sort of snuffling grunt, and turned away—with reluctance, Foxy thought. The lady took him back through the long room, into the hall, up the stairs where couples were sitting out. She threw a smile and a word here and there; her voice, Foxy noticed, was different when she talked to the guests or to her old man—higher, drawly, sort of tired; a society voice, he supposed; when she talked to him, she sounded real, younger, human.

"Why is that man dressed like Uncle Sam in the cartoons?" he asked, as they reached the first landing.

"Oh, he's an imaginative one, a smarty pants," she replied vaguely. "He represents the Capitalist Cannibals' Clique, I suppose."

A group of animated young ladies greeted her with shrill cries of enthusiasm on the next floor. As they passed on, Foxy heard his hostess murmur, "Oh my God, these meaty-faced debs and their dear little dolly voices!"

"I think *you* look a fair smasher, Lady Durbar," Foxy was moved to say.

She squeezed his hand; her mouth quivered, and Foxy saw the lovely blue eyes suddenly misted.

"Good old Foxy," she said, after a moment. "You're not so bad yourself. You from the Hill?"

Surprised, he jerked his coppery head in assent. She was a class dame all rightiyo: how come she knew the Notting Hill area by its real name?

She led him into a bedroom which made Foxy gasp. There was enough stuff here to fit out four stalls in the Portobello Road market. As she rummaged in a deep chest, he went nosing round. Lovely stuff. He took up a little Chinese jade idol, fingering it with some wistfulness.

"Do you like that?" she said over her gleaming shoulder. "Take it, Foxy ducks. I don't want it."

"What me?" He put the idol down quickly, giving her a guilty look.

"Yes, you," she laughed. "Go on. Pouch it. For a keepsake."

"Well, O.K., I don't mind—if you really—"

"Now, black your face properly with this. And your hands."

When he had done it, she wound a turban round his head, and helped him into a sort of golden robe that came down to his ankles. Then she painted two pink blubber lips over his mouth. While he admired himself in the long glass, she wrote his name on an invitation card—a whacking great ivory card with gilt edges. "Just in case any officious bloke starts asking questions," she said as she handed it to him. "Now I must go and look after my horrible guests."

This time, Foxy brought himself up to the mark. He took the divine creature's hand, bowed deeply, and put it to his lips. Here other hand touched his cheek lightly—a royal gesture. "Wander about wherever you like, Foxy. Watch the little Society victims at play." She winked companionably. "The grub's good, anyway."

As he followed her down the stairs, he heard her call out to a group of people, "Has anyone seen Alec?" So she knew the bastard. But he could tell her a thing or two about the bastard she didn't know. Obscure emotions battled in his breast: jealousy—there had been something in her voice when she said "Alec"; an impulse to protect her, not to spoil her evening; a desire to make the most of this fabulous opportunity which had fallen into his lap. Ah, what a story he'd have for the Martians tomorrow! And what a hope of getting the skeptical Copper to believe it!

Foxy went to the long room where the grub was laid out. It was pretty full now of guys and dolls; but he wriggled his way to a table by the wall and spent an interesting half hour sampling all the available dishes, in an order which caused the caterer's man to raise scandalized eyebrows. He also had a glass or two of champagne—a beverage he found himself comparing quite favorably with Coca-Cola, after the initial sensation of being asphyxiated by bubbles had passed off. Voices buzzed and babbled in his ear. Nobody paid any attention to him. This was High Life. When he had eaten himself to a standstill, Foxy asked the caterer's man, "Got any gum, mister?"

"*Gum,* sir?" bleated the man. "Did you say gum? I'm afraid not."

"Noo gahm! The service in this joint is quate shucking," said Foxy, sneering, in upper-class tones, and walked away.

Presently he strolled out into the garden. The fairy lights twinkled among the trees; there were sparkles of jewels around him, flashes of white teeth in black faces. Foxy stood entranced; he was Aladdin, and this night was his robber's cave. Walking over to one of the caldrons, he discovered that the fire beneath it was an arrangement of red paper and electric bulbs, and the caldron itself a sort of bran tub.

"May I ask to see your invitation card, sir?" said the cannibal in attendance.

"Granted."

Foxy produced his card; then thrust a hand into the caldron, withdrawing from the bran a small, hard object in tissue paper. It was a cigarette lighter, and a posh one. Rapidly pricing it at three nicker, he put it away in his pocket, under the gold robe, together with the jade idol his hostess had given him. Oh boy, what a night it was! And there were four or five more caldrons. As this grasping thought came into his mind, Foxy looked up and saw Alec Gray's eyes upon him. Panic spurted out, like a match struck in the darkness. Foxy seized, for self-defense, the nearest available object, which turned out to be a dusky maiden in hula-hula skirt, brassière, and little else, and whisked her into the dance.

"This party couldn't be more heaven, don't you think?" she said; her voice was flat, unexhilarated, and Knightsbridge.

"Smashing."

"I don't think we've met, have we?"

"The loss is mine," replied Foxy, with the feeling of one who had got well into the swing of things, and took a tighter grip on the judy. "Do you know Alec Gray?"

"Vaguely."

The champagne, churned up by the dance, rose to Foxy's throat in a rush of bubbles. He removed a hand from the maiden, to cover a belch. "Pardon. He's on the crook," said Foxy, confidentially.

"On what?"

"Let it ride, let it ride."

"You mean—Hesione?" A spark of animation momentarily gleamed in the young woman's eye as she put two and two together. "I say, are you one of Hesione's kid brothers—the ones she keeps dark?"

Foxy drew himself up to his full four foot three. "I am a friend of Lady Dunbar's," he declared, treading mercilessly upon his partner's toes.

"Ow! You horrible little—!" she began, but the turbaned imp had glided away.

From the corner of his eye, Foxy had seen the unspeakable Gray again. He was properly up a tree if that b— had penetrated his disguise. But up a tree seemed the safest place, at the moment, to be; darting behind a bit of shrubbery, away from the crowd, he tore off his hampering gold robe, then swung himself into the leaves of the nearest tree. Footsteps were approaching. A voice he seemed to have heard before began to speak, softly.

"Oh, there you are, Alec. I've been looking for you. Did you bring him?"

"He's in the study. I locked him in, with a bottle of rye."

"Good man." The voice was lowered. "What about the other matter?"

"It's a washout. We got the piece of paper, but it's the wrong paper."

"I don't follow you."

"I showed it just now to one of these newshounds. What was written on it didn't make sense, anyway. He said it had been torn off the *News of the World*."

"Well?"

"The *News of the World* happens not to be the paper that D. W. was reading," said Alec Gray in a whisper Foxy could only just catch. "The kid with the boat was pulling a fast one: practical joke, more like."

"You're a fool, Gray. Why should this boy substitute one message for another?"

"Perhaps someone told him to," said Gray in his cold, careless, public-school voice. "Perhaps the police told him."

"And what *was* written on the piece of paper? The wrong piece that you so cleverly acquired?"

" 'Halibut twelve all set. X 520. Pass on.' Penny-dreadful stuff. I wouldn't give it another thought."

"No doubt you wouldn't." There was a pause, a grunt from Gray's companion. "The boy has got to be questioned."

"That's all right. He was followed home. Produce him for you any moment."

"I don't want the boy. I want the information. See to it, please. I'm going to talk to our friend now."

"Here's the key. And keep away from you know where; the concert party'll be on the job any moment."

The two speakers began to move away. Peering after them, to establish the identity of the second, Foxy lost his balance and fell noisily out of the tree.

4

Model for an Emergency

Nigel Strangeways let his eye rove along the line of miniature horses ranged on the sill of the great studio window. Their simplified forms, their muzzles tapering to an open *o* like hose nozzles, were curiously restful. As other people might doodle, or play with a length of string, so Clare Massinger's restless fingers shaped these little clay horses, almost unconsciously, when they had nothing else to do. At present she was engaged upon a portrait head of Nigel. He sat immobile and anonymous as the doltish clay mass over there from which Clare was beginning to conjure his likeness. To her, he thought, I am just an interesting arrangement of planes and lights; or an idea in the mind, which she can only realize through that lump of clay, like the Creator when he brooded over Chaos. He smiled faintly.

"No! Don't make faces!" said Clare Massinger. "I'll put in the expression, thank you."

"Just a little embryo in the womb of your genius," Nigel murmured, resuming the utterly passive role. His mind returned to the story, printed in an early edition of the *Evening Standard* which he had bought on the way here. Big Robbery at Millionaire's House. The crime wave Blount had spoken of was piling up already. That woman, Durbur, must be a fool: a party to which half the guests came in fancy dress with their faces blacked—it was asking for trouble; anyone could walk in, move freely around, take his time, take his pick. And a nice haul it had been, by all accounts.

Clare Massinger patted, slapped, pummeled, gouged away at the clay. By a sort of sympathetic magic, Nigel felt as if he himself was undergoing a violent facial massage. She leaned away, prowled round him, returned to her stand, meditated for a little, strode aggressively up to him and glared into his face from a distance of six inches, then withdrew again: the ritual dance of the sculptor.

That boy, thought Nigel uneasily. Where is he? What was the message Dai Williams gave him? He had spent most of the previous day wandering in Kensington Gardens, by the Round Pond, hither and thither through Notting Hill and Notting Dale, keeping his eyes skinned for a small ordinary, bespectacled boy. Might as well look for one particular rabbit in a warren.

"Don't frown," said Clare sharply. "I want that light on your left temple."

Presently she glided toward him and appeared to have designs upon the lobe of his right ear.

"Don't bite the exhibits," said Nigel.

"Do you know, I believe you're lopsided," she announced interestedly. "You really have a very peculiar face. Very odd indeed. Never mind; I dare say we shall make something of it."

She opened a pair of calipers. "Shut your eyes," she said. "I'm just going to drive these through your eyeballs."

He felt the tips of the calipers touch his eyelids in a butterfly kiss, tremble faintly upon them, and withdraw. Opening his eyes, he saw the same operation performed upon his *alter ego* of clay.

"You've a wonderfully steady hand."

"Not this morning. I was at a party till the small hours."

After another ten minutes, Clare groaned heavily.

"You can come down, Nigel. I'm no good today. We'll have some coffee."

"Where was your wild party?"

"At the Durbars'."

Nigel whistled. "It was, was it?"

"I don't go much for these bloody silly parties," she said, a little on the defensive, "but Hesione Durbar is sitting for me. A commission. So I thought I'd better turn up."

Nigel studied her as she bent over the gas ring in the cluttered studio: dead pale face; coal black hair streaming down her back, released now from the peaked cap she wore when working; strong, stubby fingers; a thin body, curled up like a spring now on the floor, immensely resilient. Like a cat's, her body could suggest utter relaxation and extreme tension in one and the same pose.

"They were burgled last night, you know."

"Oh, were they? I never read the papers," she replied vaguely. "Two lumps?"

"Thank you. Tell me about the party."

"It was hell. Supposed to be a cannibal party. I ask you! Pretentious and silly. No expense spared, and a waste of shame. The usual obscene gang of debs and nobs and snobs. I don't know why Hesione does it; she's rather a golden girl, really; sensible too; beautiful bone. Where she got it from, I can't imagine. As she always says, her husband took her out of the gutter." Clare yawned and stretched like a cat. "Oh such a dull party! The only rewarding feature was when the boy fell out of the tree. How vile this coffee tastes. Have some more."

"Just a minute, Clare. A boy fell out of a tree?"

"Yes. Then someone—Alec Gray, I should think—started making hunting noises, and they all joined in—it gives you rather a line on the clientele, doesn't it? But the boy dodged through the crowd and got away over the garden wall. Hesione was furious when she heard about it."

"Had he pinched something? What was he doing there?"

"Hesione'd picked him up somehow. I couldn't quite gather. No, she was furious that they'd chased him out. I heard her giving Gray hell."

"Who's he?"

"The present incumbent. She's mad about him, actually. God knows why. He's one of the most noisome bits of sub-

Tatler riffraff you could hope to find. A neighbor of mine, too, curse it.''

"Going back to the boy—did you see him yourself? What he looked like?"

"When he ran away, his turban fell off. Hesione dressed him up, I believe. He had bright red hair. Why?"

Nigel got up, and rummaging on a littered table, found pencil and paper. "I know you can't draw. But just do me a crude impression of this boy, will you?"

"But damn it, his face was blacked."

"Never mind. Let's have the skull beneath the skin."

Nigel hardly knew why he made this request. Clearly, it had not been the same boy; but he had no trace of a clue to the one he was seeking, and now a second boy had cropped up; perhaps one boy would lead to the other.

Clare was sketching the head in thick, swift strokes, and chattering on about the party. There had been another incident, later, when some of its rowdier elements had taken over the saxophone and drums from the band, and started up a swing version of "The Red Flag." They had moved on to the "Internationale," with a number of tipsy guests giving a raucous, vocal caricature, when Sir Rudolf Durbar, hurrying out of the house, put a stop to it.

"I don't know why he took on so. If he will ask that sort of people, what does he expect?"

"Of course, if you never read the papers, my poor love, you wouldn't. The Durbars' house is well within earshot of the Russian embassy."

"Oh, is it? I see. International rudery. Undiplomatic."

"Who started the ruction?"

"I don't know. The Gray creature was playing one of the saxophones."

At that moment there came a frantic banging on the door. Nigel opened it, and a boy shot in—a boy with white face and carroty hair.

"Hide me!" the boy sobbed. "He's after me! I must hide." His eyes flickered desperately round the studio, as if he were looking for some hole into which he could disappear. Nigel reacted instantaneously. Dumping the boy into the chair on the model's throne, he fetched a stand, with a lump of clay impaled on its upright, from a corner of the studio.

"It's all right, son. Sit tight and don't talk. Go on, Clare. Get to work on it."

Clare Massinger began kneading the clay, frowning, her lower lip stuck out. She could hear footsteps crossing the courtyard which led from Number 34, Radley Gardens, to her studio at the back of it.

"Who's after you?" asked Nigel quietly.

"Mr. Gray."

"Good-oh," murmured Clare.

"Now listen. This lady is Miss Massinger, and she asked you to sit for her. Got that? What's your name?"

"Foxy."

The door bell rang. It did not just ring, and stop. The man outside kept his finger on the bell push till the door was opened. It was Nigel's first taste of Alec Gray—a very nasty taste indeed.

A round-headed, sleek-haired young man, in Norfolk jacket and tight Edwardian trousers, stood at the doorway, his finger still on the bell push.

"Is the house on fire?" asked Nigel.

"Not that I know of," said Alec Gray, brushing past him. "Yes, I thought he must have come in here. I want to have a talk with this lad."

"Well, you can have it some other time," said Clare, her dark eyes flashing. "We're busy just now."

"Ah. Spitfire type. Carry on with the art work while I interrogate, then." The man's effrontery was formidable; it created an area of positive disquiet all round him; Clare Massinger's fingers were trembling.

"Shall I throw the young gentleman out, Clare?"

"I wouldn't, if I were you," said Gray, leaning against the wall. "I was in the Commandos, and they taught us some horrible tricks, you know."

"I'm sure they came naturally to you," said Clare.

Gray studied her, as if seeing her for the first time. A flicker of interest disturbed the veiled insolence of his gaze, which slowly moved up her, from foot to head.

"I've caught this brat snooping, twice now. I'm going to teach him a lesson."

In the model's chair, Foxy froze cowering like a small animal, and Clare made an involuntary movement, as if to protect him.

"Snooping?" said Nigel. "He was simply trying to find Miss Massinger's studio. She'd fixed up with him to sit for her this morning."

"Really? Now *I*'d be surprised if Miss Massinger had ever set eyes on him before."

"As you're here, you'd better make yourself useful," said Clare unexpectedly. "Get me the six-inch ruler out of that cupboard, please."

While Gray was rummaging, his back turned, she rapidly sketched in Foxy's mouth on her drawing: she'd had to leave it blank before, since at the party it was concealed by the blubber lips which Hesione Durbar had painted over it. When Gray straightened up again, she was back at the stand.

"Now, to return to the brat here. Last night he gate-crashed a party at the Durbars'; and by a strange coincidence she had her jewels stolen."

"Here! I didn't take any—" protested Foxy; then suddenly broke off, remembering the jade idol and the cigarette lighter. They could pin it on him for that. Who'd believe that the lady had given them?

"I'm not supposing the brat swiped Hesione's jewels," Alec Gray was saying. "But these gangs do have lookout men, and such-like; and it'd be quite bright to employ an innocent-looking cheeild for the purpose. So when I find him snooping round my premises—"

"I *wasn't* snooping," cried Foxy.

"Pipe down, kiddo," said Clare. "Now, once and for all, Mr. Gray, I saw this boy in the Gardens the other day, took a fancy to his face, and asked him to sit for me. In fact, I did a rough sketch of him at the time. Perhaps this will dispose of your delusions that I'd never seen him till this morning.''

She handed Gray the sketch. It was fairly certain, from the way he had spoken, that he was not aware she had been at the Durbars' party.

''Well, I know nothing about art, but I know what I like,'' he said, his eyes moving from the sketch to Clare's body. He seemed, for once, a shade disconcerted. ''So we let the brat off with a caution? Next time you come, you come *straight* here, not via my staircase, sonny. Got that?''

''Yes.''

''Yes what?''

''Yes, sir.''

''When you've finished impressing the boy with your regimental personality,'' said Clare, ''the door is behind you.''

''Now we've met at last, we mustn't drift apart,'' said Alec Gray with a long look at her. ''What about—''

''Next time you pay a visit, ring me up first, and I'll arrange to be out.'' Anger made Clare quite exceptionally attractive—which, under the circumstances, Nigel thought was not altogether desirable. ''Now, *clear out*, you insufferable little twerp! I'm busy,'' she said.

A flush came over his blond face: his eyes, with their congested look, went narrow; and he started toward her. Nigel was out of his chair in an instant; but, before he reached the young man, Clare had thrown the lump of clay she was kneading, with unerring aim, slap across his eyes. He picked it slowly off, standing there.

''Rough games end in tears,'' he said. It sounded absurd, somehow, in that public-school voice of his, and Clare went off into a peal of laughter. Alec Gray, head lowered like a young bull, looked dangerously about him, and his eye lit on Nigel.

''Did I hear you laugh?'' he said to him.

''You really must try to grow up and behave yourself,'' Nigel replied. ''Clare and I are not impressed by subaltern's mess antics. By the way, let me introduce myself. My name is Strangeways. And I believe we have, or rather had, an acquaintance in common."

"I doubt it."

"A chap called Williams. Dai Williams."

Nigel, his eyes fixed sleepily on Gray, did not see Foxy's start of surprise. But Clare Massinger did. Gray's face went quite blank. If the arrow Nigel had shot at so wild a venture had struck him, he certainly did not flinch.

"Dai Williams? The only Dai Williams I've ever heard of is the chap who was killed near the Round Pond the other day. They gave his name in the papers this morning."

"He talked about you quite a lot, the chap *I* mean," said Nigel. "Called you 'the toff.' ' "

"Never heard of him. You're off the beam. Must've been some other Gray."

Without another look at Clare, the young man departed.

"And now," said Nigel to Foxy, "you'd better come clean. What *were* you doing, gum-shoeing around Mr. Gray's premises just now?" . . .

After breakfast, Foxy had gone round to Copper's house. He described with a wealth of detail—exaggeration being neither necessary nor possible—the events of the previous night, and put in as evidence the little jade idol, which had already become a mascot for him. Copper was finally convinced. Neither of them, at this point, knew about the robbery at the Durbars'; had they done so, Copper's law-abiding tendencies might have produced a different course of action. What seemed the nub of it all was the conversation Foxy had heard from his hidingplace in the tree. It clearly indicated the man, Gray, was Public Enemy Number One. Gray was behind the attempts to get back from Bert Hale the piece of paper: Gray had seen through the fake message they had written on the substitute paper; Gray knew which newspaper it was that Dai Williams had been reading just before he was killed. Ergo, Gray was the killer, or at least had laid on the murder.

Unfortunately, Foxy had not been able to get a glimpse of his accomplice—the man he was talking to under the tree. The voice had been vaguely familiar, but he could not place it. Then there was the problem of the third man—the one with the gangster's gait, who had accompanied Gray to the Durburs'. This was surely the man Gray had referred to during the conversation beneath the tree: "He's in the study. I locked him in with a bottle of rye." Why lock him in? Presumably, so that none of the family or the guests should see him: Foxy had been thrust into Gray's coal closet for the very same reason. And why must no one be allowed to set eyes on him? The only reason could be that he was the killer of Dai Williams—or so Foxy argued. Copper cast doubts on this theory. It didn't make sense, bringing the murderer to the Durbars' house, locking him in Sir Rudolf Durbar's study, so the Gray's accomplice could have a talk with him. What a crazy risk to take!

Then Foxy had his bright idea. Suppose he'd been right at the start, and this man had come with Gray to burgle the house. Gray had got him into the study, locked the door to prevent interference, and left him at work; "bottle of rye" was some code expression then, and the chap who talked to Gray under the tree was another accomplice in the robbery. Copper thought this a much more likely solution, if in fact it turned out that there had been a robbery. They decided to go and discuss it with Bert, picking up an early edition of an evening paper on the way.

It was at this point that the commercial traveler arrived. They heard Copper's mum open the front door: they popped out into the passage to see who it was. A jovial, red-faced man, with a case of samples under his arm.

"These your nippers, ma'am? Fine lads. Got three of my own at home, and the wife expecting another addition."

"This is mine," replied Copper's mum. "Foxy here is a friend of his."

Copper glowered at the hearty visitor, who was now patting him on the head.

"And is this all the quiverful, ma'am?"

"Him and his little sister."

"T'ck, t'ck. Well, plenty more where they came from, I always say."

The red-faced man looked, however, a shade less genial. Copper and Foxy faded. When they were alone, Copper said, "You know what? He's after Bert, bet you anything. That spiv yesterday saw Bert coming in here, and the gang've sent this chap along to reconnoiter."

They could hear the commercial traveler outside, talking to Copper's mum: he was traveling a line of cheap leather belts for boys, and he would be grateful for the names and addresses of any of her friends, who had young nippers. That had torn it. "Come on!" said Foxy, and they rushed past the red-faced man, out of the house, to warn Bert.

A quarter of an hour later, peering from the basement window of Bert's house, the two of them saw an old Morris draw up outside and the red-faced man step from it. A ticklish moment. Bert had previously left by the back door, but there was no knowing what his mother might not give away. However, though she was wax in Bert's hands, Mrs. Hale was granite to commercial travelers: they heard her, on the steps above, repelling in no uncertain terms the traveler's blandishments. Presently he retreated down the steps again. Before driving off, he gave the house a long scrutiny, and marked a cross in his address book. Foxy, watching through a chink of the curtains, felt a disagreeable qualm; the man's face was very far from jovial at that moment; it was unlikely that they had seen the last of him.

However, Bert was safe for the time being, and his friends decided to carry on with the investigation of the bastard, Gray. The next step, they agreed, was to try and trace the man who had visited Gray's flat the previous evening and been taken by him to the Durbars' party. Either he was staying in the flat, or he would be likely to visit it again soon. The flat must be kept under observation: they tossed for the first watch, and Foxy won; Copper would relieve him at midday.

So once again Foxy found himself in Radley Gardens. The

Bentley was not standing outside Number 34, but the radio still blared through the open top-floor window. After watching for ten minutes or so, from the gateway of the For Sale house, Foxy began to get bored. His personal grudge against Gray bubbled up in fantasies of hurling stones or firing rockets through that open window up there, but neither stones nor rockets were available. A postman came past, and put some letters into the letter boxes of Number 34. It gave Foxy an idea. He waited a few minutes; then, darting round to the door, rang the bell of the second-floor flat. The door buzzed at him, and he went in. He scooped up the couple of letters which lay in the letter box of Flat 3, saw they were both addressed to Alec Gray, and pocketed them. A woman's voice called from above, "Who is it?" Foxy said nothing. Footsteps were descending. He noticed a door on the right of the entrance hall where he was standing, and went through it. He was in another passage, leading to a little courtyard, with a low building beyond it. When the woman's footsteps went upstairs again, Foxy emerged into the hallway. He opened the front door. The Bentley stood there now, and Alec Gray was stepping toward him.

A quick, cold smile flicked over Gray's mouth. "You're for it now," was all he said, as he sauntered, not hurrying his pace, toward the boy. Foxy felt a jag of fear, like a knife in the stomach. Giving a little whimper, he slammed the front door in Gray's face, ran through the door on the right of the hall, closed it behind him, sped across the courtyard toward the only possible sanctuary. . . .

"What *were* you doing, gum-shoeing around Mr. Gray's premises just now?"

Foxy had had time to get his wits back; but, in spite of having been rescued by this lady and gentleman, he was on the defensive. Things you couldn't understand made you uneasy, suspicious. How could the lady have done a drawing of him when she'd never clapped eyes on him till ten minutes ago? And all that palaver about fixing up with him to sit for her—it had come too pat for his liking. As one who was seldom if ever at a loss for a plausible untruth, he was filled with suspicion that these two should have rigged the tale so cleverly to help him out. Why? What was behind it?

As if reading his thoughts, the gentleman said, "I don't know what it's all about. But we're on your side: you can trust us."

Something in his voice carried conviction. Foxy opened his mouth to tell the whole truth and nothing but the truth. But, as he shifted in his chair, he heard a faint crackle from his pocket: the two letters he had swiped; and in the other pocket lay the jade idol which no one would believe he had not swiped. If he told the true story, he'd find himself in the cooler.

Under the mop of red hair, in the pale, sharp face, Foxy's green eyes opened wide, guilelessly. "It was like this, see?" he said; and leaning heavily upon the few frail facts he dared produce, told them he'd called on Mr. Gray the previous day for a subscription to the Scouts, been kicked downstairs, returned this morning to ask subscriptions from the other flats, and—

"Oh well, if you won't tell us, you won't," interrupted Nigel.

Foxy swelled with indignation. "I *am* telling you! Show you the bruise, if you don't believe me."

"God forbid!" said Clare. "Look, here's five bob. That's your fee for the sitting. Come again tomorrow at this time, and you'll get the same."

Foxy thanked her, leaping from his chair with alacrity. He moved to the door, then visibly wavered. Again Nigel read his thoughts, and said tactfully, "Shall I just show you the way out, Foxy?"

"O.K., mister." He'd have died rather than beg for protection through the Gray territory; but, since he was offered it gratis . . .

Nigel returned to the studio, looking very thoughtful. At the front door he had asked Foxy, on an impulse, if any of his friends owned a model speedboat. The effect of this mild question was startling: the boy froze for an instant, then darted off, leaped on a bicycle standing against the curb nearby, and pedaled headlong away. There was not a taxi to be seen, not even another bicycle, on which to pursue him. He started running after the boy, but it was hopeless; and probably a ridiculous wild-goose chase too. Had Nigel known that it was the solution to a whole mystery which now swerved round into Church Street, way ahead of him, he would have run faster and farther. As he strolled back, he fingered in his mind the pieces of the puzzle which had come into his possession:

1. Dai Williams was nosing after "a toff" when he got killed.
2. Alec Gray is a toff. Mention of Dai Williams at any rate caused Gray abruptly to leave the studio without making another pass at Clare.
3. Gray was at the Durbars' party: Lady Durbar is apparently his mistress. Last night there was a big robbery at the Durbars', which had required inside information.
4. Dai Williams had claimed he was getting a lead, through a certain "toff," to Sam Borch. Scotland Yard suspected Borch of being a receiver of stolen goods.
5. The boy, Foxy, somehow got into the Durbars' party; and this morning, not for the first time, was caught hanging around Gray's premises.
6. Foxy streaked off at inquiry about a friend with a model speedboat.

Clare Massinger was looking pensive too, when Nigel returned.

"What an out-and-outer your neighbor is, to be sure."

"It *did* happen, did it? I feel as if I'd been dreaming," said Clare slowly. "That boy. And then—who's this Dai Williams you were talking about?"

"You really must subscribe to a daily paper, my dear."

After a silence, she said, "I must confess I do rather see Hesione's point. Yes. That absolutely armor-plated type of cad does fascinate us girls."

"You feel an urge to reform him, do you?"

"Gracious no! He's quite past that. No, we want to find the weak joint in his armor, or unbuckle it and see what's underneath. A combination of sex and curiosity on our part, no doubt."

"I wouldn't be surprised," said Nigel meditatively, "if you got an opportunity soon to pursue your researches."

5

Nice Morning, Mr. Borch

Mr. Samuel Borch, throwing a genial word to the lift attendant, stepped out into the vestibule of Alhambra Court. He purchased a red carnation from the girl in the flower booth and drew it carefully through the buttonhole of his light gray suit. He looked round for a moment, approvingly, before leaving the place; his fat face crinkled with pleasure, the small eyes and rosebud mouth almost disappearing into folds of flesh. The soft pile carpets, the discreetly gleaming mahogany, the delicate pastel drapes and hangings—they spelt luxury to him, and he stood there positively inhaling it. Sam Borch liked luxury, all the more because he had come to it the hard way, from small beginnings and grim poverty in Eastern Europe. He liked his comforts, and he had no intention of giving them up: he wanted everyone to be happy, but Number One came first—that was only right and natural, the law of life.

"Nice morning, Mr. Borch," said the commissionaire at the door. Something of Mr. Borch's relish in life imparted itself to the commissionaire; his vocational smile became almost human. Mr. Borch waggled his gold-banded Malacca at the man, and passed out into the sunshine, beaming.

Sam Borch had reached his present affluence, though not without ups and downs, by unremitting attention to the laws of supply and demand. Gentlemen in South America, or in Mayfair, required female companionship: Mr. Borch saw no reason why they should not have it, and was in a position to gratify their very natural inclinations. Other gentlemen, who had come into possession of valuables, jewelry, furs, objects of art, and wished to dispose of them, he was no less willing to accommodate. It all made for the general satisfaction, no less than for the particular good of Mr. Borch. In his way, he often thought, he was a public servant; but, first and foremost, he was a businessman.

As such, he had prospered by close observance of a few simple rules. First, only the best is good enough: whether in female flesh or in the other commodities he dealt with, prime cuts were a *sine qua non* of satisfactory service. Second, don't spoil the ship for a hap'orth of tar: Mr. Borch gave good prices for what he was prepared to buy, just as he demanded good prices for what he had to sell. Third, all transactions of a certain nature to be strictly cash. Fourth, the personal touch is the secret of success: Mr. Borch made a point of being always accessible to his contacts, was always willing to listen to their hopes, their fears, and their plans, to offer advice when asked for it, to give credit where credit was due—though, as a sound judge of character, he chose his contacts very carefully indeed. Fifth and last, a little of what you fancy does you good; but never, never tell a pretty woman a secret.

A picture of euphoria, Sam Borch walked up Park Lane, humming in a rich baritone warble "Land of Hope and Glory." Business had been particularly good lately. There were competitors, of course; but Sam felt no resentment against them: monopoly had never been an ambition of his.

Mr. Borch moved toward a newsvendor; then, with a polite "After you, sir," made way for another man who had arrived simultaneously at the newsvendor's pitch. The stranger made no acknowledgement of this courtesy, but asked for some comics. Sam Borch, who was an observant man, noticed that the stranger spoke in an American accent but did not wear American-cut clothes; he also noticed, with disapproval, a waft of a rather sickly violet smell as the stranger moved away, walking with a neat, economical cat-like gait, to enter one of the luxury hotels nearby.

Hailing a taxi, Mr. Borch got in and opened his early

edition of the evening paper. A headline caught his eye. He chuckled richly: so they'd brought that off, too. Things were going very nicely—he could look forward to yet another satisfactory deal; it was almost embarrassing, the amount of business which was piling up. Still, the boom would not last forever, and one must make all the hay one could while the sun shone. Sam Borch turned to another column, and his expression changed: he had not forgotten what happened to his family in Poland during the first year of the Occupation.

The taxi drew up at the entrance to The High Dive, the nigh club which was one of Sam's interests; not the well-concealed back entrance where Dai Williams had heard the scrap of conversation that led to his death, but the almost aggressively prim front. Mr. Borch let himself in, gave an exuberant "good morning" to the cleaners, and proceeded upstairs toward his manager's flat. Within, talking to the manager, were two men whom Mr. Borch instantly recognized as police officers. With unfaltering stride, he crossed the room toward them and held out his pudgy hand.

"Good morning, gentlemen. Everything in order, I hope."

Mr. Borch knew damned well everything was in order, as far as The High Dive was concerned. He paid George Antrobus, the manager, £1,500 a year to ensure that: the Recording Angel himself, he was wont to say, could not find a blot on its copybook.

"You are Mr. Borch? Mr. Samuel Borch?" said one of the officers, making it sound ominous.

"That's me. I don't think I've had the pleasure—"

"No, we're new faces to you. I am Divisional Detective Inspector Wright, and this is Detective-Sergeant Allen."

"Nothing wrong, I hope, gentlemen."

"We've been making some routine inquiries, in which Mr. Antrobus has assisted us. And now I should like a word with you, sir, in private.

"Certainly, certainly. George, if you will—" The manager departed, after a glance which Mr. Borch interpreted to mean that nothing, so far, was amiss.

"I am investigating the murder of Dai Williams, who was

stabbed in Kensington Gardens last Sunday,'' said the senior officer, his eyes fastened upon Mr. Borch in an alert, unblinking stare. Mr. Borch raised his eyebrows inquiringly; he never, unlike most criminals, made the mistake of talking too much, showing righteous indignation, or being too helpful; but Wright sensed a faint relaxation in his attitude.

"Have you ever come across this man?" asked Inspector Wright, producing a photograph. Sam Borch studied it for a moment, then flipped it aside onto his desk.

"No, never. Who is he?"

"Herbert James. Known in some circles as 'the Quack.' He's an ex-medico: got a stretch some years ago for wounding—a race-gang affray. He's also a dope addict."

"Well now, Inspector, I come across some queer cards in my line of business, but—"

"Your various lines of business, Mr. Borch."

"You are very kind."

"A man answering to the description of Herbert James was seen leaving Kensington Gardens, five minutes after the murder of Dai Williams. We should like to check up on him."

"But he has disappeared?"

"Just so. We'd be grateful if you could keep your ears open, sir. You are in a position to pick up odd bits of information; and even in the best-regulated night clubs, as you say, you get some queer customers."

"I'll bear it in mind," said Mr. Borch, and pursed his rosebud mouth. "But I don't think any of our clientele here move in that sort of circles."

Inspector Wright studied Mr. Borch attentively. Wright had never before felt so chafed by the rules which govern police investigation and questioning. He was a man of brilliant gifts, whose unorthodox mind cried out for unorthodox methods: how else could one shake this Borch, this greasy basket sitting so pretty behind his prepared defenses? Wright had taught himself the patience, the refusal to try short cuts, which is the good detective officer's most essential quality. But today circumstances were exceptional and time was se-

verely rationed. After what he had been told by Strangeways
and by the men investigating the robbery at Sir Rudolf Durbar's house, Wright was itching to take the short cut.

In the meantime, at a sign from him, Sergeant Allen had
engaged Sam Borch in a series of "routine questions" about
his movements over the last few days. Wright knew—and
knew that Borch knew he knew—what was Borch's main
source of income: it was a moral certainty that he would profit
from this week's outbreak of large-scale robbery, and at least
fifty-fifty that he had something to do with the organizing of
it. But the ordinary police methods had never succeeded in
discovering his lines of communication.

Mr. Borch, puffing at a cigar, beaming co-operatively or
wrinkling his brow in thought, replied happily to Sergeant
Allen's questions. He was on very safe ground now, and he
enjoyed an opportunity to exercise his talents as an actor.

"Well, much obliged to you, sir. I think that is all," said
Inspector Wright, his watchful, lantern face relaxing. "Oh,
just one more thing. You know a Mr. Alec Gray."

Mr. Borch's pudgy fist, enclosing the cigar, came slowly
toward his mouth; the knuckle of his thumb rubbed up and
down against the pendulous lower lip.

"Mr. Gray? Oh yes, he comes here often. He's an old
member of the club. A very high-spirited young gentleman."

Inspector Wright stood by the door, as if in thought, saying
nothing. It was the ordeal by silence; and after a minute a
bead of perspiration came slowly trickling down Sam Borch's
forehead.

"He's not in any trouble, I hope?" said Mr. Borch, a note
of solicitude in his rich voice. He switched on an electric fan.
"Damned stuffy today."

"Yes, it is, sir. And I dare say it'll be getting warmer
before long. I suppose Mr. Gray brings guests here from time
to time?"

"He does. Lady Durbar comes quite often with him.
And—"

"Is Mr. Gray a personal friend of yours, may I ask?"

Mr. Borch took a moment to reply. "We're on good terms, Inspector. But of course I'm not intimate with him, if that's what you mean."

"May I see your visitors' book, sir, please?"

"You're welcome, Inspector."

Mr. Borch rang a bell and the manager was sent to fetch the book. Inspector Wright noted that, on his last visit a week ago, the high-spirited Mr. Gray had brought four guests— Lady Durbar, Miss Felicity Smythe, G. Fawkes, Esq., and J. Stalin, Esq. He pointed to the two last names, remarking austerely, "This won't do at all, Mr. Borch."

"I quite agree. Mr. Antrobus, how was this allowed to happen? You know my instructions." Mr. Borch was almost wheezing with anger. "You know perfectly well we don't allow any funny business here."

"I'm exceedingly sorry, Mr. Borch. I'll speak to the doorman about it."

"And who, in fact, were the persons who adopted these pseudonyms? Do you remember them?"

Tapping his desk, Mr. Borch looked sharply at Mr. Antrobus, who was only too willing to oblige. Messrs. Fawkes and Stalin turned out to have been two young sprigs, one a Guardee, the other on Lloyds, whose faces were familiar to him through the pages of the *Tatler*.

Outside in the street again, Inspector Wright waggled his little finger at a man who was killing time on the opposite pavement. Then he remarked to Sergeant Allen, as they walked off, "Well, my lad, what did you make of him?"

"A smooth customer, sir."

"I don't mind telling you," said Wright in a spurt of cold violence which made the Sergeant glance up sharply, "I'd like to stamp him into the pavement."

Well, they'd stirred him up. And, if Strangeways' hunch was correct, Borch would soon try to get in touch with Gray. The Exchanges would have a record of telephone calls at either end—Wright had arranged for this. And, if Borch paid a visit in person, Jones would be on his tail. At this point, with luck, they might find a link and begin hauling in the chain. If there was some criminal association between the two, Borch would be bound to warn the other about the police inquiries.

Sam Borch questioned Mr. Antrobus as to what the police officers had said before his arrival, then dismissed him. His hand went to the telephone, but he withdrew it. Walking downstairs, he passed through the empty kitchen, and down another flight of steps to the cellars. He took a bunch of keys from his pocket, opened the door, entered, locked it again behind him. Stooping, he went up to a wine bin, whose racks of bottles stretched from floor to ceiling. Absent-mindedly he stroked one of the bottles; it was a vintage which did not find its way to the tables upstairs, but was reserved for use in his own private room. Mr. Borch bent down, fiddled a moment, then swung the whole framework of racks away from the wall, on its concealed hinge. Behind it lay a door in the wall, itself invisible except to an expert searcher. Mr. Borch passed through this into a narrow, vaulted passage, up some steps, unlocked another door, and was in the back room of a second-hand clothes shop. He whistled a few bars of a merry little tune. A respectable-looking woman entered from the shop, betraying no apparent surprise at finding Mr. Borch in her back room.

"You want to go out, sir?" she asked, in an accent not English.

Mr. Borch nodded. The woman, returning to her shop, glanced out from behind the clothes hanging in its window, left and right along the alley.

"All clear, sir," she said.

Mr. Borch went out into the passage, and sallied forth through the private door which lay to the right of the shop window. This was his escape hatch—a secret known to none but himself and a few of his contacts. It was still sunny outside, but Mr. Borch was not quite the little ray of sunshine he had appeared, earlier this morning, to the employees of Alhambra Court. He walked rapidly up the alley. There was a telephone booth just where this joined the street, but Mr. Borch ignored it; instead, taking a twopence ride on a bus, he telephoned from a booth at Oxford Circus, the best part of a mile from his club. Attention to detail was one of Mr. Borch's watchwords.

Ten minutes later, he re-entered the second-hand garment shop, went up to his room in The High Dive, lit another cigar, and emerged in due course from the front door of the club. The plain-clothes man, Jones, bored stiff with reading books from the one-shilling tray of the shop opposite, followed Mr. Borch at a respectful distance. Mr. Borch was well aware he was being followed. Pursing his rosebud mouth, he began to whistle: it was a cheering thought, that the dick would report him as having stayed in the club for half an hour after Inspector Wright had left, and then having strolled along to the Ivy. It was even more gratifying to consume a large and lengthy lunch there while the dick, outside, consumed his soul in patience. . . .

That same afternoon—it was Thursday, August 5th, the day after the scene in Clare Massinger's studio—Nigel Strangeways was talking to Inspector Wright. Like every other senior police officer in London, Wright was feeling the strain of conducting an abnormal number of investigations with depleted forces: he had to hold a line which the enemy attacked at many different points, and attacked in an unusually audacious manner. Moreover, though the safety of the Russian delegation was specifically the affair of the Special Branch, the Soviet Embassy's being in Wright's district did not lighten his task, for its officials were prickly, somewhat exacting, and difficult to deal with.

After many hours of inquiry at the Durbars' house and among those who had been guests at the party on the 3rd, it was established that the robbery could only have been brought off by inside information of a very special kind. Briefly a concealed safe in Lady Durbar's bedroom had been opened, some time between seven o'clock that evening and three-fifteen the next morning, when she went to put away the jewelry she had worn at the party, and valuables to the amount of some £50,000 had been stolen. The safe was not forced; so the criminal must have known, not only its position, but the combination of the lock. There were no suspicious marks on the window sill, the wall, or the ground below; no fingerprints, except Lady Durbar's and her husband's, on the safe. What made the investigators'- task still more difficult was her statement that no one but she and her husband knew the combination. Her personal maid, and the rest of the staff, had all been with the family for some time, so little or no suspicion could be attached to them.

It was true that a highly skilled operator could hope, by trial and error, and with unlimited time at his disposal, to discover the combination; but the only two criminals, known to the police, who possessed this extraordinary sensitivity of touch and hearing, and could break combinations by listening to the fall of the tumblers, were safely in jail. Besides, unlimited time was an article the criminal could least of all rely on; for the bedroom was not locked (a criminal piece of negligence, Wright grimly commented), guests were wandering all over the house, and some of them on their own admission had peered in to catch a glimpse of the room's fabled splendors. One of the police's most backbreaking tasks had been to compile, by interviewing each of the two hundred odd guests, a list of the approximate periods during which the bedroom had been empty.

"Whose idea was this farcical party?" asked Nigel, when Wright had given him a résumé of the investigations up to date.

The Inspector gave him a quick, approving grin. "Just what I asked myself. Sir Rudolf said it was his wife's. *She* thought it was his; but she's a vague, scatter-brained type. A shocking bad witness."

"You know that Gray is rumored to be her lover?"

"It has come to my ears," replied the Inspector dryly. "So he'd be apt to know the combination of the safe?"

"And she to protect him by saying he didn't. Also, he'd be in a position to suggest to her the idea of a party for which the guests wore black faces with their fancy dress. Does he fit in with any of the other robberies?"

Inspector Wright nibbled at the inside of a forefinger. "Gray is what used to be called a young-man-about-town. He has been a guest, more or less frequent, at four out of the five big houses where we've had robberies this week. But so have a good many other people. They're a sort of Inner Circle, that set—always going the round of the same stations."

"And the same hostesses, don't forget. Gray is clearly attractive to the sex."

"Oh, we'll take him apart, don't you worry, if we're reasonably sure there's anything to find. A link with Borch would've been enough. But I reckon we've fallen down on that one—there's been no communication between them since I interviewed Borch."

"You're sure of that?"

"Nothing's sure in this world. But Sam B. has been behaving like the driven snow ever since. He stayed in the club for half an hour after we left; no telephone calls from there. Had lunch at the Ivy, alone, no telephone calls—my chap verified that. Returned to Alhambra Court, etc., etc. You'd think he'd taken a pledge against using the instrument. Same the other end: Gray has had a few calls, but nothing suspicious."

"So now what?"

"So now you find that red-headed boy you let trickle through your fingers," said Inspector Wright, unsmiling. He was not a man to gloss over incompetence—his own or anyone else's. "Lady Durbar seemed a bit gone on him: she'll probably give you a reward."

"The boy who knows the boy who owns a model speedboat. Or does he? He didn't turn up again this morning at Miss Massinger's studio, by the way."

"You frightened him off," said Wright sourly. Then, with a surprisingly intense appeal in his voice, the dark eyes boring into Nigel as if he were trying to hypnotize him, he added, "Find him, Mr. Strangeways. We've got to reach that boy Dai Williams passed the message to. He's bound to be in danger. His life is—" the Inspector's hand, palm downward, tipped over rapidly from side to side, like something trembling in the balance. . . .

In his luxury apartment, Elmer J. Steig put away the street map of London he had been studying and began to clean and load his revolver. The new instructions he had received, though unexpected, were not unwelcome. Inactivity bored him; and while he was far from being a sociable character, it irked him to remain for so long at a stretch in his apartments, however luxuriously appointed. Even the comics had begun to pall—not that the comics amounted to much in this goddamned, crummy little country. Now, he could keep his hand in, and earn an extra premium. Mr. Steig was a very highly paid executive indeed.

He examined the magazine of his automatic, gave a faint smile like a glint of sun on an icicle, and reached out for another violet cachou.

6

A Home from Home

"Breaking and entering," said Copper severely. "It won't do, chummies."

Foxy made a rude noise.

"But we've planned it this way. And it wouldn't be breaking," argued Bert. "I mean, there's no glass left in the windows. All we do—"

"Loitering with intent," said Copper.

"With intent to do what, my good man? You know there's nothing left to steal in those houses, so how could I be loitering with intent to steal?"

Copper was shaken for a moment by this logic. The he said, "You might be going to commit willful damage to the premises; or arson; or a nuisance."

"Keep it clean, mate," said Foxy.

"Well, what do you suggest? Isn't this why we chose the house? Have you any better ideas? The meeting is thrown open to discussion."

"I'm just telling you, that's all," said Copper stolidly.

Foxy snapped his fingers. "So what? If the Brain does get pinched for loitering or any of that crap, what's it matter? He'll be safe enough in the cooler, see—safer than in that bloody old ruin."

Bert rapped on the table. "No expletives, gentlemen, if you please. That's all very well, Foxy, but my mother wouldn't like me to be in prison."

"Your mother wouldn't like it if you were kidnaped, or they cut your throat."

"You've got something there," said Copper. . . .

His legalistic objections were to a plan that Bert should go to ground for a few days in one of a row of detached, bomb-damaged houses off Campden Hill Road. Things had been getting hot for the president of the Martian society. The bogus commercial traveler had not returned; but yesterday, a few hours after his visit, another man had come to the house, inquiring about lodgings. There were none vacant, Mrs. Hale told him. She did not tell him that he was, in any case, the class of lodger for whom she preferred not to cater. Unfortunately, his persistence got him into her sanctum on the ground floor—a sanctum adorned with photographs of Bert. As the visitor left, Bert, peering up from his den in the basement, caught an eyeful of him: it was the second of the two men who had accosted him in the Gardens—the unpalatable character with the knuckle-duster, called Fred.

No doubt, at this point, Bert should have told his mother the whole story. Left to himself, he would have done so. But by this time his fellow Martians had succumbed to a virulent attack of detection fever; and Bert, together with a boy's limited sense of realities, had a boy's exaggerated fear of betraying fear to his friends, particularly when he is their accepted leader. He knew that his influence over Foxy and Copper was one of brain rather than brawn, and that at any grave sign of weakness on his part they would very likely depose him or even gang up against him.

Bert's decision to hide out had been made only a quarter of an hour ago, and was the result of information brought to him hotfoot by his friends. Quite by chance, they had seen the red-faced "commercial traveler" walk out of a pub early this afternoon. They tracked him, at a respectful distance, from Notting Hill Gate up past the water tower along Campden Hill Road. Presently he turned left, and walking beside a row of bomb-damaged houses, stopped opposite one of them to light a cigarette. He then moved on, and caught a bus in Church Street, evading further pursuit.

On this being reported to Bert, he conceived a plan which

should, at one stroke, alleviate his own considerable trepidation about the red-faced man and establish himself in his friends' opinion as a tough and daring type. He would have insisted even more firmly on the necessity for his own temporary disappearance, had his friends been able to report a conversation which took place in the pub not long before they saw the red-faced man leaving it. He had, by tact, bonhomie, and plentiful treating, elicited from one of Mrs. Hale's lodgers a number of useful facts about the house—amongst them, the position of Bert's bedroom.

So now, Copper's objections (which were, as his father might have said, a purely routine matter) being swept aside, the three worked out ways and means by which Bert should be secreted and kept supplied in one of the derelict houses. The Martian Society had had its eye on the houses for some time, as a good hideout area in case of emergencies. The house in which they had decided to seclude Bert that evening was one they had previously chosen as ideal. It was concealed from the road by a shrubbery, and friends of theirs had often used it as an illicit playground, since it was the easiest house of that derelict row to break into. It was, in fact, easy to get into, as Foxy had proved, as a test. Across the waste ground at the back of the house there was a small, accessible, and unboarded window, which led into a pantry. Foxy had nipped in and out and had reported that there was nothing to it and that the place was suitable as a retreat place.

They would commandeer blankets and provisions from Bert's own house. Foxy would help him to get in the pantry window, after nightfall, while Copper kept *cave* outside.

"What'll your mum say?" asked Copper dubiously. "She'll raise hell when she finds you've run out on her, won't she?"

It was a thought which had occurred to Bert already. He was fond of his mother, and had no wish to cause her unnecessary anxiety.

"I'll leave a note to say we've gone to Battersea Pleasure Gardens and I'll be back late. Not to sit up for me."

"Yes, but what about tomorrow?"

"I'll give you another note, to leave in the letter box early tomorrow. I'll say—" Bert brooded a moment— "I'll say I've run away to sea."

"Don't be soft," remarked Foxy. "Why not say you've gone to the moon on a rocket? Just about as likely."

"You pipe down, Foxy, me lad," said Copper, who was apt unexpectedly to take Bert's side. "When you have the nerve to stay all night in a haunted house, you can talk."

"Haunted?" said Bert, after a pause.

"Well, I expect there was sudden death there. The land mine. Proper blew the lights out of those houses. It looks a spooky place, anyway. Just like that house in the flick we saw—*The Ghoul of Muttering Grange.*"

"Tactful, aren't you?" was Foxy's comment.

Up to this point, the scheme had been for Bert a bold, pleasing fantasy. Now he realized he was expected to go through with it, and the reality did not feel so agreeable: shades of the haunted house began to close around the growing boy. However, assuming an expression at once resolute and insouciant, he said, "I'll tell her I met Uncle James at the Pleasure Gardens and he invited me to stay with him a few nights. I've been there before."

No sooner had he said it than Bert perceived he had hit upon the perfect let-out. Although he had indeed stayed once with Uncle James at Wandsworth, he knew that his mother would at once make inquiries, and finding him not there, go to the police. The whole story would then have to come out, but in such a way that his friends could not possibly accuse him of having been windy; honor would be saved and peace of mind secured at one stroke. Bert looked up a little guiltily at Foxy and Copper, but they were regarding him with ill-concealed admiration.

"The Brain's got what it takes," said Copper.

The meeting then returned to the problem of Mr. Gray and his mail. Of the two letters Foxy had pinched the previous day, one was a printed announcement from a night club called The High Dive; the other was more enigmatic: type-written, without address or signature, it said:

> D. *street party off. Too hot. All laid on for Kingsway.*

The Martians stared at this message again, utterly baffled. It could not be innocent—otherwise it would have a signature at least.

"Look here," said Bert at last. "Suppose this chap is a master criminal. . . ."

Before the great bomb came gently swaying down on its parachute, the house had been a charming example of early Victorian domestic architecture, a small eligible property in a quiet road, embowered behind laurels and flowering shrubs, wisteria trained up its white stucco façade, with a veranda facing south at the back. The blast had taken off most of the roof, twisted into different, insane patterns the once elegant wrought-iron of balcony and grille, sucked out the window panes, and cracked the walls. Outside, the shrubs had grown dense and weeds proliferated: within there was a pervasive dankness, as though the house were still sweating with the fear of that terrible night.

Such of the furniture as was worth salvaging had long since been removed by the tenants. Children, playing on the waste ground nearby, where the rubble of the direct hit had been cleared away, had dared one another to enter the house and from time to time dismantled it further. The landlord being dead and his affairs in confusion, negotiations had only recently been concluded through which the house and its rickety neighbors were scheduled for clearance by the Borough Council.

It was this house which had been chosen by the red-faced man as a very temporary domicile for the murderer of Dai Williams. He, too, had realized that it was the best concealed of the derelict houses. It was less clean than ordinary condemned cell, but hardly less homey; and it had the advantage that a dead body could lie there for months with little risk of discovery. The red-faced man was only an intermediary, a link in the chain. He had received orders to find a suitable spot and arrange that the Quack should be there at a given time; he did not even know who the executioner would be. All he knew was that the Quack had outlived his usefulness to the organization, and indeed, now the police were hunting for him, could be a deadly danger to it—as great a danger, perhaps, as the man he had murdered. At any rate, Camden Town was too hot to hold the Quack just now; it had been decided, at short notice, that he must be moved—first moved, and then removed for good. What better place could there be for this final removal than a derelict house in a road of detached, derelict houses, where no one could overhear the Quack's last words? One with a lot of nice shrubs around it.

The red-faced man had been pleased with himself this afternoon—first, to have found the ideal spot on which the Quack could be put; and second, because it looked as if no trouble could be coming now through the Hale nipper. If the nipper, he argued, had gone to the police with his story, the police would be taking a keen interest in Mrs. Hale's lodging house and any strange visitors there. But he himself and Fred had both gone there without being picked up by the flatties. It had been a risk, of course, but they were paid well to take risks; they were less frightened of the police than of their own organization; and in any case, the police would have hell's own job proving they had done anything more than try to buy a boat from a nipper.

They were one jump ahead of the police, then, in knowing the whereabouts of the boy who had received Dai Williams' last message. It only remained to get hold of that message—the real one, not the phony screed which the little bleeder had fobbed off on them—to get hold of it one way or another, and he and Fred could indulge in a period of well-earned retirement. A quiet chat with young Hale was long overdue: Mrs. Hale's house would not be the most convenient one for the purpose, so the nipper would be taken elsewhere. It was all lined up. . . .

The Quack settled down in what had been the dining room of the derelict house off Campden Hill Road. It looked out upon the garden at the front—or would have looked out if the window had not been shuttered. He had got in after nightfall, without difficulty, through a window at the side—the boards nailed across it had worked loose—and selected his present room because it gave him a peephole onto the street and felt less damp than the others on the ground floor. His last shot of dope and the prospect of a new life filled him with exhilaration. An hour or two in a rotting house was a small price to pay for safety, let alone the future in another country which the organization had planned for him. Now that the police description of him had appeared in the papers, it was obviously time to fade. He would be picked up here, given papers and money, smuggled out of the country. He could leave all that to the organization, in which he had implicit confidence: indeed, he felt toward it as he would have felt, when a child, toward his father, had his father not died before he was born. It appeared to him all-wise and all-powerful; it made stern demands on him, which had to be obeyed, not questioned; it provided a sort of framework for his erratic, disintegrating life; it looked after him. When he was told to be here at a certain hour, without any identifiable possessions in his pockets, he accepted it for a wise, if slightly mysterious, piece of paternalism.

As an ex-public-schoolboy, the Quack retained the vestiges of a certain code—an attitude of mind which quite barred out the idea of betrayal by one's associates. It was his reassurance, and his undoing.

Copper had been sent to case the joint that afternoon to make sure everything was in order. He had eeled his way into the pantry and noted that the kitchen taps produced no water, that a tread was missing from the stairs which led up to the first floor, and that, on the damp-stained plaster of the kitchen wall, among other, less reticent writings, was an announcement "Dudley Jarvis goes with Rita Bloggs." He found the side door to the basement. It was not locked, but heavily bolted. He treated the bolts with some bicycle oil he had thoughtfully brought with him, but found it impossible to shift them. After nosing around a bit—the house had a disagreeable, charred smell, as though someone had started a fire which the damp had presently extinguished—Copper wrote on the wall "Foxy loves Lady Durbar," and took his departure.

Some five hours later, Bert and Foxy entered the house from the back. Copper himself was keeping *cave* in the road outside; he would give them five minutes, then go home. They lit a storm lantern which Foxy had acquired, laid out the blankets on the tiled floor of the kitchen, and opened the haversack. It contained four bottles of Coca-Cola, a loaf, two tins of pilchards, some cakes with vermilion icing, a slab of chocolate, and a science-fiction work—enough to last Bert till they refueled him tomorrow night. Foxy had agreed to stay with him for an hour, so that he could get acclimatized.

"Lovely place you've got here, Sir Albert," said Foxy. "Ring for the butler and let's have some champagne."

"Wish we could light a fire," said Bert. He was shivering already, though not entirely with the damp chill of the room.

"Plenty of loose wood about. Why shouldn't we?" said Foxy, shining his torch round the bedraggled room.

"Don't be a fool. They'd see the smoke."

They were still speaking in hoarse whispers, as though there might be someone else in the house.

"What's that?" asked Foxy. His torch beam had picked out a ledge and panel in the far wall.

"That's a serving hatch. Must be the dining room the other side."

"The idle rich. Our mum dishes up in the kitchen. I wonder what them Durbars are eating off their gold plates tonight," said Foxy dreamily. "Smashing judy, Lady Durbar is. I could go for her in a big way."

"Wasn't she in pantomime or something? My mother said—"

"Lady Durbar on ice. Bet she knocked 'em."

"Women are all right. But I shan't get married. It'd interfere with my scientific studies. A man's got to put his career first."

"I could do with one of those fancies. Makes you hungry, camping in a haunted house."

"You can have half," said Bert, breaking a cake. "It's my iron ration."

"Iron! You've said it," Foxy exclaimed, after biting into the delicacy. "Bent my best pair of false teeth on it."

They both giggled; then a sighing, strumming noise from outside began to fill up the silence—rain tapping and strumming faster on the dry leaves of the laurels. A loose board in a window somewhere gave one loud, peremptory rap.

"Postman's late tonight," said Foxy.

"Turn it up. That was the wind."

"So's this," said Foxy, belching resonantly. "Don't strike a light, there's an escape of gas!"

Presently Bert's resolution broke down, and he began to devour the food, ably assisted by Foxy. When they had eaten half of it, Bert looked at his watch. To his dismay, he realized they had been here less than an hour: it seemed ages, and the rest of the night stretched before him like an eternity.

"Well, I'll be drifting," Foxy said.

"Let's explore the house first." Anything to keep his friend with him a little longer, in this dark, dank tomb.

Bert took up the storm lantern: they sallied forth into the passage, and climbed the stairs, stepping carefully over the missing tread which Copper had reported. On the first landing, Bert stopped abruptly, with a little gasp of fear. The faint glow of the lantern had shown a door, and the door had moved—swung and stopped.

"See that?"

"It's the wind," whispered Foxy, with less than his normal confidence. "Drafty old dump, this."

The wind had indeed risen, flinging handfuls of rain

against the window shutters and sending drafts like scurrying rats along the passages. The boys pushed each other forward into the room whose door had swung open. It had been the drawing room once, long and elegant, three tall sash windows looking out over the top of the veranda onto the garden, where ladies in bustles, moving with the heraldic dignity of peacocks, had played croquet.

"Funny smell," said Bert.

"Corpses," said Foxy.

He shone his torch round the walls. The faded but still too exuberant patterns of the wallpaper, relic of some Edwardian tenant, writhed under the torch beam; here and there the paper had been torn away from the wall and hung like flaps of stained, flayed skin.

"If you're starving, you can always eat them things," said Foxy heartlessly, indicating some baleful-looking fungi growing on the skirting board in a corner. "Let's go."

They examined two little rooms on this floor, which yielded nothing but emptiness and rot. The staircase to the next floor was so rickety that they decided to go no farther; indeed, up here, it felt as if the whole house was swaying and tilting like their own shadows on the landing wall. Foxy executed a few jive steps, admiring his shadow, causing the floor to creak and the drawingroom door firmly to close itself. They started downstairs.

"Change and decay in all around I see," sang Foxy in a throaty contralto. The next moment, forgetting the missing tread, he had tripped, and tumbled down the remaining stairs into the hall. The hollow house clattered like a smithy; some flakes of plaster fell; then silence returned in a backwash so powerful, so engulfing, that Bert's heart seemed to stop beating under its influence. He opened his mouth to ask Foxy if he was hurt, but the silence stifled his voice.

And worse was to come. Foxy had picked himself up, jerked his head at the dining-room door.

"What's in there?" he said.

Bert tried the door. It gave a little, then stopped giving: in fact, it was almost as if it had pushed against him. He swallowed hard, before he could speak.

"No good," he said, "it's stuck," and quickly led the way back into the kitchen. He knew that he could not stay the night here now, until the mystery of that almost human pressure, on the other side of the door, had been solved. It must have been his imagination. "Bert's such an imaginative boy," his mother was always saying.

"Try that sliding panel, Foxy. The serving hatch thing. You can see into the room through it, if it'll move," he whispered.

Unlike the dining-room door, the panel did not stick. If flew open with alacrity. Foxy's torch beam, darting through, stopped dead on a dead-white face, two yards away from his own; a mouth hanging open, with a little saliva dribbling from one corner; eyes that seemed all whites, like a corpse's, glaring at him.

Foxy recoiled with a yelp of terror, bumping into Bert who was just behind him, and knocking the lantern out of his hand. By the time they had picked it up, and were halfway toward the window through which they had entered the house, a voice close behind them said, "Just a minute, boys. What's the hurry?"

A hand fell on Foxy's shoulder. He wriggled under it, then stopped wriggling; for in the man's other hand was a razor.

"Take it easy," said the man. "We'll have a nice, quiet talk. And when I say quiet, I mean quiet."

The razor carved the air caressingly, a foot from the boys' faces. Not that either of them had the breath to cry out: there was something about those pinpoint pupils, that hoarse, edged voice, which deflated their lungs. The man made a gesture, and they preceded him into the room whose door had so strangely resisted Bert's effort to open it. Bert became aware of a smell, different from the dank, charred smell of the house, yet also a smell like decay; he knew he had smelled it before, but he was too frightened to remember where, he did not want to remember where.

"Sit down, boys. Against the wall there. And put down your lantern in front of you. That's right."

The man receded into the gloom, between them and the door.

"You're not frightened of me, are you?" he said, his voice cajoling now, almost uncertain.

"No, sir," replied Bert.

"What were you doing in my house?"

"Camping," said Foxy. "Didn't know it was yours. I mean, we thought it was empty, see?"

"Ah, a boyish excapade. Doing it for a bet, were you?"

"Yes, sir."

"I heard one of you fall downstairs, didn't I? Not hurt, I hope? I used to— I'm a doctor, so if you've any cuts, sprains, bruises, you've come to the right shop. Is there a doctor in the house? I expect the last thing you thought you'd find in the house was a doctor."

The man gave a little giggle. Huddled together, backs to the wall, the boys felt each other trembling.

"Yes, sir. No, sir, I mean," quavered Bert.

"Where are you at school?"

Bert told him.

"I was a *public*-school man myself: before I became a surgeon, of course. Funny thing, you know, I always wanted to be a surgeon. Even at school. They used to call me 'the Quack.' Have you two got nicknames?"

"I'm Foxy and we call Bert 'the Brain.'"

"Ah. Clever type, eh? What's your subject?"

"Well, I'm keen on science, sir."

"Good show. There's a future in science. I remember a beak saying to me. . . ."

What shook Foxy to the wick, as he told Bert afterward, was the way the man went on talking: he just couldn't stop; it was like listening to a mad, boring scoutmaster palavering over a campfire. The chap was obviously nuts—you could see it in his eyes, which were wildly excited yet didn't seem to look at anything, and in the way his face sagged and twitched. Well, the only thing was to humor him. He couldn't go on forever.

Bert's reactions, meanwhile, were different. His fright temporarily ebbing, allowed his mind to work again. And the first thing it fastened on was the idea that the man must have been as scared by them as they were of him. Why, otherwise, should he have stayed lurking in this room while they were moving about overhead? Why hold the door shut just now? Perhaps it was sheer relief that made him go on gassing away like this. The man had clearly not wanted them to discover his presence in the house; but, now they had discovered it, he was taking good care they shouldn't give the alarm. No doubt he was relieved to find that the people he had heard moving about were only two boys. The man must be hiding up here, just as Bert was: he couldn't be just a tramp; he was—

And, in a lurid flash, Bert realized who this man was. The smell in the room was the same smell, stale and rancid, which he had noticed, on his way to the Round Pond last Sunday, when a man with a prancing gait had brushed past him. That encounter had been quite forgotten. Even the picture in the paper this morning, of a man whom the police wished to interview in connection with the murder of Dai Williams, had not rung a bell with Bert. But now, covertly glancing at the Quack as he talked on and on, reminiscing about school days and hospital days, Bert realized that he was in a room, in a derelict house out of human call, with a murderer.

He tugged Foxy's sleeve. The man's apparently unseeing eyes caught the movement.

"Don't fidget!" he said sharply. He was fidgety enough himself, though, Bert noticed: as he talked he pranced up and down the room; or leaned against the door, his head jerking, the hand which had held the razor plucking at his lower lip. He was like a restless marionette.

Bert did not dare whisper to Foxy. The knowledge he dared not impart swelled in him painfully, till he felt he must yell it out or burst. At last, when the man stopped his flow of talk for a minute, Bert put up his hand, as if he were in class, and said, "Please, sir, may we go home now?"

"Not yet, boys. I've got a friend coming to fetch me. Be here any moment now. Like you to meet him. I expect you're wondering what I'm doing here. Well, chaps—Brain and Foxy—I'll tell you." The man's tongue flickered over his lips. "I used to live here, you see. Happiest days of my life. When I was your age. I'm going abroad, you see. Going to start a new life. And I thought I'd pay a last pilgrimage to the old place, before I left."

"Were you here when the place was blitzed?" asked Foxy. Anything to humor this crackpot.

The man started talking again: bomb stories now. Foxy relaxed. Not so, Bert. Bert could feel his nerve fraying, fraying, as if the secret within him was sawing at it. Suddenly, as the Quack's to-and-fro pacing took him away from the door, Bert heard himself whimper, was on his feet, making a dart for it. An arm, that seemed to elongate like a shadow, shot out and hurled him back across the room. His head struck the wall. He thought he was going to be sick.

"No you don't, my Brain." The man's face, gray-white as a fungus, hovered over him. There were streaks of light in the gloom, which Bert's swimming eyes could not at first identify.

"Stop waving that razor about, you bastard," said Foxy, loud and clear. It diverted the Quack's attention, anyway. He turned on Foxy.

"Have you every had a tonsillectomy?"

"Come again."

"Have you had your tonsils out?"

Foxy shook his head.

"Well, you will, damned soon, if you and your young friend don't behave. Without anesthetics."

In the silence that followed, a seed of sound began to germinate. A car engine. The car must be coming up Campden Hill Road. Then the car stopped, some way off.

"I dare say that'll be my friend. If it is, we shall have to lock you in here. If you keep *quite* quiet, we shall only lock you in. I prescribe absolute silence, you understand—before, during, and after. Otherwise I shall have to operate."

Bert and Foxy froze. They could feel the pulses in their temples ticking as loud as giant clocks. After another eternity, there came a tap on the shutters—a light tap, but it made the boys start as if it had been an explosion.

"Remember what I said? Not a move. Not a sound."

"Yes, sir."

The man was at the window, fingering the shutters. Through the chink, he muttered something they could not catch; it might have been a password.

"O.K., Quack. Open up," came a low voice from outside; not too low, though, for the boys to miss the American accent of the speaker. The Quack, with one threatening glance at them, folded back the shutters. They saw a cylindrical object poke in suddenly out of the night. They heard it give a quick, thudding cough. The Quack's hands gripped the shutters, as if against a whirlwind blowing into the room. His head was punched back on his shoulders: it seemed to have gone out of shape. Then, slow as the start of a landslide, he began falling to the floor.

7

Rapiers and Bludgeons

It was the morning of Friday, August 6th. Nigel Strangeways strolled toward Clare Massinger's studio, chewing over what Inspector Wright had just told him. Four boys had been reported missing in the London area since the murder of Dai Williams, but three had already been found and none of the four corresponded with the boy Nigel had met in the Gardens; he was sure of this, after studying their photographs. The inference seemed clear. Either Dai Williams' murderers had found the boy, and terrorized him into silence after getting possession of the message; or else they were still looking for him. The former was more likely. Dai Williams would surely have indicated in his message that it should be passed on to the police. Why had the boy not done so, then, unless he had been frightened off it? Well, perhaps he and his young friend were trying some amateur detection: the lad called "Foxy" might be in it; but Foxy had not returned to the studio after the rencontre with Alec Gray.

More to Inspector Wright's immediate purpose was the disappearance of the Quack. Every policeman in the country had his description: his photograph was in the papers; his movements had been traced to a Camden Town lodging house. But this he had left two days ago, and the trail petered out. There was just the "information received" from a member of the general public, who had seen a man leave Kensington Gardens shortly after the murder, been struck by his peculiar walk and appearance, and identified him from the

Scotland Yard files. But the Quack had vanished off the face of the earth.

Remembering his recent interview with Sam Borch, Inspector Wright was uneasy. He relied, more than he would admit to himself, on intuition. When he had questioned Borch about Herbert James, known to some as "the Quack," he had received no impression of fear, guilt, or protective reserve on Borch's part. It was Wright's experience that, if you touched a criminal on his sore spot, you always got some perceptible reaction: it might be an outburst of crude bluster; or only a sort of slight drawing in, as it were, of the sensitive horns. Mention of Alec Gray had produced this reaction from Borch; mention of the Quack had not. Yet there ought to be a tie-up between Dai Williams, Borch, and Gray. Why else had Williams been killed?

Chewing it over now, Nigel found himself mentally biting on a piece of grit. Dai Williams, nosing after Sam Borch, had got onto a character he called "the toff." Gray fitted in with this character: at least, he was a young man about town who had been in an excellent position to give inside information about households where burglaries had, in fact, recently taken place. Borch was suspected of being a receiver. Gray frequently visited Borch's night club. So far, so good. But did the murder of Dai Williams really fit in? A gang, or more than one gang, was active on these thefts; but gangs concerned in burglary did not, as a rule, carry violence to the point of planned murder. They would cosh a night watchman: they might certainly terrorize a suspected informer—beat him up or razor him. What seemed unlikely was that they should use a dope-fiend ex-doctor to kill this informer. The method of Dai Williams' murder ruled out any chance that it had been intimidation which accidentally went too far. Was it not possible, then, that Dai Williams' secret related to something quite different? that, following up one kind of criminal, Dai had fortuitously stumbled over a more sinister, a far more dangerous kind?

When Clare Massinger let Nigel into her studio, he found

the throne occupied by a regal figure. Lady Hesione Durbar had put on weight, perhaps, since her theater days: but she had the gift of vitality in repose; her deep blue eyes were unclouded by the petulance or ennui of the rich, spoiled woman, and the merciless north light could find no fault with her shoulders, bared for the sitting, shapely and pure as snow-drifts. She was a great enjoyer of life, evidently; and, Nigel quickly realized, a frank enjoyer of male company. She began to flirt with him almost as soon as they were introduced—to flirt in the grand manner, like a stage queen with the ambassador of some major foreign power. The great eyes opened wide to engulf him, the lovely blond head lifted and consciously poised itself for his admiration.

"Don't forget," said Clare Massinger sharply. "You've lost the pose. Head down a little, please. That's better."

Hesione Durbar gave Nigel an arrant wink, revealing the gamine beneath the stately façade. He noticed that Clare was pummeling and thwacking the clay with more than her usual aggressiveness. Her sharp, narrow-eyed scrutinies of the sub-ject had something witch-like about them.

"Be careful you don't give me a thick ear, darling," said Lady Durbar. Then, to Nigel, "You've tried this, Mr. Strangeways, haven't you? Face massage by proxy?"

"Yes, I'm sitting for Clare now. It's an odd experience, watching one's double emerging out of a lump of clay. Have you seen Foxy again?"

"Foxy? Oh, that angel child who gate-crashed my party. You've come across him too, have you?"

"You know he gate-crashed in here, the morning after it? Pursued by a boor?"

Clare shot Nigel a warning glance, which he refused to accept. "Yes, a young neighbor of Clare's. What's his name?"

"Gray," said Clare abruptly.

"Not Alec? What was he doing here?"

"Oh, I'm sorry. You know him, Lady Durbar? He seemed to be suffering from a delusion that this Foxy was spying on him. He was remarkably aggressive. Clare had to throw a lump of clay at him. Why *should* he think he was being spied on?''

"You never told me this, Clare," said Hesione.

"Well, no," Clare uncomfortably replied.

"Now I must get this straight. I'm pretty well a moron, so just please explain in simple words what happened, Mr. Strangeways, will you?"

Mr. Strangeways explained. Lady Durbar listened attentively, her red mouth a little open, showing the small, regular teeth.

"But how utterly weird! What can Alec have been thinking of?" she said, when Nigel had finished. Her voice now sounded artificial, synthetic—the accent of the actress overlaying her natural tones. She seemed, thought Nigel, more disturbed than the story warranted, and it gave her face a stupid expression.

"I think we'd better stop." Clare said, laying down her tools. "I can't work if we're going to have a *conversazione*."

"Sorry, love. It's my fault. Look, will you come to lunch, and bring Mr. Strangeways with you?"

"Well, actually—" began Clare.

"We'd simply love to. It's most kind of you, Lady Durbar," Nigel broke in, administering to Clare a sort of covert, ocular kick.

"Now what are you up to?" Clare asked, when her patron had swept out. "First you ruin a sitting for me, and then you involve me in a lunch party I just haven't time for."

"I'm interested in the glamorous Lady Durbar."

"So I noticed."

"You look very beautiful, prowling up and down with your hair swirling, and spitting with rage."

"I must say you put your flat feet in it all right. Didn't you know Alec Gray was her Ladyship's fancy man?"

"Of course I knew. I've intrigued her. That's why she asked a total stranger to lunch on the spur of the moment."

"You flatter yourself. Well, I suppose I'd better get on with you, as you've driven out my millionaire client. But you really are maddening, Nigel."

Presently, as he sat on the chair vacated by Hesione Durbar, and Clare Massinger was scraping little slivers of clay from the head, he surprised her by saying, "You're inordinately interested in the Durbars' burglary."

"Am I?" Clare absently replied.

"Yes. You're going to be quite a bore about it at lunch. You simply won't be able to keep off the subject."

"Why?"

"Because Nanny says so. It's a star part I am offering you. The beautiful, slinky *agente provocatrice*."

"Chin up a little. Head a shade to the left. What is this nonsense you're talking?"

"I'm going to plunge you into reality, my little Ivory Towerist. Full instructions will be given you presently."

"Bossy old bastard," she grumbled. . . .

Over the top of his Martini, Nigel studied Sir Rudolf Durbar. The great man was leaning back at one end of a sofa, being immensely agreeable to Clare Massinger. He had charm—no doubt of that; but one felt it was cultivated rather than innate: it was not exactly turned on, but as it were laid on, like all the other amenities of this fabulous house—part of a pattern of life which would include, for example, Nigel imagined, Sir Rudolf's instructing his secretary to choose a suitable present for Lady Hesione's birthday. To the general public, Sir Rudolf was a man of mystery; his yacht, his magnificent houses, his wife and her parties, the huge yet unobtrusive philanthropies—all these were familiar to anyone who could read a newspaper. But only a very small circle knew about his origins, or the exact nature and extent of his ramifying "interests" in Europe, the United States, and the Middle East, while fewer still had any intimate knowledge of the man himself. Behind the façade of wealth and power, he worked as anonymously as a revolutionary. He did not, in the traditional manner of his kind, call attention to himself either by personal asceticism or exorbitant ostentation. His appetites, no less than his opinions, seemed to be moderate. The word "cosmopolitan" fitted him as well as any other, if it can be taken to define the man who is at ease everywhere and at home nowhere, who has innumerable contacts but no allegiance. He did not appear to make a fetish of work or a business of pleasure. Nigel was not the first student of human nature to find himself wondering what made Sir Rudolf Durbar tick.

A secretary came in, whispering discreetly to his employer, "New York on the telephone, Sir Rudolf."

"What? No, not now. Tell them I'll call back after lunch. No, wait a minute—you handle it, Charles. You know the set-up."

It was rather impressive—the informality, the decentralization, the light, quick tones of the resonant voice. Nigel toyed with the fantasy of some gigantic merger, tottering in the balance like a caber, tossed to the gratified secretary to deal with.

"No wonder we're nearly bankrupt," Lady Durbar whispered to him, a certain affectionate pride in her voice. "Rudolf hates people ringing up at mealtimes."

"Drake hated people who interrupted his game of bowls."

Hesione slapped him on the arm; it was a habit carried over from her unregenerate days; one expected a whoop of shrill, coarse laughter to go with it. "Oh, Drake was an old pirate," she protested.

Meaning, thought Nigel, that she fancies Sir Rudolf as a bit of an old pirate himself.

Sir Rudolf was giving Clare his attention, arguing animatedly with her about the technical merits of a recent work by Epstein. His broad, square shoulders; the head, with its strong nose and deep-set eyes, firmly set upon them; the bronze complexion—all contributed to a sculptural effect, an effect of mass, weight, solidity—of something carved out of one block, primitive yet subtle. Nigel wondered how Hesione Durbar could have found an acceptable substitute for this in the crude, brutal Alec Gray, and wondered still more that Sir Rudolf should permit it. One could not for a moment imagine him being hoodwinked; nor, on the other hand, did his attitude to Hesione give any grounds for supposing that their relationship was extinct, or that he despised her and was beyond caring what she did.

At lunch, when Clare opened up a vein of chatter about the robbery, Nigel was conscious of Sir Rudolf's eyes turned speculatively upon him: their gaze was a little arrogant and extremely shrewd; one felt that Sir Rudolf could quite effortlessly keep a jump ahead of any rival, and would make a formidable adversary.

"But, my dear," Hesione was saying, "anyone'd think it was me who'd committed a felony. Those wonderful policemen of ours keep nagging me about having had a cannibal party at all. They say it was asking for trouble."

"So it was, darling," said her husband pleasantly.

"And they've asked me fifty times, if they've asked me once, whose idea it was. And now the insurance people are being beastly about it too."

"They have to go into these things."

"You mean," said Clare, "whoever suggested that sort of fancy-dress affair, with blackened faces, may be an accomplice of the burglars?"

"Exactly! And it's quite idiotic. It was either Rudie's idea or mine—niether of us is quite sure which."

"Then the police started up about Alec. Did Alec put the idea into my head? Did Alec know the safe combination?"

"Oh come, my dear, they didn't put it quite like that."

"Well, it was obvious who they meant. Any intimate friends of the family, or frequent guests—you know—the usual patter of big boots."

"And did he?" asked Clare in her forthright way.

"Did who what?"

"Did Alec know the combination? or anyone else?"

Lady Durbar sipped her Moselle, holding the glass cupped in both hands, like a child. "I've no notion," she said carelessly.

"You really are impossible, Hess," said her husband, laughing.

Clare remarked, "I do believe you rather admire your wife for taking it all so lightly."

"Perhaps I do."

"Rudie has been wonderful about it." Hesione exchanged a long glance with her husband.

"Well, they were your jewels, after all," he said.

There was a lull in the conversation, while another course was handed round. Then Clare began again. "It must be queer, having policemen on the premises. What do they do?—take everyone's fingerprints?"

Sir Rudolf's quick, deep voice bore in. "You should ask Mr. Strangeways. He knows all about police work, Miss Massinger."

Clare's surprise was none the less convincing for being quite genuine. And a good thing too, thought Nigel.

"*You* know all about *police* work?" she said to him, in great astonishment.

"Not all. A little."

Both women were gazing at him with the bright, encouraging look of aunts who have discovered an unexpected talent in a rather moderately endowed small nephew.

"Why have you never told me this?" pursued Clare.

"Mr. Strangeways," remarked their host affably, "hides his light under a bushel."

"But not from you, apparently," Clare said.

Nigel observed, "Sir Rudolf is a very well-informed man."

"You know, Hess, you ought to get Strangeways to investigate this robbery of yours. If he's not too busy now. He's pretty hot, by all accounts."

"Well, of course. But—" There was a puzzled look in

Lady Durbar's liquid blue eyes. "I mean, do you do it for a sort of hobby?"

"Oh no. I get paid."

"How much?" asked Clare, and the others broke into laughter.

The talk turned to the visit of the Soviet delegation. Sir Rudolf again proved himself an exceptionally well-informed man. He had friends in high place, from whom he had gathered much—perhaps rather too much—about the scope and course of the negotiations. He talked knowledgeably, incisively, and, for a man to whom communism must represent everything he held least sacred, dispassionately. He summed up shrewdly the personalities of those who were leading the discussions, though beneath the surface there was a faint undertone of brusqueness, contempt almost—the attitude of the business mogul toward politicians who pretend to be directing the world's affairs but are themselves pawns in the hands of a higher power. One inferred that this higher power was history, operating through the almighty dollar. Sir Rudolf and Lady Hesione, it came out, were going to a reception this evening at which the Russian Minister would be present.

"Yes," she gaily said, "you could have knocked me down with a feather when Rudie accepted. It's like the Archbishop of Canterbury gracing a garden party at a brothel."

"Oh, do they have garden parties?" asked Clare.

Sir Rudolf was not amused. His heavy, bronze-brown face flushed darker, and he said to his wife, "Don't be a fool, my dear." Then, less brusquely, "You don't understand these things. One can't always choose one's company."

"Rudie has a Watch-Committee streak," she said, after a slight pause, to her guests. "He still finds me rather shocking sometimes. But he likes it really—don't you, my pet?"

"I suppose," said Nigel presently, "that any successful moves toward world peace—a plan for progressive disarmament, for instance—are bound to create new economic problems."

Sir Rudolf gave him a heavy-lidded, skeptical look, but said nothing. Nigel went on, "Look how the steel and nickel markets slumped last year, just at a breath of a possibility of better international relations."

His host bit the end off a cigar, then sighted it at Nigel. "You study the markets?"

"I notice they're as sensitive as prima donnas."

Sir Rudolf gave a couple of noncommittal grunts, applying his cigar to a massive table lighter.

"And," Nigel continued, "particularly, just now, at the idea of peace. You only have to mention it, and they go off into a swoon. I suppose that's why the newspapers insulate the world 'peace' with quotation marks—to prevent the poor dear markets getting a shock."

"The poor, dear financiers, you mean?"

Nigel shrugged. "Disarmament would hit some of them pretty hard, I imagine."

Sir Rudolf gave him a cursory look, which seemed to measure him and throw him back into the water.

"The work 'peace' is insulated, as you put it, because all these so-called 'peace movements' are a fraud—Communist-inspired—to weaken moral resistance and political co-operation in the West."

"*All* of them? Including the P.M.'s invitation to these discussions that are going on now?"

"Oh, that's quite different. Nobody in his senses could object to them."

"Then there must be a lot of people out of their senses."

Sir Rudolf was glowering at him. "I don't understand you."

"All these incidents that have been taking place. They're obviously organized, don't you think?"

"I dare say. Organized by a few crackpots. They mean precisely nothing." Sir Rudolf dismissed the crackpots with a wave of his cigar, and rose from the table.

In the drawing room Lady Durbar, beckoning Nigel to a sofa beside her, turned upon him the full voltage of her deep blue eyes.

"What about it?" she asked. "Will you come and find these burglars for me?"

"But, you know, the police are infinitely better equipped for that sort of thing."

"Even when it's what they call an inside job?"

"Do *you* think it is?" he asked, after a little pause.

Her eyes glanced aside from Nigel. He noticed the handkerchief, balled tight in her left hand, and a delicious waft of perfume. "I just don't know," she helplessly murmured. Then, lower still, as if to herself, "I don't mind losing the jewels, if I don't also have to lose my faith in—" Her voice trailed away altogether.

"Your faith?" Nigel prompted. "You do suspect somebody? Well, it'd be better to know, one way or another, than to go on worrying, wouldn't it?"

"Yes," she repeated childishly, "I want to know. I simply must know."

"Well then—"

"But I'm not—I can't go sicking it all up to the police." Her voice had become rich and vibrant again, and there was the faintest stress on the last word.

"What are you two conspiring about?" asked Sir Rudolf from the other side of the room.

"I'm trying to interest Mr. Strangeways in a valuable robbery."

"And is he interested?"

Nigel smoothed back the tow-colored hair from his forehead, looking worried. "I am. But I've got a rather full-time job on my hands just now."

"Oh, do tell us about it," said Hesione. "Or must it be a secret?"

"I'm looking for a boy."

"Has he been kidnaped or something?"

"Not yet."

"How very sinister this sounds!"

"Do you mean that boy Foxy?" asked Clare.

"No. It's a boy who has come into possession of some knowledge which might lead the police to a murderer."

Nigel paused. His audience were all attention.

"Oh, poor little boy," exclaimed Hesione.

"Has he disappeared, then?" her husband asked.

"Not exactly. But it's difficult, trying to find one boy among the whole population of London."

Sir Rudolf leaned forward. "You mean, I take it, that you're the only person who could identify this boy?"

"The only person on the side of the Law, yes. There's a couple of thugs after him too, who know what he looks like." Nigel proceded to tell them, with certain reservations, the story of the boy he had rescued in Kensington Gardens. When he had finished, Sir Rudolf slapped his knee.

"That must be the murder you read out to me in the paper the other day, Hess. What was the fellow's name? Williams. Dai Williams. But I thought they knew now who'd done it, Strangeways. They published a description of a fellow they want to interview, didn't they, yesterday?"

"Well, this message the boy received—the police think it may be the key to—to a very considerable conspiracy which they've got wind of."

"Why don't they advertise for the boy, then?"

"Afraid it might lead to *his* being bumped off, I suppose."

Clare's eyes, dark velvety as pansies, were regarding Nigel strangely. "And what about you?" she said. "This is all absurdly melodramatic; but I should have thought you were in danger yourself."

"I expect I am," Nigel equably answered.

At this point, the secretary came in to say that Sir Rudolf was wanted on the telephone.

"Oh, it's Marchbanks, is it? I'd better talk to him. Will you excuse me a few minutes?"

When Sir Rudolf returned, Nigel and Clare got up to say good-by. But their host pressed them to stay a little and look at some of his pictures. He would send Clare back in his car, so that she could resume work on schedule. They refused this offer, Nigel saying he would escort Miss Massinger home after they had inspected the pictures. These, in a long gallery on the first floor, proved rewarding enough, though none was quite the equal of a superb Van Dyck which Sir Rudolf fetched from another room.

"Can't think why the burglars didn't lay hands on this, while they were about it," he said.

"Too difficult to get rid of, I imagine."

As they walked back along Church Street, Clare was rather silent. At last she said, "It's fantastic. I've known you off and on for four years, and I had no notion you—"

"My dear, why should you? You're an artist. You're interested in everything to do with that, and you shut everything else out. Very right and proper. The artist has quite enough distractions nowadays without—well, anyway, I don't want you dabbling in crime."

"But that's just what you made me do, isn't it, putting me up to be inquisitive about the Durbars' burglary?"

Nigel laughed. "Oh, that's not crime. That's chickenfeed."

"Well, if you won't tell me, you won't." Clare pouted, looking much younger than her twenty-six years. Presently she said, "You don't seem to be doing much about this boy you're supposed to be searching for."

"That remains to be seen," was Nigel's somewhat enigmatic reply.

In one sense, it did not remain long. As the pair emerged from the passage into Clare's courtyard, a hand was clamped over her mouth, and a cosh fell with hideous force upon Nigel's head. Clare saw the man who had struck him bend over Nigel to strike again. She managed, wriggling convulsively with all the strength of her wiry body, to wrench herself from the man who held her, and went tooth and nail for Nigel's assailant, screaming at the top of her voice. She had never known she could go berserk like this. Seizing a dustbin lid, she stood, like some Amazon in a classic battle frieze, over Nigel's recumbent body. Both the attackers had handkerchiefs covering the lower part of their faces. Screaming for help still, she kicked out viciously at one and bashed the dust-bin lid at the other's eye.

It was over almost as soon as it had begun. Help came—

from an unexpected quarter. Alec Gray leaped out into the yard, sent one man reeling with a savage blow to the side of the head, and closed with his comrade, who broke free after a brief struggle, and the two shot away through the door, with Gray in pursuit.

"No good," he said, returning in a minute. "The blighters had a car outside. Clean getaway. Did they rob you?"

Clare shook her head mutely, pointed at Nigel, and to her own fury burst into tears. They put a coat under Nigel's head—his heart was beating, though faintly—and Gray went to ring for a doctor and the police. Dark hair streaming, eyes streaming with tears, Clare knelt beside Nigel. Her mind felt wispy, empty. The attack might have been a bad dream. She heard someone say, "Please, God, don't let him die," over and over again, and discovered that it was her own voice.

One's reactions were all so unimaginable. When Alec Gray returned, and they had satisfied themselves that Nigel was still breathing, Clare's first words were, "You've caught the sun badly."

"What? Oh yes. I drove up from Southampton this morning. Just got back for lunch. In the nick, as they say, of time."

Gray's shirt had been torn in the struggle, and Clare had seen a bright-red triangle of sunburn to the left of the base of his throat; the inside of his right forearm was the same color. It's the sort of thing I *would* notice at a time like this, she thought. Bloody, self-centered artist. My little Ivory Towerist. Oh God! that's what Nigel called me. Observing the pigmentation of skin when a man—when he is lying there, dying there perhaps.

"Don't glare at me like that, my poppet. *I* didn't do it."

"Sorry," said Clare, kneeling beside Nigel, her fingers trailing against his face. "It wasn't meant for you."

"I'm going to get you a stiff drink," said Alec Gray.

8

The Aftermath

On this same Friday morning, after Nigel left him, Inspector Wright had been trying to catch up with a mass of routine work. Among other reports which he was perusing, one specially caught his attention. At eleven forty-nine the previous night, in answer to a call, a Flying Squad car had proceeded to a house off Ladbroke Square. The occupant, a widow named Hale, had been sitting up for her son, a boy of twelve, who had gone with two friends to the Battersea Pleasure Gardens. At about eleven-thirty, hearing movements on the floor below, she left her room, thinking it was her son returning. He had a key to the back door. Going down the basement, where his bedroom was, she called out, "Is that you, Bertie? You're very late." There was no reply. She tried the bedroom door, but found it locked. She then woke up one of the lodgers, to help her break down the door. However, when they had got downstairs again, they found the door unlocked and the bedroom empty. Investigation shortly discovered a window at the back of the house which had been forced open. Mrs. Hale then telephoned for the police.

What caught Inspector Wright's eye in the report on this apparently trivial occurrence was Mrs. Hale's statement, corroborated by the lodger, that on entering the bedroom they had noticed a faint smell of chloroform. The Flying Squad men asked her if any articles were missing. None, it appeared, but some blankets from the boy's bed and a few tins of meat. The natural inference was that a vagrant had broken in, and been surprised. Mrs. Hale was in some distress that the boy had not yet returned, though he had left her a message not to wait up for him. However, following the policeman's instructions, she had rung up Divisional H.Q. today, saying that her son was safe at home; he had returned in the small hours, tired out, having missed the last bus and been compelled to walk all the way, with his friends, carrying the blankets and a haversack of food which he had taken, so he said, for a picnic at the Pleasure Gardens.

Inspector Wright raised his eyebrows momentarily at this last part of the statement; but the ways of small boys are sometimes past understanding, and he let it go. What interested him was that whiff of chloroform—a commodity not usually carried by vagrants. As the boy had been out of the house for several hours when his mother entered the bedroom, it could not be accounted for by his love of chemistry; nor had the Flying Squad men found a leaky bottle or impregnated rag in the room. There was just one chance in a hundred that a kidnaping attempt had been made.

So Wright instructed a detective-sergeant and sent him off to Mrs. Hale's house. He also rang up Nigel, found he was out, and left a message for him to call back as soon as he got home. Afterward, the Inspector never quite forgave himself for not following up this hunch in person. Yet it would be difficult for anyone else to blame him—a tired-out man fighting one sector of a crime wave with depleted forces—because he deputed to a subordinate officer a task which, by all the odds, would turn out a wild-goose chase.

Unfortunately this officer, though a worthy and conscientious individual, had two disqualifications for his present job: he lacked the particular kind of imagination which can enter into a boy's responses and thought processes; and years on the beat, before he graduated to the detective branch, had given him a ponderous, formidable professional manner.

His first remark, when he entered the room where Bert Hale was still in bed, frightened and feverish, properly tore it.

"Well, son," he said, kindly at heart but Jehovah-like in manner, "you been in trouble?"

For a boy who had spent hours in that rotting house off the Campden Hill Road, been frightened out of his wits by the obscene Quack, and then stunned by the spectacle of the man shot before his eyes—the head blown out of shape, the blood everywhere—this question was paralyzing. Bert knew, of course, that he had not, in fact, murdered the Quack. But he felt himself involved: the blood, the guilt, the anxiety of it had seeped into his mind like a thick fog. His mind, struggling hard to maintain its balance, selected one real, though trivial, aspect from the whole irrational pile of guilt which weighed upon it—namely, his having broken into a house and lied to his mother. He could feel bad about this, reproach himself for it; and as long as he concentrated upon it, he could keep the major horrors at bay. But the appearance of this policeman seemed to reopen the flood gates. Bert was sure he had come to arrest him for breaking into a house, for murder perhaps. Cowering under the bedclothes, he said, "No. No, sir."

"Out on the tiles last night, weren't you, son?" said the Sergeant, in what he fondly imagined was a jovial tone, though to Bert it sounded like the crack of doom.

"Yes, sir. I—we missed the last bus."

"Your mum was very worried about you, I expect."

Bert's lips quivered at this unconsciously devastating thrust. He could not answer.

"Well now, Bert—Bert's the name, isn't it? I've not come to talk about that. Let bygones by bygones, I always say." Sitting on the bed, the Sergeant theatrically relaxed. "You're a bit of an engineer, I hear. Model boats, and such-like, eh?"

"Yes, I'm keen on models," replied Bert suspiciously.

"Sail 'em on the Round Pond, I suppose?"

Bright and frightened as a guinea pig's, Bert's eyes regarded the Sergeant from above the bedclothes. He nodded.

"Now what I've come to ask you, old man—we've had complaints about two rough customers trying to steal boys' boats from them. Wondered if you'd had any trouble of that sort."

The Sergeant smiled, in self-congratulation on this splendidly tactful approach. To Bert, it looked like the grin of a ravenous alligator. The whole dire chain of events rose up in his mind, ready to bind him hand and foot if he admitted one link of it. He just could not be sensible about this. He felt absolutely certain that, once he had told this bobby about the speedboat, everything else would come out; and from such revelations he shrank with all the accumulated fear of his small being.

"Oh no, sir," he said.

"You're quite sure, son? No need to be frightened. We wouldn't let 'em do anything to you, if that's what worries you."

"Quite sure," lied Bert, swallowing hard.

"Any of your young friends been pestered?"

"No, sir."

The Sergeant asked him a good many more questions. But Bert had begun to feel some command of the situation; with a schoolboy's deadly instinct for a teacher's weak spot, he now sensed that there was no real confidence behind the Sergeant's interrogation. Had this worthy man taken Bert into his confidence, told him that the whole police force of London was looking for Dai Williams' message and that maybe Britain's fate depended upon it, Bert would have seen himself as the hero of the piece, and come clean. But the Sergeant had no vein of fantasy; nor would he ever rid himself now of the orthodoxy that a detective's job is to ask questions, not to give information. He had a short talk with Mrs. Hale, borrowed her most recent photograph of Bert, and took his departure.

Bert lay back in bed, feeling very shaky again. The events of last night kept passing, like a stage army, before his inward eye. Had they left any clues behind? After the shot had been fired and the horrible man had crumpled at their feet, Bert and Foxy froze for minutes, expecting the unseen murderer to enter the house. That was the worst part of all, because, once he found them there, he'd be bound to shoot them—he just could not afford to have two eyewitnesses of the crime left alive. But minutes, that seemed hours, passed, and no fatal footsteps did they hear—only snatches of gusty rain against the half-open shutters, the house corruptly muttering to itself, wind moaning like miniature air-raid sirens through keyholes and under doors. Presently the pair had plucked up courage, and crept out of the room, Foxy bearing the storm lantern, into the kitchen. Without a word to each other, they repacked the haversack, picked up the blankets, and left the house by the way they had entered.

But now Bert was remembering the crumbs they must have left on the floor, the empty Coca-Cola bottles they had certainly forgotten to remove; and the fingerprints. On their way back, Foxy had sworn him to silence. Foxy would write an anonymous letter to the police, telling them where to look for the body, but beyond that he was not sticking his neck out.

Mrs. Hale came in. Her son looked feverish, sort of haunted. She hoped he had not caught a chill from getting so wet last night; the thermometer only showed a slight rise of temperature, however. The best thing would be to pack him off to her sister in Essex for the week end, to get some country air and farm produce. For once, Bert showed considerable enthusiasm at the project. Mrs. Hale, after absently smoothing his hair, went off to telephone; she was a worried woman: it did a landlady no good, having the police in and out; and last night—what with the tramp breaking in and Bert giving her such a fright—had upset her terribly. Well, Bert was like his poor dad: secretive, never told you anything till his lordship thought fit—no use nagging at him. She never knew half what went on in that funny head of his. But he was straight—she'd take her oath on that, against all the coppers in London.

When Foxy turned up, early that afternoon, he was told that Mrs. Hale had taken Bert to a relation in the country, and would not be home again herself till suppertime. He considerably startled the daily by saying to her, "Don't you tell no one where he's gone, see? It's important. Specially no smoothies that come to the door."

"We had a cop here this morning," she informed him. "Ever so nosy. And a burglar last night."

"Coo, aren't you seeing life, Madeleine! Now remember what I told you. Not a word to anyone about Bert, or I won't answer for the consequences. Be seeing you."

The daily gaped after him, dim-witted, but seriously impressed. . . .

Clare Massinger was not to get any work done this afternoon. First there had been the doctor, who did not seem at all happy about Nigel; it might be only severe concussion, but there might be a lesion of the brain. Then the ambulance came, and Nigel was borne off to hospital, still unconscious. A policeman was taking down, in a notebook and slow motion, her account of the affray. Neighbors, conspicuously absent while it was in progress, now swarmed around them, excitedly questioning one another, theorizing, or gaping at Clare. The policeman, requesting the chief witnesses to stay put in Clare's studio, got to work on the telephone. Alec Gray fidgeted about picking up Clare's little clay horses and putting them down, till she could have screamed at him. He had behaved pretty well, she had to admit; but she could think only of Nigel, the damp-cold feel of his face as he had lain there in the sunny little courtyard, among the bay trees in their green tubs.

A hatchet-faced man, neatly dressed, his features drawn with fatigue but his eyes sharp as augers, now came in with the policeman, and introduced himself as Detective-Inspector Wright.

"Miss Massinger? I'm very sorry to hear about this. Don't worry too much. He's a hardheaded chap, Mr. Strangeways."

Clare smiled at him gratefully.

"And you are Mr. Alec Gray?"

"Right first time."

"Lucky you were on the spot, sir. You must have moved fast."

"I do, when I have to." Gray's public-school drawl was very pronounced.

"You were in your flat, I take it, when you heard this lady call out for help?"

"You take it correctly."

"Your flat is on the top floor?"

"My flat is on the top floor. And I'd like to return to it, with your permission."

"By all means, sir. If you'd find it convenient, I'll come and have a word with you in half an hour."

Alec Gray flipped his hand at Clare, and departed.

"A very self-possessed young man," commented the Inspector.

"That's one word for it. But, you know, he did save Nigel's life. Those men were out to kill. They'd have hit him again—" Clare broke off, shuddering.

"If you hadn't fought them off for a bit." The Inspector smiled attractively. "Oh yes, Constable Smithers here has told me your account of the affair. Quite a dust-up, it must have been. We're grateful to you. We think quite a lot of Mr. Strangeways."

"I'd no idea he'd anything to do with police work—not till Rudolf Durbar came out with it at lunch."

"Sir Rudolf? You were lunching there just now? Both of you?"

"Yes. And it was the first time I heard about this boy Nigel is looking for. I seem to be catching up on my general knowledge today."

The Inspector was frowning. "You mean, he talked about it at lunch? Who else was there?"

"Just the Durbars and ourselves. Why?"

Inspector Wright got up, absently removed the cloth from

the portrait head of Nigel, stared at it, frowning still, as if awaiting some explanation from the clay lips, then sat down again.

"Have you a good memory, Miss Massinger?" he asked, with a sudden incisiveness that momentarily disconcerted her.

"A good—? Well, fair to middling."

"Will you try to tell me what everyone said at this lunch party?"

"Everything everyone said?" she asked, in dismay.

"Don't get anxious. It's not so difficult. You're a sculptor. Start with their faces, then. Shut your eyes, concentrate on their faces. Mouths opening and shutting, expressions, words coming out. Right? Off we go, then," said the remarkable man. And, to her amazement, haltingly at first, but soon with increasing fluency, Clare found herself repeating the talk at the lunch party. Inspector Wright helped her out with questions, from time to time. She did not understand the point of them all, particularly when he pressed her closely about the end of their visit.

"So Lady Durbar didn't accompany you when you went to look at the pictures? How long were you in the gallery?"

"Oh, about twenty minutes. A bit less, perhaps."

"But she saw you off?"

"Yes."

"Any change in her demeanor then?"

"I don't quite—".

"Was she distraight? Politely eager to get rid of you? Unusually talkative? Anything like that?"

"No. I didn't notice any change in her."

"It was definitely Sir Rudolf who invited you to look at the pictures? After he'd returned from telephoning?"

"Yes. Yes, but Hesione did say something to him—I didn't hear what—when he came back into the room. She might have been suggesting he should tour us round the pictures, I suppose."

"Now let me see if I've got these movements quite

straight. After lunch Mr. Strangeways talks about the boy he's looking for. Sir Rudolf is called out to the telephone. Returns. Invites you to look at pictures. Spends some twenty minutes with you—he *was* with you all that time?''

"Yes. No. He nipped out for a couple of minutes to fetch a Van Dyck from some other room.''

"And then you went back to the drawing room, where Lady Durbar was still sitting, and said good-by?''

"Yes.''

"Well, it's time for me to say good-by too. I'm most grateful to you, Miss Massinger.'' He held her hand for a moment, adding, "Don't worry. He's having the best attention. I'll see you get the report from the hospital, as soon as they've finished their examination.''

An hour later, Wright was in conference with Superintendent Blount at Headquarters.

"So there you have it, sir,'' Wright was saying. "There's more coincidence knocking about the world than people give credit for, but I can't swallow this as a coincidence—Strangeways getting bashed on the head half an hour after he's announced that he's the only person who can identify the boy we're looking for.''

"Just so. But you're not suggesting that Sir Rudolf Durbar organized it, are you?'' Blount gave a wry grin. "You're going to run into a packet of trouble, if that's the way your mind is moving. You'd be safer accusing the Governor of the Bank of England—''

"No. It's his wife, Lady Hesione. She had the knowledge, the opportunity, and a motive.''

"A motive?''

"Her liaison with this fellow Gray. Why, unless she's under his thumb, does she refuse to admit that he knew the combination of her safe? She's protecting him.''

"Even after he's stolen her jewels?''

"She can only *suspect* him of that, sir, at the worst. And you know the way a woman—an infatuated woman—will shut her eyes to a reality that's staring her in the face, and pretend it's not there.''

"Uh-huh. Well?"

"As soon as Sir Rudolf takes his guests off to see the pictures, Lady Durbar rings Gray. We're finding out if she did put through any calls. He's asked her to keep him posted about Strangeways. Or maybe she just gossips. Anyway, he knows now that Strangeways is a danger to him, and he has plenty of time to lay on his countermeasures.''

"And then ruin them by charging to the rescue before his thugs have finished Strangeways off?"

"That was just a blind," said Wright, rather nettled, "and not a very clever one. He's a powerfully built fellow, an ex-Commando, yet he let them both get away from him. And it was all too pat, the way he turned up. About ten seconds after she first screamed for help, Miss Massinger reckons; and she'd not have been able to hold off two men much longer than that. Ten seconds to get down three flights of stairs and along the passage. I don't believe it. I reckon he was waiting about, much nearer.'' Superintendent Blount scratched his chin, sighing heavily. "It's all very well, Wright. But there are too many unknowns in the equation. We've no proof that Gray is the man Dai Williams was after; no proof that he's behind these robberies; nothing to link him with the men who tried to get hold of that boy's boat, or criminally with Sam Borch.''

"I know that, sir," Wright broke in impatiently. "But you can't get away from this attack on Strangeways. Why did it happen *when* it did? Because of what he deliberately let out at the Durbars'—there's no other reasonable explanation. And you can't tell me that Lady Durbar—or Sir Rudolf, for that matter—has a gang of cosh boys on tap, just waiting for a telephone call. We've been through their friends, during the investigation over the burglary, and the only one we've a shadow of a reason to suspect is Gray.''

"But there's no proof, either, that Gray has criminal associates.''

"We've got to find proof," said Wright keenly.

They discussed the steps which had already been taken in this direction, but admittedly led nowhere. Gray's dossier was not, so far, very revealing: a good public school, war service, both parents killed in a motor accident some years ago, a legacy from an uncle, the flat in London, and a cottage on a Hampshire estuary, where he sailed. He appeared to be a rich playboy, without a profession, whom everybody in a certain social milieu knew, but no one—except the women he had lived with, and possibly lived on—knew well. Strained as their resources were at present, the C.I.D. had not yet been able to check Gray's career at every point, or examine it deeply. His standard of living seemed to be higher than the income from his legacy would permit; but he might be living on capital as well as on women.

It was out of the question to apply yet for a search warrant. Gray would be kept under surveillance, as far as this was possible. Wright would interview Lady Durbar again, in an attempt to turn Gray's flank from that direction.

"And," he said, "I think we must take the risk now, sir, and issue a public appeal for the boy to come forward. Now Strangeways is out of action—"

"Which shows how far they're prepared to go, to prevent us getting hold of Dai Williams' message."

"I know, sir. That's just the point. We only held back from making a public appeal because we did not wish to emphasize the value we set on the message. That reason's gone, now we know the importance the other side—whoever they are—attaches to it."

"Very well. I agree."

"I was hoping I'd got onto it this morning," said Wright. He told Blount about the affair at Mrs. Hale's house, and his Sergeant's visit. "But it turned out a dead end. We've got a photograph of this Bert Hale, just in case. But why should he have denied all knowledge of the affair, if he was the right boy?"

The two set to work, drafting appeals for press and radio. The telephone rang.

"It's for you, Wright. From Division."

Wright took up the receiver. "What's that?" he exclaimed in a moment. "Just hold on." He took out paper and pencil. "All right. Repeat it."

When he had taken down the message, given some instructions, and rung off, he handed the paper to Blount. "Just come in by the last post. Anonymous."

The message ran:

Body of Bloke alias the Kwack to be found at 6 Belvedere Street, W. 8. He was murdered last night. Go to it, chummies.

Part
Two

9

Wanted—A Boy

The police surgeon had made his preliminary report. The body had been photographed, searched, and removed. Fingerprint men were still at work. The D.D.I. leaned against a wall of the derelict kitchen, watching Detective Sergeant Allen carefully scoop some crumbs from the floor into an envelope.

"You know what I was talking about to Superintendent Blount just now, when you rang me up at H.Q.?"

"No, sir."

"Coincidences."

"Yes, sir?" the Sergeant replied, politely but abstractedly, as he scribbled on the envelope.

"Now we've got another." Wright jerked his head in the direction of the adjoining room. "Yesterday morning we ask Sam Borch if he knows anything about the Quack. Last night, the Quack is murdered."

"Fishy, sir."

"No doubt we'll find Borch has a lovely alibi for last night."

"Put him and his alibi through the mangle."

"Mind you, the Quack's description was in all the papers by then. Somebody was afraid he'd be found, and squeal. That somebody doesn't have to be Borch."

"You think he'd been hiding here some time, sir?"

"Use your loaf, Allen. Nothing in his pocket, but a razor. No blankets. No overcoat. No money."

"There are these traces of food, sir. And the empty Coca-Cola bottles."

"We'll come to them in a minute. But I lay you a month's pay it's not his dabs we'll find on those bottles. Nah, it won't do! Who'd pick on a broken-down dump like this to hide up in? It's an eligible residence for one kind of tenant only. A dead man. How d'you reconstruct it, Allen?" Wright was popular with his men—the ambitious ones, anyway—because he encouraged them to think for themselves, to learn.

"From the blood on the floor, he was shot in that room next door, not brought here dead. Position of body, plus recent footmarks on the earth outside, suggest he was shot by someone firing through the window. Well now, sir—"

"The open shutters?" Wright prompted.

"He'd not open up to anyone he wasn't sure of. Therefore he must have been expecting a confederate."

"What for, Allen, what for?"

"Well, sir, not to bring him supplies—not if you're right that he didn't intend to stay long. I'd say he was expecting someone who'd get him away from here—out of the country, perhaps. And this bloke double-crossed him."

"Good enough, Allen."

The Sergeant, gratified, began to embroider the theme.

"The Quack thought it was a transit camp, but it turned out a terminus."

"Cut the literary trimmings, Allen. Or have you started writing your memoirs already?"

The Sergeant looked sheepish.

"These other traces of occupation," continued Wright. "The small footmarks upstairs, etc. What do they suggest to you?"

"Kids breaking in, sir."

"About the murder, I mean."

Allen thought for a few moments. "He's not a local man, or he'd know there was a danger of kids finding the body. Or else, he didn't much care whether it was found or not. Just picked this spot in a hurry, as isolated—fairly safe for his purpose."

"Safe, M'm. Maybe he was unlucky, though. Another of these coincidences. Or was it?"

"Sir?"

Wright's keen face had the alertness of a terrier at a rat hole. "I'm interested in three things. The bolt of the side door, which has been oiled but not drawn back; that rim on the floor, where someone has recently put down some sort of paraffin lamp; and these traces of food. Try your teeth on them, Sergeant."

"Well, it doesn't seem likely the Quack would have brought a storm lantern with him, as he didn't bring anything else," said Allen slowly. "I've got it! A confederate of his broke in—the night before; oiled the bolt, so that the Quack could make a quick getaway if necessary; left some food and a lantern for him."

"And a box of matches?"

"Beg pardon, sir?"

"Matches, Allen: there were none on the body. There's not a box in the house. And where's the lantern? Would the murderer waste time getting into the house and removing the lantern, after he'd shot his man?"

Allen grinned. "I reckon I'm off the beam this time."

"But suppose a gang of kids decide to camp out here, for a dare. That'd account for everything—including the door bolt, which they oiled but hadn't the strength to force back. And it must have been recently. Last night, maybe. They may have heard the shot—been eyewitnesses, even. Those crumbs are still fresh. And then there's the writing on the wall."

Sergeant Allen started and looked up where the Inspector's thumb had pointed, as if he half expected to see a moving finger write.

"Up there. 'Foxy loves Lady Durbar.' Foxy's that boy Strangeways told us about. And Foxy didn't know Lady Durbar till he gate-crashed her idiotic party, three nights ago.

Foxy, or one of his young friends, more likely, must have written that.''

"Another coincidence, sir?''

"Coincidence be damned! Wherever we move in this case, we find boys under our feet.''

"Turn a stone and start a cherub's wing, sir.''

"Cherubs! Blasted little arabs,'' said Wright bitterly. "And I told you to lay off the literature.''

"Sorry, sir. You were saying?''

"I said, coincidence be damned. Who wrote that anonymous letter? The murderer? One of his gang? Not on your life. It's the way a boy would write. We've got to find this Foxy now—or one of his dear little playmates.''

A few streets away the police were making their inquiries, when Alec Gray turned on the six o'clock news. There was a police message; and the millions listening in had never heard a stranger one. Would the boy who was sailing a model speedboat on the Round Pond on Sunday afternoon, August 1st, and was later approached by two men with a view to purchasing his boat, etc., etc.

Alec Gray switched off the radio, stood for a moment in thought, then hurriedly changed into his dinner jacket and rang for a taxi. The plain-clothes man, Jones, heard him give the address of The High Dive to the taxi driver. Jones caught a taxi himself, a few minutes later, in Church Street, and arrived at the night club just after Gray had entered it. Gray's taxi man informed Jones that his fare had stopped on the way to telephone from a public call box. Jones instructed a policeman on the beat to put through a call for him, then settled down to watch the club entrance, and wait for his relief. He was properly browned off with all this hanging around, but he was a disciplined man and did not relax his vigilance.

Alec Gray found Mr. Borch on the premises. They had a brief conversation. Presently Mr. Borch escorted Gray through the cellar up into the room behind the second-hand clothes shop: there were no guests in the club yet, and Mr. Borch took care that the few waiters who had so far arrived should not see his companion's departure. Putting on an overcoat and hat, borrowed from the shop's stock, Gray walked out into the alley, turned left, and opened the door of the car which was waiting a hundred yards away. He gave the driver some instructions, then untied a parcel lying on the back seat. The parcel contained a policeman's uniform, complete with regulation boots; and it contained one or two other items, also suitable for fancy dress.

Although the attempt to grab Bert Hale last night had failed, the organization had not failed to follow the subsequent move which had deposited Bert in Essex. The police appeal on the radio rendered it imperative that the boy should be dealt with. This time, there must be no mistakes; that was why Gray had taken on the job himself. Of course even now it might be too late. But farmers were slow-moving people: suppose the boy had heard the first radio appeal, and come clean to his uncle and aunt, there was still a fair chance they would not contact the police till tomorrow morning. But what Gray chiefly banked on was that, since the boy had presumably not yet told even his mother about the speedboat episode—otherwise, she would surely have gone to the authorities—he would not tell his uncle or aunt now.

The car shook itself free of traffic, and accelerated along Eastern Avenue toward Chelmsford.

Bert Hale had indeed heard the radio appeal on the six o'clock news. His uncle was out milking, his aunt was laying high tea, when it came through. The appeal roused conflicting emotions in Bert's bosom: he felt like a hunted criminal, and imagined the row he would get into for having lied to the policeman this morning; he felt rather grand, at the thought of the B.B.C. appealing to him, Bert Hale, to disgorge his secret; he felt, above all, an overmastering sense of relief that soon this secret would no longer be hanging round his neck like the albatross in the poem.

"You're looking pale, my dear," said his aunt. "You must eat a good supper and go to bed early."

Bert opened his mouth to speak, thought better of it, and crammed in a buttered scone instead.

"That's a funny message on the wireless, isn't it? Wonder what he's been up to. Something bad, I'm sure, or they wouldn't wireless for him."

Bert choked over a mouthful of milk, then bent down to stroke the cat, and conceal the guilt which must be written on his face. His aunt's comfortable, basket-chair voice creaked on: she was lonely on the small farm, and it was nice to have someone to talk to, though young Bert didn't seem as bright as usual.

Presently they heard Bert's uncle at the back door, taking off his Wellingtons and washing his hands in the sink. The aunt fetched a hot dish for him out of the oven. As he ate, she told him about the radio message.

"You're one for model boats, eh, boy?" he said to Bert; then, winking at the boy, "we'll not let on to the coppers, though, shall us?"

Bert went scarlet, grinning uncertainly. Every moment that passed seemed to make it more impossible for him to come out with his secret: it was like having to confess to—a murder. The thought brought flooding back all the horrors of the previous night, which he had kept dammed up at the back of his mind for the last few hours.

At eight-thirty his aunt sent him to bed. He was glad enough to go, for he had determined to own up next morning, and in the meantime it was no fun sitting with his aunt and uncle, expecting all the time that they would recur to the subject of the radio appeal. Bert did not undress immediately. He looked out of the small, low window at the farm buildings, the rooks fidgeting in the ash trees, the deeply rutted track which led through flat fields to the farm gate.

Up this track, a few minutes later, he saw a uniformed

policeman walking. The farm dogs barked; the rooks flustered in the elm tops. Daylight was fast on the ebb.

"Oh, bother!" said Bert, but halfheartedly; he was certain the policeman had come for him, and glad on the whole that the initiative would be taken out of his own hands.

Bert's aunt answered the knock on the door.

"Mrs. Johnson?" asked the constable—a youngish man, freshfaced, with a blond mustache, and very nicely spoken, as she afterward described him.

"You have a small boy staying her, madam—name of Hale—I believe."

"Yes. He's not got into trouble, I hope. He's my nephew."

"The police have reason to believe he may be the boy for whom an appeal is being broadcast. Perhaps you heard it, madam?"

"Yes, we did. But Bert'd have—" she broke off, looking uncomfortable as she remembered how Bert had reacted to the radio appeal. Her husband came to the door beside her.

"Your nephew didn't say anything to you about the broadcast? Or to you, Mr. Johnson?"

The farmer and his wife shook their heads.

"Made no comment at all?"

"No. It's not like him, I said to myself. He's usually such a talkative little chap."

"I'd like a word with him, please."

"Oh but he's gone to bed. Wouldn't it do tomorrow?"

"I'm afraid it's rather an urgent matter," said the constable, adding drily, "we don't make broadcast appeals otherwise."

Mr. Johnson called upstairs, and Bert was down in a moment, still fully dressed.

"The constable wants to ask you a question," said Mr. Johnson. "Don't be frightened of that, my dear."

"We've had a message from London, asking us to inquire—"

The constable did not have to proceed further. White-faced, but standing straight up to it, Bert declared, "Yes, I'm the boy you're looking for. I heard the broadcast. I was going," he lamely added, "to tell Uncle in the morning."

"Well, fancy that now!" exclaimed Mrs. Johnson, a little shrilly, her gaze groping toward her husband.

"I'm afraid I must ask you to let me take your nephew into Chelmsford. The Super wants some information from him. Don't worry yourself, madam. We've a car in the lane—didn't like to bring it down this track—and we'll have him back here in an hour."

"But look here," said Mr. Johnson. "What's this all about? How do we know?"

The constable, beckoning him aside, muttered in his ear, "It's a murder inquiry, sir. The boy has unwittingly come into the possession of some information which may be of vital importance."

Uncle and Aunt watched Bert receding along the track at the constable's side. He swung his arms, looked almost jaunty—as well he might, with such a load off his mind. He turned once, and waved to them. The constable turned, too, raising his hand in cheerful salute.

"Very decent young fellow, that seems."

"Yes. Not a local man, though, I reckon."

"Whatever'll Lily say when she hears of this? You know the way she spoils him. Too soft with him, I always say."

"The way you talk, anyone'd think Bert was being arrested. They only want some gen about a murder."

"A murder, Bob?" exclaimed Mrs. Johnson with a faint shriek.

Bert got into the back seat, beside the friendly constable, and the plain-clothes man at the wheel drove off. The lane, heavy with its late-summer leaves and the lowering twilight, was deserted. The constable asked Bert if there'd been a message on the bit of paper in his boat.

"Oh yes, rather," said Bert enthusiastically. "That's what those two blighters must've been after."

"What did it say, son?"

"Well, that's the extraordinary thing. It just had my name and age written on it."

"Go on!" remarked the constable.

"Honestly! And I tried it for invisible writing. Must have been in code, don't you think?"

"I suppose it must. Let's have a crack at it—I'm quite hot on codes." The constable produced pencil and notebook. "Write it down here—exactly what was written on the bit of paper: it's easier if you can actually see the words."

Bert began to write. The motion of the car made it difficult, and at one point of the message the pencil jerked, altering a letter. He finished, then surveyed what he had written.

"Jees!" he exclaimed. "Look at—"

But what the constable was to look at remained unspoken. Bert, feeling the car brake hard, glanced up. They had just rounded a bend, and there was another car ahead of them, stationary, almost blocking the narrow lane.

"It's a stick-up!" squeaked Bert.

"Get down on the floor, and keep quiet," the constable ordered. Bert did so, having first, with great presence of mind, torn the sheet from the notebook and put it in his mouth. As he frantically chewed at it, he listened for the sounds of battle. None came. What did come was a pair of blue serge sleeves from behind him, a pair of hands which slapped adhesive plaster over Bert's mouth and a scarf round his eyes. He felt himself lifted out of the car, carried, thrown down again, his hands and legs trussed: then the ground on which he was lying jerked violently, and he realized it must be the floor of a car—the other car. It all happened with such dazing swiftness that he had no time to be frightened. He had not even had time to swallow the paper. It was agonizing to move his jaws, with the adhesive plaster binding his mouth, but he finally got the paper swallowed.

Not till he had done so did he realize that it was a useless gesture; for, now that he had collected his wits, he remembered vividly the blue serge sleeves. It was the friendly "constable" who had betrayed him, gagged and blindfolded him;

and he had seen the message which Bert had copied out in the notebook—had time to see it, anyway—just before the fake stick-up. Well, of course it was not a stick-up at all. For some reason, Bert clearly perceived, it had been prearranged by the gang that he should be transferred to another car. The "constable" and the original driver would now be speeding back to London, or wherever they had come from, with Dai Williams' secret in their possession.

Bert's reasoning was correct. A little before eleven P.M., dressed in his dinner jacket and borrowed overcoat again, Alec Gray unlocked the door beside the second-hand clothes shop, passed through into The High Dive, and made for Sam Borch's private room upstairs. An hour later, Jones' relief saw Alec Gray emerge from the front door of the club, assisted by a doorman and at an advanced stage of intoxication, to be driven off in a taxi.

Meanwhile, Bert had begun to worry—not so much about his own predicament as the effect his disappearance would have on his aunt, uncle, and his mother. He did not think the gang would kill him; they could have done so before, if they'd wanted to. There object, he thought, must be to prevent him communicating Dai Williams' message to anyone else. What they did not know was that Foxy and Copper shared the secret; no doubt his friends would go to the police as soon as they heard of his disappearance, but on the other hand they did not understand the significance of what Dai Williams had written on that piece of paper, and it might well escape the police too.

The car, which had been winding this way and that along a bumpy road, now moved faster, straighter, on a smoother surface, and other cars from time to time whirred past. They must be on a main road: but Bert had not the faintest idea whether they were traveling north, south, east, or west. He wriggled again with wrists and feet, but he had been lashed up too efficiently. There seemed to be no one else in the back of the car; and if the driver had a companion, he must be dumb or asleep, for not a word was spoken. This silence began to get on Bert's nerves. It was like being in an empty car, a runaway car, tearing through the night: sooner or later it must hit something, it would catch fire, and he would not be able to get out.

Bert, momentarily overwrought by this appalling fantasy, tried to yell. The adhesive plaster cruelly nipped his mouth, and he gave a loud whimper instead.

"Pipe down, kid," came a man's voice. "Not far to go now."

The voice was not harsh, was almost reassuring. Bert's mind threw up a sort of composite figure of all the rugged jailers in history and fiction, softened by the appeals of their young captives. But he could not appeal till this filthy thing had been taken off his mouth, and it seemed ages of darkness and pain before the car stopped, a gate was opened, and then they moved forward again with the wheels bumping over a rough track.

He was picked up, still in silence, carried up some stairs, along a passage, and finally put down on a bed. Footsteps came and went. Hands untied the scarf from round his head, and the ropes. A woman was bending over him, vigorously massaging his wrists and ankles, clucking to herself—a homely-faced old woman, utterly different from the gangster's moll he had expected.

"I'll get some hot water, ducks," she said, "and that plater'll come off easier. A cruel shame, I call it."

For a moment, Bert wildly thought he must have been rescued, not kidnaped. But then he heard a key turn in the lock after the old woman had gone out, and saw that the window of the room was barred. The next thing he saw, by the light of the shaded bulb overhead, was a rocking horse, its red nostrils sneering at him from a corner of the room. The wallpaper had a pattern of Noah's arks and animals; on a Prussian blue cupboard sat an array of golliwoggs and teddy bears. He was in a nursery.

Whatever effect, if any, his captors might have intended by this, Bert's environment provoked him to seething rage. The indignity of putting him, the president of the Martian Society, in a room full of kid's toys—all of them brand new too, it seemed, as if the room had been fitted out for him! Who the hell did they think he was?

His indignation carried him through the painful business of removing the plaster, and it was tears of rage rather than grief which came to his eyes. The old woman, entering with a basin of hot water, had said,

"Now, Master Bert, before we take that horrid thing off, you must promise me not to call out or do anything silly. No one will hear you, so you might as well save your breath to cool your porridge. Your word of honor, Master Bert. Nothing naughty."

Precluded from speech, Bert nodded his head. The unpeeling operation was performed, with only a few stifled moans from the boy. The woman produced a bag of sweets from her apron pocket.

"That's a good boy," she said. "You can have a sweetie for being so brave."

"Who are you?" asked Bert, sucking the sweet.

"You can call me Nanny" she said, in a cozy, creaking voice which reminded him of his aunt's. Bert suppressed the glare of indignation he was tempted to bestow upon the silly old hag. She was obviously touched in the head; and Bert's instinct for playing up adult weakness was at once aroused. If the old fool has delusions that I'm a kid, let her keep them; maybe it'll put her off her guard. Assuming an infantile tone which made him sick to the stomach, he said, "Where am I, Nanny?"

"Ah, that'd be telling, ducks. Ask no questions and you'll hear no lies," she crooned.

"Why have I been kidnaped?" Bert persisted.

"Now, Master Bert, that's a very naughty word. I don't like to hear that sort of words from my babies."

Bert shuddered strongly.

"The poor little chap's feeling cold," she said. "A nice warm supper in his little tum-tum—that's what he wants."

"Gug, gug, gug," said Bert, slightly overplaying his part.

The old women retired, locking the door again, and presently reappeared with a tray of very tolerable grub. As Bert consumed it, he asked if he could write a letter to his mother; she'd be worrying about him; just to tell her he'd arrived safely.

"We'll see," the woman replied, a momentary look of bewilderment in her old gray eyes. "Tomorrow, perhaps, if you're a good boy."

When she had gone out with the tray. Bert inspected his prision. Admirably stocked as it was for infant tastes, it offered precious little for his own recreation. He took a book from a shelf. Like the toys, it was brand new; but, discovering it to be a nauseating tale about some flopsy bunnies, Bert put it back. He tried all the books—not for reading purposes now, but looking for clues. Not one of them, however, had an owner's name on the flyleaf.

Bert felt very sleepy. Perhaps he was asleep—had been asleep for hours: the whole thing was like a dream, vivid and mad. He started undressing. The bed had been turned down. On the pillow lay a nightdress of sorts. Bert lifted it, and a spasm of fear shook him. The nightdress was less than two feet long—a baby's. He took a grip on himself. Either he was dreaming, or not; he couldn't do anything about it, either way; and at least he was alive. He found a basin behind a screen, splashed his face with cold water, and got into bed in his pants.

He went to sleep without difficulty. He dreamed that he was an aged Nanny in old-fashioned cap and apron, being pursued through Kensington Gardens by a horde of naked and infuriated babies, all shooting from the hip. As he stepped into his model speedboat and accelerated across the Round Pond, leaving the naked babies dancing with rage on the shore, the engine blew up, and Bert awoke to daylight, with the noise of an explosion still ringing in his ears. He rubbed his eyes. Propping himself up in bed, he heard another shot, quite near. Or was it someone cracking a whip?

10

Brisk Business in the
Portobello Road

At about the same hour as Bert woke up in his nursery prison, Nigel Strangeways awoke in a private room of the hospital. He had recovered consciousness the previous evening, but soon gone off into a natural sleep. Apart from the sensation, when he attempted to move, of an inexpert carver at work inside his skull, he felt reasonably himself again. It was a time for thought rather than action, so he lay still, patiently groping for the bits of the puzzle which yesterday's assault had swept off his mind, and piecing them together. The result was curiously interesting. On the other hand, like the result of a falsely conceived proposition, it seemed fit only to be labeled with a final "Which Is Absurd."

A nurse came in, took his temperature, and departed, poker-backed and poker-faced. Presently the doctor arrived, accompanied by a sister. Nigel's bandages were removed, his head carefully inspected and several tests taken. Absorbed by his problem, Nigel was hardly aware what they were doing.

"You'll be all right," said the doctor finally. "A few days' rest, then go slow for a week—"

"I've got to see someone," said Nigel.

The sister gave him a disapproving look, the doctor a very keen one; he had been told a little of the background of this case.

"I think Mr. Strangeways might have a visitor. Say ten minutes. Who do you want to see?"

"Miss Clare Massinger."

Sister said, "She has rung up to inquire about you. Also Lady Durbar."

"And if Inspector Wright turns up, I must see him too."

Sister bridled at the patient's authoritative tone. She was accustomed to patients taking orders, not giving them. But the doctor only said, "If you're prepared to risk a set-back, Mr. Strangeways."

"I have to take risks just now."

"I understand. We'll fix it up for you."

At ten-thirty a magnificent floral tribute arrived, with Lady Durbar's card on it. Half an hour later, Clare Massinger was shown in.

"Oh, Nigel, you look like Lazarus risen from the dead," were her first words. She just touched the bandages swathing his head, and sat down beside him. "Are you really better? Where did all those vulgar flowers come from?"

"Lady Durbar."

"Oh."

"Listen, Clare, we've only got ten minutes. I want you to tell me exactly what happened when I got coshed."

"Aren't you glad to see me?"

"Yes, my dear, of course. But—"

Clare turned away her head. "Well, you might have said so. If you really are ill, you oughtn't to—"

"Darling Clare, why are women always so irritable when their—when men are ill? Exasperated, brusque, and skeptical?"

She paused a moment; then, still looking away, came out with, "Because we're afraid you might die. You give us a fright, and fright for—for someone you're fond of—always makes you irritable afterward."

"The doctor said I'd be all right, if I followed his instructures closely. He said I must be sure to kiss the first visitor who arrived."

"Did Hesione bring those vile flowers in person?"

"No. I still require the prescribed treatment."

Clare's lips on his were like moths, trembling and velvety. Two tears fell on his face.

"Now, you ministering angel, tell me what happened."

"I do love you when you're being business-like and bracing," she said dreamily. Then she told him about the fight in the courtyard and Alec Gray's intervention.

"So you saved my life?"

"I suppose I did."

"You and the unprepossessing Mr. Gray."

Absently, she played with Nigel's fingers. "I've been thinking," she said. "When the fight was over, I made an idiotic remark to him about his sunburn."

Nigel began to laugh, but it sent a knife through his head.

"He accounted for it by saying he'd driven back from Southampton that morning. The inside of his right forearm was red with sunburn; and there was a triangle of it at the base of his throat, with one side of it running up the left side of his neck. So he must have been lying, mustn't he?"

"I'm sorry. My head can't be working properly."

"In the morning, my poor slow-witted sleuth, the sun is moving from east to south."

"The sun doesn't move."

"Shut up. You know what I mean. So, if you were driving an open car, with your shirt sleeves rolled up, from Southampton to London, it would strike the *right* side of your neck and the inside of your *left* forearm."

"By Jove, Clare, you're right! You're a wonder. To get sunburned in those places, he must have been driving from, let's see—" Nigel sat us in bed, grasping an imaginary steering wheel—"from the East coast direction. From Norfolk or Suffolk. He didn't say when he'd started?"

"No. But he told me he'd just got back for lunch."

"It'd take several hours to produce sunburn that bad. Whatever bit of no good he was up to, he must have come at least a hundred miles—probably more. If he started from somewhere in Suffolk after breakfast, at ten o'clock say, he'd get back to London for lunch."

"But he could have been driving all night as well—from Stockton-on-Tees."

"Don't be depressing. I'm an invalid. Has there been anything in the papers about a spectacular robbery in the Constable country—or Stockton-on-Tees?"

"Well, actually I did buy a newspaper this morning," said Clare, with the proud but dubious tone of a suburban housewife announcing to hubby that she has purchased some exotic delicacy for his supper. She rummaged in her bag, gave Nigel a folded paper, and moved away to look at the card which Lady Durbar had sent with her flowers.

Wishing you a speedy recovery. Must see you soon, it said.

Clare turned round, to see Nigel, gray-faced, staring at the front page of the newspaper.

"Darling, what is it?" She was at his side in one swift movement.

"They've got him." Nigel indicated a photograph. "This is the boy I was looking for. He's been kidnaped. From where he was staying, with an uncle and aunt, near Chelmsford. Essex. But it was *last* night."

The sister came in, to say that Miss Massinger's ten-minute visit was up.

When Inspector Wright looked in, at lunchtime, the newspaper was still on Nigel's bed.

"So you've seen it, sir."

"Yes. That's the boy all right. We've missed the bus."

"And we had our hands on him yesterday morning," said Wright bitterly. He told Nigel about his hunch, and the Sergeant's abortive interview with the boy. "Someone must have followed him and his mother down to Essex. Then, when the radio appeal went out—yes, we decided to broadcast for the boy yesterday—they knew they had to move fast. Chap dressed up as a policeman arrives at the farm; inquires for boy. Young Bert admits he's the lad in question—why the hell he should lie to my Sergeant in the morning but come clean the same night, I don't know. Bert had said nothing about it to his uncle or aunt. Phony cop says the Super at

Chelmsford wants to ask boy a few questions. Police car at end of lane. Fetch him back in an hour. Hour passes. No boy. Uncle rings up Chelmsford police. Curtain. A blasted smooth bit of work, so now, what?''

"Find the other boy instead. Foxy. I'm convinced he knows this Bert, and he may know about Dai Williams' message. No doubt the gang, whoever they are, have extracted it from Bert by now. That's all the more reason for us to get hold of it.''

"Foxy. Yes. Mrs. Hale must know him, if he's a friend of her son's. She's gone down to her sister in Essex this morning.'' The Inspector told Nigel about the discovery of the Quack's body, and the writing on the wall. Nigel informed him of Clare's detective effort.

"Where was Gray last night?'' he asked.

"At The High Dive, from six-thirty till about midnight. A pity, because—apart from the mustache—he roughly answers to the uncle's description of the phony cop. But we'll put his alibi through the mangle, and we'll investigate his movements on Thursday night as well. That was a clever bit of work by Miss Massinger. Any theories, sir?''

"We've got to assume there are links between Dai Williams, the Quack, Gray, Bert Hale, and Foxy. Otherwise we'll go mad. Now, we know Gray was in London on Thursday afternoon. That evening, or night, he must have driven the best part of a hundred miles out of London—far enough to allow for his getting badly sunburned driving back the next morning. He says it was Southampton. We think it was not. O.K. If Gray is the man Dai Williams was after, Gray was behind his murder. He must have some sort of organization, which duly bumped off Dai's murderer when he looked like becoming a danger to it. I don't think Gray shot the Quack himself; he'd hardly drive a hundred miles just to throw his revolver into the North Sea. But he might well have driven the actual killer out of London that night—down to Harwich, say, where he could catch a boat for the continent or Scandinavia.''

"We'll have to arrange for you to be coshed at regular intervals, sir," said Wright, with his attractive, brief flash of a smile. "It seems to clear your mind. Well, I think I've got all those points. Enough work to keep fifty men busy, and I've got—" The Inspector shrugged. "Time you had your sleep, sir. I'll be off."

"When you find Foxy, let *me* see him. I've done nothing yet. You know, Wright—"

"Yes, sir?"

"There must be bigger things at stake than the success of a gang of housebreakers."

"That's what has me worried. . . ."

Copper's father, the Detective-Sergeant, had been transferred a couple of weeks before to another Division. His family remained at Notting Hill till he could find a house in his new area, and he only saw them on his few irregular hours off. Glancing at the newspaper this morning, he had recognized Bert's photograph as that of one of his son's young friends. No urgent action seemed to be called for; he was going home later for the night, and would discuss it with his son then—not that the boy could know anything about Bert's disappearance.

Mrs. Hale, contacted by the county police at her sister's farm, had given them Foxy's name and address. As soon as Inspector Wright received the information from them, he sent a man to the address, who was told by Foxy's mother that her son was helping his father at the barrow in Portobello Road. She offered him one of her innumerable brood, a redhead of eight called Gloria, to take him to the pitch and identify Foxy.

Earlier in the day, Foxy and Copper had foregathered, to deal with the situation arising from the newspaper accounts they had read of Bert's disappearance. Unaware that he had been betrayed by Copper's *jeu d'esprit*, written upon the kitchen wall of the derelict house, Foxy advocated a policy of masterly inaction. Foxy's general attitude toward the constabularly was that, if they could not be confined to barracks, they should be confined to directing traffic and other such harmless necessary pursuits: having in his possession now the letters he had stolen from Alec Gray and the jade idol, he would certainly be accused of stealing from Lady Durbar; having been guilty of housebreaking, and, in Copper's view, of withholding information about a murder he had witnessed—if not of being an accessory after the fact (the anonymous letter could only be considered as a slight palliative of his guilt), Foxy was more averse than ever to any contact with the police. Besides, he had argued to Copper, how could it help Bert now? Foxy had said at the start that Dai Williams' message was a warning to Bert that he would be kidnaped. Well, he had been kidnaped. So what?

So they ought to tell the police about the red-faced man, the spiv outside the Post Office, the young gent with the buttonhole, protested Copper. They needn't say any more; but the above characters must be mixed up in the kidnaping—they were, or ought to be, Wanted Men. Foxy said that one thing would lead to another, and if you started spieling to the dicks, the next thing you found yourself in the cooler. Copper, who had a healthy respect for his dad, began to waver. His initial skepticism about the Dai Williams' message had recently returned. It was too much to swallow, that a dying man would write down the name and age of a boy he had never met, and give the paper to the boy. Bert must have made it up. It wouldn't have been the first time Bert's powerful imagination had hypnotized his friends into crediting the incredible. Copper decided privately that he would tell his father about the "message," and strongly put forward his own view that Bert must have substituted it for the real one he had received.

After their midday meal, the two boys walked along to Portobello Road. On a Saturday afternoon, the Portobello Road ceases to be a thoroughfare and becomes a dense cross section of London life with the animation of an Oriental bazaar. The upper end is lined with booths at which are sold antiques of every degree of modernity, Victorian jewelry, cutlery, bits of lace and silk squares, clocks and watches, books, vases ranging in aesthetic quality from the hideous to the inconceivable—a long array of junk in which the occasional elegant piece shines out, to the connoisseur's eye, like a diamond on a dunghill.

Here, the crowd is as variegated as the articles for sale. Engaged couples looking for a bargain; Americans bemused by the wealth of the genu-ine antiques; ballet students in stovepipe trousers; hairy young painters and their sloppy-looking mistresses; aged, eccentric ladies—decayed gentlewomen from Bayswater bedsitting rooms—padding along in plimsolls, with all their wardrobe on their backs, muttering and crazily peering ahead into some unfathomable vista. Sprinkled amongst the throng, one saw the drape suits and eye-searing ties of the wide boys. Children, avoiding collisions by some instinctual radar, pursued one another through the crowd. At their stalls sat the dealers, inscrutably eyeing prospective customers, separating the sheep from the goats—the real buyers from the finger-and-pass-on brigade—with the skill of long experience.

Foxy and Copper threaded their way down the curving hill toward their objective. As one descends, the market changes character: the decorative gradually gives way to the purely utilitarian, knickknacks to household necessities, obese vases to second-hand corsets. The boys stopped for a moment to watch some entertainers, performing in a side street for the benefit of a row of children who sat on pavement and railings. The entertainment consisted of a fiddler, a drummer, a cornet player, and the life and soul of the party—a tiny, dark-faced man dressed in a top hat adorned with feathers, a clergyman's collar and frock coat, riding breeches and plimsolls, who capered indefatigably, chaffed the audience, told jokes unsuitable both for it and his collar, and led them in community song. The childern were eating it. Foxy and Copper gave the show a dirty look and passed on.

Now the crowd was thicker than ever. All the housewives

of London seemed to have congregated here. The fruit and
vegetable barrows were doing a roaring trade. At the next
intersection a Communist Party meeting endeavored to com-
pete. The speaker, watched by two yawning constables and a
Special Branch man impenetrably disguised as a spiv, was
thundering to an audience of at least twenty that they, the
irresistible working classes, the heirs of the future, must express their solidarity with their Russian comrades in this time
of sharpening capitalist contradictions and demand that the
Tory government take a stand against the American warmon-
gers, and clear out of Africa ("What about Scotland?" asked
a stentorian voice from the crowd), and throw in their lot with
the glorious Soviet Union whose representatives were now in
London ("What about Churchill?" "What about freedom of
speech?" "What about Father Christmas?" bellowed several
British workers).

Foxy, somewhat impressed by the oration, bought an ice-
cream cone, elbowed his way to the rostrum, and placed the
cone on the palm of the speaker, which was outstretched in a
rhetorical gesture.

"Good for the choobs, chum," he said.

The boys now repaired to the fruit barrow owned by
Foxy's father. An apparently infinite succession of red-haired
children—Foxy's brothers and sisters—emerged from the
press, like a recurring decimal, to greet him. His dad flipped
a hand. Foxy set to work weighing out orders for the customers, and Copper bagged them up. Foxy was a well-known
figure here: barrow boys winked at him, or made the arcane
gestures of their calling; passers-by recognized the hoarse,
shrill voice he lifted to advertise the family wares. It was
during a lull in business, some twenty minutes later, that
Foxy, lighting a cigarette butt and glancing up the street, saw
his sister Gloria approaching, hand in hand with a character
whom his trained eye instantly recognized as a plain-clothes
Busy. Foxy dived underneath the barrow.

He heard the Busy inquire after him, and his father's puzzled voice, "He was here a minute ago." The Busy said he

would wait. Foxy became acutely conscious of the little jade idol in one pocket, and in another the letter he had pinched from the Gray bastard; also, a wasp was turning its attention from a squashed plum to Foxy's nose. It was time to scarper. He wriggled from under the barrow, at the end opposite the Busy's boots, and merged into the crowd, followed by a yell from the unspeakable Gloria, "There he is! Hey, Foxy, you're wanted!" Snatching the cap from the head of a gormless lad who was gazing at a nylon-and-brassière display, Foxy put it on the conceal his carroty hair, and moved smartly up the hill again, bumping and boring through the crowd.

Mr. Borch, too, was a familiar figure in the Portobello Road market. Like many another person who, by his own unaided efforts has risen from poverty to affluence, he loved bargaining for its own sake and was wont to chaffer interminably for an article which he did not really want and could have afforded to purchase by the gross. He was something of a connoisseur, besides; when Sam Borch approached, stallholders abandoned their usual patter and prepared for a stiff tussle. But, here as elsewhere, Mr. Borch combined pleasure with business. Antisocial types could rely on finding him here at certain hours; and a few muttered words exchanged, in the thick of a crowd, while the speakers were examining objects on a stall, were a safe and often fruitful method of communication. This was all the more so just at present, when Mr. Borch, fully aware that the police had turned on the heat, had felt it advisable to close down certain other channels of communication for a while.

This afternoon, Mr. Borch was in search of information rather than *objets de vertu*. Things had been happening in his world, or on its fringes, which puzzled him. Notably the murder of the Quack. He was not interested in the Quack professionally; but it had disconcerted him that this individual should have been ironed out so soon after the police had inquired at The High Dive about him. That sort of thing aroused nasty suspicions in the official breast. Indeed he had already been interviewed on the subject; and the fact that he possessed a genuine, guaranteed alibi for the hours in question did not altogether remove his uneasiness. He felt, in short, that things were rather less under control than normally.

They were far less so than Mr. Borch apprehended. An observer—and the C.I.D. were keeping him under observation at this very moment—noting Mr. Borch's large, genial face, his pearl-gray Homburg and suit, his Malacca cane, might well have supposed that here was a man on top of the world. Equally, one might admire the solidity and opulence of a table which is actually infested by white ants and will soon crumble to dust before its owner's eyes. The C.I.D. had been burrowing for some little time now into the structure of Mr. Borch's interests. His downfall, however, was to be brought about, not by the forces of abstract Justice, but by those passions which, as the poet correctly tells us, spin the plot.

Mr. Borch sauntered toward the pitch where the clerical-collared man and his band were entertaining the children. As their voices rose in song, Mr. Borch exchanged a few words, his lips barely moving, with an unwholesome-looking character who had also drifted that way. He then moved back into the market, for he had seen a red-faced man, of the commercial-traveler type, making an almost imperceptible sign in his direction. His progress did not go unmarked, and his presence at the market on other occasions had been noted, too. So that, just as Mr. Borch was approaching this person, he felt a violent concussion which sent him reeling and knocked off his hat. A boy had run into him full tilt. Mr. Borch's expression changed. He lifted his cane and slashed the boy viciously across the buttocks. Foxy let out a howl of anguish.

In an instant the crowd was pressing round them. The few who had seen the incident were hostile to Mr. Borch, the rest were all ready to take sides as soon as they knew what it was about. Mr. Borch picked up his hat, saying, "Let me pass, please," and tried to move away.

"What's the hurry?"

"Who the hell do you think you're pushing?"

"He hit the boy. Give him some of his own medicine!"

"The arab knocked his hat off. Serve the little bleeder right!"

"You think so? You want to make something of it?"

The red-faced man had now worked his way into the ring, with several of the wide boys behind him.

"Lay off it," he said menacingly. "Let this gent pass."

Foxy, white-faced with pain and fury, pointed to the new arrival, yelling at the top of his voice,

"Get that ———! He tried to kidnap Bert Hale. He's in the snatch racket!"

Copper, turning up that moment, also recognized the "commercial traveler" who had hung around Mrs. Hale's house, and sang out, "That's right! He's wanted by the police!"

"Cut it out, you little—!"

"What's he say?"

"Bert Hale. Kid in the papers who's disappeared. That chap done it."

The wide boys had whipped out their razors and bicycle chains. They formed a tight round Mr. Borch. It was the last think he wanted—this sort of publicity. And there was worse to come.

The red-faced man shot out his hand and gripped Foxy. Copper, snatching up a hugh vase from a stall, swung it at the man's knees; he roared with pain, and released Foxy. A police whistle sounded from the higher end of the street. It was the C.I.D. man who had been shadowing Sam Borch, but found it impossible to break through the milling crowd. The mobsters began to move away from the sound of the whistle, down the hill. Mr. Borch, willy-nilly, had to go with them. Intimidated by the razors and whirling chains, the crowd pressed back to the sides of the street. Several stalls were overset and wrecked by the pressure. Their owners began to bombard the wide boys with their stock-in-trade, and at once the bystanders joined in: a fusillade of tomatoes, plums, cabbages were directed against the enemy.

Mr. Borch's Savile-Row suit was soon ruined. He had been protesting vigorously if incoherently, and the crowd now got the idea—not altogether unfounded—that he was being carried off by the mobsters against his will. Some of the hardier spirits advanced to rescue him, closed with his apparent captors, and an ugly hand-to-hand fight started. This was Foxy's opportunity. He had got it in for Mr. Borch, and when Foxy's blood was up, there was no holding him. Streaking through the melee, closely attended by Copper, he hurled a tomato full in Mr. Borch's face, snatched his Malacca stick and gave him a ferocious blow across the buttocks. Mr. Borch, who now resembled the losing end of a heavyweight contest, staggered away, to be tripped up by Copper's outthrust foot. Foxy jumped up and down on Mr. Borch's stomach, preparatory to doing him a permanent injury, but was knocked sprawling by a clout from the "commercial traveler." The latter, though hampered by the bash across the knees he had received from Copper, was still very much in the fight. He made a limping dash. Copper, who had learned jujitsu from his father, interposed and sent the red-faced man flying, on his own impetus, in a graceful parabola which landed him on the much-enduring Mr. Borch's kidneys.

Police whistles now sounded close at hand and the crowd began to melt at its outer edges. Dizzy with the blow he had received, Foxy nevertheless retained enough sense to know he must get rid of the incriminating articles in his possession, lest the police should nab him. Mr. Borch and the red-faced man, inextricably mingled, were struggling to get to their feet, buffeted by the reeling, milling figures around them. They were in no condition to notice it when Foxy's creeping up to them, transferred certain objects from his own pockets to theirs. For good measure, he gave each of them a powerful kick where it would hurt most, then darted back to the pavement.

The two policemen who had been watching the Communist meeting, together with the plain-clothes men detailed to shadow Mr. Borch and pick up Foxy, had now got the situation under control. Three of the mobsters were already in custody. Mr. Borch and the "commercial traveler," both groggy still, were arrested for disturbing the peace. A Black Maria, with reinforcements, soon arrived, and the tedious business began of getting statements from eyewitnesses, some of whom needed medical attention. The battle of the Portobello Road was over. Whistling innocently, looking like battered cherubs, Foxy and Copper strolled away from the battlefield.

11

Hospital Visitors

There was a gleam in Inspector Wright's eye when he came to visit Nigel the next morning.

"Things are moving at last," he said. "We've got that oily old basket, Borch, where we want him."

Wright told Nigel of the fracas in the Portobello Road. A number of arrests had been made: three small-time mobsters, and two bigger fish—Sam Borch, and a man called Percy Chalmers, who designated himself as a commercial traveler. Both men were searched. In Borch's pocket was found a small jade idol. This object had not been listed among the articles stolen at any of the recent robberies; but Wright had sent a man round to make inquiries from the victims. He had drawn blank at two houses. Then Lady Durbar's personal maid (her master and mistress were out to dinner) identified the idol as one which had stood on a table in Lady Durbar's bedroom. The room was full of knickknacks, and the maid had not noticed before that this particular object was missing; nor, presumably, had its owner.

"We can get a search warrant on this. We're holding Borch, and we'll go through The High Dive and his private apartments tomorrow."

"What does the great Borch say about it?"

"Full of righteous indignation. Accuses us of framing him. Says he'd never set eyes on the niddy little idol before."

"Had he set fingers on it?"

"He's a receiver, not a thief."

"I mean, were his fingerprints on it?"

The Inspector gave Nigel a long, long look. "Now, sir, what awkward questions you do ask." His quick smile flashed once, like an Aldis lamp.

"So they weren't?"

"Oh but they are. Sam—er—handled the object when he was confronted with it at the Station."

"I see. How resourceful our police are. So the theory is he'd just been carrying a piece of stolen property round in his pocket? Though he must have known he was under observation?"

"Sam is a bit of a connoisseur. Perhaps he'd fallen in love with the piece, and couldn't bring himself to part from it. Ugly little brute—that idol. But I never did like *chinoiserie* mascots, and they tell me it's valuable enough."

"Mascots," said Nigel in a speculative tone, remembering the guilty look on Foxy's face at a certain point during the episode in Clare's studio. "Was the boy Foxy mixed up in this Portobello Road affair?"

Inspector Wright's eyes sparked again. "He was. I'd sent a man to look for him. He was directed to a barrow owned by Foxy's dad. Foxy had been there a moment before. And eyewitnesses of the fracas said it began with a red-headed boy accidentally running into Sam Borch and getting a whack across the bottom with his cane."

"And Foxy had the run of the Durbars' house on the night of the burglary. And boys have a passion for mascots. But he'd want to get rid of it if the police began crowding him too close."

"Looks like we shall have to interview him again—*after* we've got Sam Borch tidied up," said Wright with a meaning intonation.

"You've seen him then? Foxy?" Nigel's voice was eager.

"Oh yes, sir. We caught up with him last night."

"And you've got Dai Williams' message?"

Inspector Wright sliced the air before him with the edge of his hand. "We've drawn a blank there."

He had extracted the boys' stories when Foxy and Copper

were brought to the Station—how Bert had shown them a piece of paper, how they had set up on their own as detectives, put a bogus message in the boat, and palmed it off on the crooks. The original "message" had been destroyed. But they had both seen it. "Bert Hale, 12." Copper was convinced now that Bert had been pulling their legs—had substituted for the piece of paper Dai Williams gave him one on which he had written a more interesting, mystifying message. Bert was quite capable of it—both boys agreed.

"Do you agree?" said Nigel.

"Well, it doesn't make sense otherwise, does it? I showed the boys a specimen of Dai's handwriting. They admitted that, as far as they could remember, it was like the writing on the bit of paper Bert showed them. But Bert could have roughly copied the writing of the real message."

"So we're no further till we've found Bert?"

"I wouldn't quite say that, sir. We have much stronger links with Gray now. Your Foxy believes he saw Gray receive the fake message they'd concocted from the spiv Bert failed to sell his boat to. That's what set them off shadowing Gray."

"When Foxy followed him into the Durbars' party?"

"Yes. Foxy was unforthcoming about the party itself. But he gave me a description of a man who accompanied Gray to it—and of a conversation he overheard between Gray and some other unknown man which suggested to him that Gray's companion did the robbery. It doesn't quite suggest that to me."

The Inspector repeated the conversation which Foxy had heard from his hiding place in the tree.

"My word!" exclaimed Nigel. "So he heard Gray talking about the fake message in Bert's boat and the need to get the real message out of him? It seems to me we've got Gray cold." Nigel paused, and added, "You're not going to be precipitate and arrest him, I hope?"

"Not on your life, sir. I shall be asking him some carefully chosen questions this afternoon—give him a mild shock and plenty of rope, and see where he leads us.''

"He's got to lead us to Bert. I'm worried about that lad. The character Foxy described—the one who came with Gray to the cannibal party—"

"Walks like an American gangster. Has violet-smelling brilliantine, or sucks violet sweets. That's about all Foxy could tell me. Chap's face was blacked for the party. *But—*" the Inspector paused, "the man who shot the Quack speaks with an American accent. Of course, half the young toughies in this country affect American accents and walks—"

"Where did you get this from?"

"Your friend Foxy again. He and Bert were present at the liquidation of the Quack. Foxy wrote us that anonymous letter about where to find the body. His chum, Copper, made him come clean about it."

Wright passed on the whole story. "And what made them choose that particular house for Bert to go to ground in? Their damned detective game again. They were shadowing a red-faced man who had been making sinister inquiries after young Bert. He stopped outside this house, not many hours before the Quack was murdered there, to light a cigarette. No doubt he was prospecting. And this red-faced man has now been identified as Percy Chalmers." Wright sketched a gesture of a wheel coming full circle.

"You're making my head go round," said Nigel. "Who is this Chalmers, then?"

"Bad type, Mosleyite before the war. Done a stretch for extortion. Commercial traveler, plausible, sex appeal, bored housewife or pretty daughter goes a bit too far with him, anonymous letters presently—pay up or I'll tell hubby or dad as the case may be. He's a newcomer to my manor. We found this letter on him."

Nigel read it: *D street party off. Too hot. All laid on for Kingsway.* "Translate, please," he said.

"Chalmers isn't gaffing. Put on an act he'd never seen it

before. Like hell he hadn't! It's a stone ginger the message is about these political demonstrations. I've passed it to the Special Branch. Downing Street demonstration called off. Everything ready for Kingsway Hall—there's a big peace meeting there on Tuesday night, and I suppose they're going to break it up."

"Some staff work behind this."

"You've said it. The Special Branch are hopping mad. Their plans for the Downing Street reception were very comprehensive and very secret. Whoever's organizing these demonstrations must've been tipped off from high up that Downing Street wouldn't be healthy."

"And this Chalmers is one of the ex-Mosleyite scum. I wonder what clubs our friend Gray belongs to—apart from The High Dive."

"We're digging into his past."

"Good luck to the archaeologists. I shall do a bit of spadework myself presently. Lady Durbar is coming to visit me...."

At midday Hesione entered, dressed as if she were going on to a Royal Garden Party. She swooped toward the bed, releasing a gust of *Femme* and a torrent of solicitousness about Nigel's injury; then sat down, crossing the famous legs which had drawn full houses at Drury Lane and in the provinces. She took out a cigarette, put it away again, turned over a book on the bedside table, inquired after Clare, cast surreptitious little glances at the mirror.

"First-night nerves?" murmured Nigel.

"You wicked man!" She slapped his forearm lightly. "You see too much. Well, I am nervous. I never did like these places since I had my appendix whipped out when I was a small girl. The public ward for me, of course, in those days. So my bedside manners are shocking. Have they found out who did it?"

"Swiped your jewels?" said Nigel, deliberately misunderstanding.

"Oh, damn *them*. No, the men who attacked you, I mean."

"Not yet. Mr. Gray saw the number of the car they drove away in, but it was a false number plate. I should be very grateful to him for turning up when he did."

Hesione was fidgeting with a ring on her third finger—a magnificent sapphire which reflected the sapphire of her eyes. Suddenly she came out with,

"He's no damned fool, you know."

Nigel refrained from comment. He did not want to rush her. She went off at a tangent. "That Inspector asked me if I'd rung Alec up after lunch—the day you and Clare came. The police do suspect him, don't they?"

"Had you rung him up?"

"I never went near the telephone. I've not seen Alec or spoken to him, since the robbery." Her beautiful, wide mouth contorted bitterly. "When I've been sold a pup, I know it all right. Cut your losses, Mum always used to say."

"You've broken with him because you suspect it was he who stole your jewels?"

Hesione's index and middle fingers chased each other along the counterpane. After a pause, she said, "Alec Gray is a boor, a cheap skate, a proper young Demon King. But he's brave as they come, and no fool; and he has what it takes. He walks straight up to you, and next moment you're on your back. Excuse my tongue—I was brought up rough. Oh, I fell for him all right. I wouldn't have cared if he'd robbed all my best friends, and tanned his dear old granny to make a pair of shoes."

"But you drew the line at his robbing you?"

"Ah, if only I knew, if only I knew!" Hesione shook her clasped hands. "But between you and me and the bedpan, I could swear *I* never told him the combination of the ruddy safe—unless I talk in my sleep. I'm not that damn silly. Of course, as I've delicately intimated, he has been in my bedroom. But— No, what put me off young Alec was the blatant way he chased other skirts in front of me, and the way he chased that boy, Foxy, the night of my party. I saw the look on his face. He'd have half killed the boy. I never did go for hunting noises and blood sports.''

"Yes. I see. But Foxy isn't an angel, you know. He pinched a little jade idol from your house.

Lady Durbar's splendid eyes opened wide. "Oh no he didn't. I gave it to him. He's not in trouble for—?''

"Will you do something for me, Lady Durbar?''

"Hess to you.''

"Don't tell anyone for a few days—anyone at all—that you gave it to him. If you're asked about it, just say you hadn't noticed it was missing. Foxy won't get into trouble, I promise you.''

"All right. If you say so.''

"Now, going back to young Gray, did your husband know about it?''

"This is where I draw myself up and say, 'How dare you, Mr. Strangeways, accuse my husband of being a complaisant cuckold!' '' She gave him the full benefit of her swaggering, theater look, then laughed infectiously. "We didn't ever talk about it, but I'm sure Rudie knew.''

"And he's in a position to make things very hot for Gray.''

"Oh yes,'' she vaguely replied. "He could make it hot for anyone, if he wanted to. But he's too big to get worked up over my little peccadilloes. Besides—''

"Besides?'' Nigel prompted.

"Well, after my baby died—it was stillborn—Rudie sort of lost interest in me, in that way.'' She was speaking jerkily, painfully now. "I can never have another. And Rudie's heart was set on an heir. We get on awfully well, though.''

Nigel regarded his visitor thoughtfully. "Why are you telling me all this?''

"I couldn't tell the police, could I now? It'd be like—like discussing one's sex life with the Income Tax authorities.''

"About Gray, I meant.''

Her eyes fluttered away from him. She gave the impression of a woman who, disconcerted, is wondering whether to lie or tell the truth—wondering which will pay her best. Then she said, with deliberation, "I don't want him messing up your Clare. From what she said to me the other—"

"Clare can look after herself," interrupted Nigel, disregarding the possessive pronoun Hesione had used, though it gave him a queer little shiver of delight.

"My poor man! 'Look after herself'—that's the cue line for trouble. No woman can. Well, leave Clare out of it if you like. I want Alec"—her clear, rich voice grew harsh—"I want Alec stopped."

"Stopped?"

"Stopped doing whatever he is doing."

There was a question in her tones which Nigel ignored. He was not here to be pumped. He said, "What do *you* think he's doing?"

For an instant she seemed about to confide something; then she drew back. She still had a loyalty—a compunction, at least.

"Oh, how should I know?" she vaguely replied.

Remembering a phrase she had come out with at the lunch party, when he talked about the boy he was searching for, Nigel decided to take a risk.

"That boy who's disappeared—Bert Hale—you've seen it in the papers—it's possible that Gray kidnaped him."

"*Kidnaped?* But why?"

"Not for ransom. To get something out of him."

Hesione was visibly trembling. "Oh, the poor little boy! But it's—I can't understand it. Even Alec. Are you sure?"

"Where would he take him? Has he anywhere in the country?"

"He has a cottage in Hampshire."

"The police are making routine inquiries there. But I mean somewhere secret—a place, perhaps, that he would take a woman to."

"Not that I know of." She lifted her beautiful head. "I used to go to his flat. Still got the key, in fact."

"That might come in useful." Nigel paused; then lightly

added, "I was hoping he might have a hideout you knew about, in East Anglia. A hundred miles or so from London. Suffolk, say."

"Suffolk? Why d'you say Suffolk?" she asked sharply.

"Oh, it'd be convenient," was Nigel's evasive answer.

Lady Durbar was gazing into her lap. "Do you know the Stour Valley?" she presently said, in her social voice. "It's beautiful country. Lush and gentle. Sort of maternal." She is talking at random, thought Nigel: like a woman trying to avoid a crucial question. Then she doubled off on another track. "Some men are absurdly maternal. More than women. When I was expecting, Rudie spent hours studying those catalogues of baby apparatus. I just couldn't have believed it. Of course Rudie's a bit of an old pasha."

"Hess, you're babbling."

She gave him an uncertain, April kind of smile, and squeezed his hand. "I suppose I am. Listen, it's nothing to do with kidnaping—at least, it can't be; but one night, about a fortnight ago, I was with Alec. He'd gone to sleep. After a bit he said, quite loud and sharp, 'Elmer Steig.' Then he mumbled something about 'a gun for sale.' That's the name of a book, isn't it?"

"Yes. But who is Elmer Steig?"

"I haven't a clue. Next morning, I told Alec what he'd said in his sleep. Do you know what he did then?"

"No."

"He knelt on my arms, put the pillow over my face, and started to suffocate me. I thought it was—well, one of our games—at first. Then I knew it wasn't. I think I must have been half dead before he stopped. He said the object of the exercise—those were his actual words—was to make sure I didn't repeat what I'd heard him say in his sleep; if ever I did, he'd go through with the exercise. I was—I don't know—just dazed, bewildered. After that, he made love to me till I didn't care any longer. I was mad for him in those days."

Hesione had been talking to herself, more than to Nigel. Her voice was panting a little before she finished, and her hands, palm uppermost, trembled on her lap, the fingers curling up like leaves in a fire. Nigel firmly and tactfully changed the subject. "Is he interested in politics?"

Her faraway eyes gradually focused him, as if she was coming out of an anesthetic. "Politics? Oh, I see. I shouldn't have thought he had any time for that."

"You never discussed with him these new peace moves— the invitation to Russia?"

"Deary me, no. He wouldn't include a woman's opinions among her charms. If he went in for politics, it'd be for what he could get out of them. Why do you ask?"

"I'm trying to get at his motive for kidnaping Bert. If he did. Does he belong to any political body, or Old Soldiers' Association? Does he work for anyone?"

Hesione Durbar sucked in her ripe underlip. "Well, once or twice lately, when he'd stood me up, he made excuses afterward that he'd been detained by work. 'The syndicate is so exacting,' he said once. I let it ride. Alec work! I assumed he'd been with some other woman."

Which is exactly what you were intended to assume, thought Nigel. He asked Hesione a number more questions—about people she had met in Gray's company, about his past, his war career, the sources of his apparently unearned income.

"Women gave him money," she said, not looking at Nigel.

"Blackmail?"

"Sometimes, perhaps. Just love, generally, I imagine. If love is the word. It's funny you should mention blackmail, though. I've often wondered, recently, if he was blackmailing Rudie."

Nigel sat up. "Why? I shouldn't have thought it'd be healthy to try that on your husband."

"No. But it was curious that Rudie should let him go on coming to the house, after he'd found out about us. Even on the night of my cannibal party, they seemed quite thick— well, I mean they weren't avoiding each other, like you'd expect." She went off into a trill of laughter. "Perhaps it's the other way round: Rudie blackmailing Alec." The idea was so droll that she bent over her knees, laughing with the demonstrative heartiness of her plebeian upbringing. Suddenly she sobered again.

"Anything I can do to help about that poor little boy— what's his name?—Bert Hale, you've just to ask me."

Bert was peering through the bars of the nursery window, sideways and downward. The previous morning, when he was awakened by the sound of a shot, he had jumped out of bed and run to the window, with a vague, wild hope of rescue. All he had seen, though, was the barrel of some firearm poking—in a way that unpleasantly reminded him of the house in Belvedere Street—through a first-floor window below him to the right. The weapon kicked, and there was another whipping crack. Automatically his eye followed a line protracted from the rifle barrel, to be arrested by a stake which had been driven into the unkempt lawn. On the stake was fastened a target. Several more shots followed. Bert's hope of rescue faded into the realization that one of his captors was indulging in target practice. Before the unseen marksman emerged to take up his target, Bert heard footsteps approaching his door. He jumped back into bed, and when "Nanny" entered with a breakfast tray, he was pretending to be asleep.

The day had passed in waves of boredom and misery. There was nothing to be seen from the window, which was high up in a large gray house, except a terrace with stone balustrade directly beneath him, then a stretch of lawn bounded by what looked like a waterless moat, and beyond this the country—a countryside resembling, to his town-bred eyes, Hyde Park, except that the trees were much taller. The view was no doubt beautiful, peaceful, rural; but it gave Bert a pain in the neck, for it was a landscape without figures. Even if he had dared to call out for help, it would have been pointless, since not one solitary human being appeared, either in the foreground or the middle distance, all day. The place was as silent, too, as it was deserted: Bert heard no sound of train or car—only the occasional, distant mooing of a cow, and the day-long complacent roo-coo-rooing of pigeons which somehow reminded him of Nanny's voice.

He had written a letter to his mother, assuring her he was well and being properly looked after, and given it to the old woman to post. It told nothing about his kidnaping or his captivity, but he had little hope of its ever reaching its destination. He found a brand-new paint box and brushes in the cupboard, and spent an hour or two coloring the pictures in one of the kids' books. But it was a dreary, interminable day, relieved only by the meals Nanny brought and her fits of gossip about distinguished babies she had once had in her charge, so Bert was glad enough when bedtime came.

This morning, waking a bit earlier than on the first day of his imprisonment, he went again to the window. The prospect before him was unchanged. The sun, mounting the sky to his left, revealed the same boring expense of sky, trees and rich, rank grass. Looking nearer at hand, however, he observed one new feature in the landscape. On the lawn below his window, about where the stake had stood yesterday morning, was set a plain kitchen chair, and on this chair was sitting the old woman who called herself Nanny. Her back was toward him, and she was either asleep or admiring the view. Bert stayed at the window, not in any positive hope of seeing other human figures—indeed, he had not even bothered to put on his spectacles—but as a castaway surveys the expenses of ocean, in a dreary self-hypnosis, and because there is nothing else to look at.

Presently, he heard the sound of a window being gently opened, below him and to his right. The muzzle of the rifle poked out. It was trained in the same direction as yesterday. Bert opened his mouth, yelling a warning to the old woman asleep on the kitchen chair. His cry was drowned by the crack of the rifle, to which, like an almost instantaneous echo, was added a sort of sharp "clock"—the sound of a cricket bat meeting a ball—and the head of the figure seated in the chair visibly jerked.

Bert scrambled back to bed, hid his face in the pillow;

then, as further shots followed, he dug his fingers into his ears, sobbing. The memory of another shot, another head jerking and disintegrating, in the derelict house, rushed back at him. The old woman was silly, aggravating; but she had been kind to him. Now, for all he knew, he would be alone in this mansion with the person who had killed her. But why had she been killed? It seemed crazy, a piece of mad, meaningless nightmare. Then Bert remembered the letter he had written. Perhaps she really had tried to post it, and been caught, and this was her punishment.

Bert was still sobbing, hiccuping with sobs, when he heard a key turn in the lock. He burrowed under the clothes, away from whoever was coming in. A hand pulled the bedclothes back. A voice said, "Now, now, Master Bert. Hiding?"

It was Nanny.

Bert stared at her, rubbed his eyes, then flung himself into her arms.

"There, there," she said. "Was it a horrid dream?"

The word touched off again his doubt and his horror. Running to the window, he gazed out. Then, putting on his spectacles, he looked a second time. He could see clearly now: the figure on the chair was a dummy, dressed in apron and gray gown: the head, Nanny's head, was a coconut, its sparse hair painted grayish-white.

"I thought he was shooting at you," the boy blurted out.

Nanny clucked cozily. "The idea! Now, eat up your breakfast like a good boy. I've brought you some lovely rusks for a treat."

"But who is he? Who's been firing at that dummy?"

"It's a gentleman staying here, ducky. He's ever so fond of a nice bit of shooting."

"But why does he?—did he borrow those clothes from you?"

"Well, he wouldn't want to ruin his own, would he? They're just some old things of mine, I don't mind if he makes bullet holes in them."

The logic of this was so unassailable that for a moment its utter irrationality was lost on Bert. When he perceived it, he was appalled.

"But—" he began.

"Little boys should keep their but's to butter their bread with."

"Look here, I do wish you'd realize I'm not a little boy. I'm twelve."

But it was no good. The old woman's eye took on the wandering, bewildered look he had noticed before. Bert began to eat his breakfast. Presently Nanny, still at the window, waved her handerchief.

"Who are you waving to?" Bert asked, getting up and moving toward her.

"No, Master Bert! Sit down at once and get on with your breakfast!" she said sharply. "Mister Inquisitive got his fingers burned."

Bert got on with it. He had never eaten rusks before, and found them quite good.

"Who else lives here?"

"There's me, and my nephew. And the gardener; but he has a cottage in the grounds."

"Do you and your nephew own the house?"

"Listen to him!" The old woman went off into a paroxysm of wheezing chuckles. "No, dearie, we're caretakers. Most of the house is shut up. We just keep a room or two ready for visitors—like you, and the gentleman who's staying. Ever so sad, I call it, when I remember the house parties and goings-on we used to have in the old days."

Bert let her ramble away. He had discovered yesterday that there were certain questions she would not answer: she would not tell him, for example, where this house was, or who had invited him—as he tactfully put it—to stay here. So now he was exercising his brains to get at the information in some devious way.

At a pause of her reminiscences he said, "It's an awfully

out-of-the-way place isn't it? Where do you get your food from? Is there a village near?''

"Well, Master Bert, when you're my age you don't want gallivantings and cinemas and that. The village is two miles away. But they send regularly from—'' she stopped in mid-sentence, a flicker of fear in her eye.

"Send what?''

"The groceries and meat and such. We have our own fruit and vegetables, of course. And the dustman comes every second Monday. It wouldn't suit everyone, mind you. The young mistress couldn't abide it. Too quiet for her. But then, she was used to racketing about in—''

Once again, Bert shut off his attention. A wheeze, a brain wave whose brilliance startled even him, accustomed though he was to the visitations of ingenuity, had come into his head. By hook or by crook, he was thinking, I must get out to where they keep the dustbins, for the day after tomorrow is the second Monday of the month.

12

Light at Eventide

Bert's apparent docility, his acceptance of the extraordinary situation in which he was placed, must have impressed his captors. On Sunday morning, when he asked the old woman if he might go out and play ball on the lawn, she said she would ask her nephew. There had been no shooting today from the first-floor window; instead, Bert heard the sound of church bells, faint or swelling on wafts of wind from the east: that way lay the village, then. The old woman returned, to tell him that her nephew would take him out for exercise in the yard this afternoon. It sounded—this curious phrase—as if he was a dog; or, for that matter, a prisoner. But the boy's heart leaped. A yard was where one kept dustbins. No doubt the yard would be a safer place than the lawn, from his jailers' point of view: it could not be overlooked; though, for all the signs of human activity around this god-forsaken place, they could have let him fire off rockets from the roof with little risk of anyone noticing it.

As soon as the old woman retired with his breakfast tray, after making the bed and pottering about with a duster, Bert settled down to write a message. He dared not make any rough copies, in case they should be discovered later and betray him; he must get it right first time. So he worked out alternatives in his head. Satisfied at last, he wrote, in large letters, on the drawing pad he had found among the children's books:

BERT HALE, THE KIDNAPED BOY THE POLICE ARE LOOKING FOR, IS
IMPRISONED IN THE HOUSE WHERE THIS DUSTBIN WAS COLLECTED
FROM. PLEASE INFORM THE POLICE AT ONCE. VERY URGENT. S.O.S.
                                                                BERT HALE.

Bert's plan was based on his observation of the London
dustman. He had often seen them, before decanting a bin into
their refuse lorry, poke about among its contents. If it contained anything of value, they set this aside; they seemed
particulary interested in wooden boxes—perhaps they were
all amateur carpenters. Having written his message, Bert cast
about for the best receptacle. It must be something he could
take out to the yard in a pocket—small enough not to create a
suspicious bulge, but not so small that it would escape a
dustman's notice. Looking through the toy cupboard, he rejected a pencil box, a carton of crayons, a cardboard con-
tainer full of draftsmen, and finally chose a small box en-
crusted with shells: it would fit into his pocket, and it would
be more likely than the others to attract attention when lying
in a heap of refuse. Into this Bert put his message. The lid
seemed fairly firm. Only when the box was safely tucked
away in his trouser pocket did he begin to think what might
be done to him if the message were intercepted.

After lunch, Nanny brought in a stalwart man of about
thirty, who proved to be as silent as his aunt was garrulous.
Bert had selected, from a number of woolly and rubber balls
in the cupboard, one whose colors were less atrociously sissy
than the rest, and now he followed the man, whom Nanny
called Tom, out of the room. They descended three flights of
stairs, went along a short passage, and entered what had once
been the servants' hall and was now a sitting room for the
caretakers. Bert, noticing a telephone on a shelf in one
corner, involuntarily slowed. It was only the slightest check,
but it did not escape the man. He spoke, for the first time, in a
voice which sounded to Bert like a rusty key turning in the
lock of a dungeon door.

"No, sonny. The blower's not for you. Keep moving."

They went through an enormous, cobwebbed kitchen, into another passage, and then Tom was unbolting the back door. What Nanny had called "the yard" was very different from Bert's experience of yards in London. It proved to be an expanse bigger than the school playground, composed of cobblestones with grass sprouting between them. On his right was a high wall; in front of him a line of buildings, which resembled a London mews: to the left lay a gateway, flanked by lichened stone pillars and giving a view of a drive curling round toward the front of the house: a stone drinking trough stood in the center of the yard. The place was desolate and anonymous, as if a plague had passed over it. Even the pigeons had been silenced by the afternoon heat. Bert jumped a little when the man beside him broke this silence.

"No funny business, see? I can run faster than you, and we don't want no excitement. Bad for you, after your nervous breakdown. And don't try your high notes, or I'll kick you in the railings."

The intention, if not the exact meaning, was clear enough to Bert. Despondently he nodded. This was not going to be like those stories in which pathetic young prisoners soften the hearts of surly jailers. The man, Tom, moved off to the left, stationing himself between Bert and the yard gateway; he had locked the back door and pocketed the key, so there'd be no chance of escaping through the house. On the other hand, against the house, between the back door and the gate, stood a couple of dustbins.

"Well, go on," said the man. "You wanted to play ball. Play!"

That moment was the nadir of Bert's young life. It sharpened the nightmare quality of his isolation to an unbearable pitch. He felt broken open, utterly exposed: tears of self-pity and exasperation pricked his eyes, and he kicked the idiotic colored ball viciously, aimlessly against the wall on his right. It slapped against the wall with a sort of elastic sound which filled the empty courtyard. Bert took a run at the ball, and kicking it again, stubbed his toe against a cobble. As he danced on one foot, in pain, the man Tom guffawed.

"You're no bloody good at this, mate," he said.

It brought Bert to boiling point.

"Bet you I can get it past you. Go on," he said furiously, "you stand between those pillars. That's the goal. If you're so damned good at football—"

"Temper, temper!" said the man. "All right, cock, see what you can do."

Stubbing out his cigarette, Tom went to stand in the gateway. He stopped a few shots from Bert, with contemptuous ease. Then the boy got one past him, and began to jeer at him. Tom was taking it in earnest now, crouching with outspread arms. Bert knew his chance had come. After a few deliberately feeble shots at goal, he pretended to lose his temper again, took an almighty kick at the ball, and sent it curling over the wall to the right of the gateway. Tom disappeared to retrieve it. Risking observation from the back window, Bert whipped off a dustbin lid, buried the little box from his pocket just under the surface of the refuse, and had replaced the lid before Tom reappeared in the gateway.

In the hospital that same afternoon, sitting up in a chair now, Nigel Strangeways fretted at his uselessness. As so often happens when the mind is both overtired and overexcited, he kept covering the same ground again and again, like a golfer searching for a lost ball; his thoughts brooded over the lunch party at the Durbars'. It was impossible to avoid the conclusion that either Hesione or her husband had ordered the attempt on his life. Hesione had denied telephoning when the others were looking at Durbar's pictures; but of course, if guilty, she would deny it. Sir Rudolf had pressed them to stay a little longer; and, on hearing that Nigel would escort Clare home, had gone out of the gallery to fetch the Van Dyck. He could have telephoned then, informing Gray of Nigel's exact movements; and previously, when the secretary called him out of the room, he could have rung up Gray, or whoever his chief strong-arm man was, to order a state or readiness.

It was incredible to Nigel that either Sir Rudolf or Lady Durbar should have a gang of thugs on tap. He could have imagined Hesione innocently telling Gray, during a telephone conversation, that her guest was searching for a boy called Bert Hale, whom no one else was in a position to identify; he could have imagined it, if Hesione were still on intimate terms with Gray. But, after the things she had told him yesterday about her exlover, this seemed out of the question. As for Sir Rudolf—well, Superintendent Blount had said to him only this morning, after hearing Nigel's suspicions, "You might as well accuse the Bank of England of cooking the petty cash. Big men like Durbar don't employ cosh boys. They don't need to. And they wouldn't know where to find them, if they did need."

This, so far as it went, was sound enough. The Superintendent, a most experienced and able police officer, could always be relied on to puncture the bubbles of Nigel's fancy: as a professional, Blount could not afford to indulge in the irresponsible conjectures which his friend sometimes threw off. Nevertheless, thought Nigel now, many crimes have been committed from behind a cover of respectability—of apparently inculpable eminence, even. Durbar was the kind of man who, if he wanted something arranged, would find the right man to arrange it, pay him well, and expect the work to be well done. He had spent hours, before his child was born—so Hesione had said—"studying those catalogues of baby apparatus": the job of buying them would be handed over, no doubt, to a well-qualified underling: Sir Rudolf would not descend into the market place himself.

And, if he wanted violence done, he would entrust the working out of ways and means to suitable hands, washing his own of the whole matter. Sir Rudolf, then, produced the ideas; his middlemen would retail them. Whatever Sir Rudolf was up to—assuming he was up to something other than doing down his business rivals in the normal, near-legal

way—Gray would be imagined as a highly effective middle-
man. But it was just here that the whole thing became incom-
prehensible. Alec Gray was Durbar's only known link with
the violent and the shady. But Gray had also been the lover of
Durbar's wife: and Durbar was "a bit of a pasha." Was it
conceivable that Durbar should use such a man as his instrument?

Yet he had not forbidden Gray the house. Even as recently
as the night of the party, the two—according to Lady
Durbar—had "seemed quite thick." Perhaps it was Sir
Rudolf himself whom Foxy, up in his tree, had overheard
talking to Gray. No wonder the latter had it in for Foxy. One
thing was certain—Durbar would only use his wife's lover
for a criminal purpose if that purpose were more important to
him than his own pride or his relationship with his wife. His
"interests," his financial empire would be more important;
and, if the present negotiations with Russia were successful,
if they paved the way toward better international relations,
Durbar's interests would suffer. Though Sir Rudolf had given
nothing away at the lunch party, he had not relished Nigel's
probing; his manner had shown that this was a tender spot.

But the incidents which were occurring during the Russian
visit, although they could be part of a campaign, could hardly
be its main object: they had been, so far, nuisances and pin
pricks, at the worst. Men were not murdered and boys kidnaped to safeguard so amateurish a guerrilla warfare as this.
Some decisive blow must be preparing—or else Nigel was off
the track altogether.

His thoughts now revolved around Hesione's curious reve-
lation. Gray had attacked her viciously because she had heard
him talking in his sleep. "Elmer Steig" and "something
about a gun for sale" were the operative words. Elmer Steig
was an American-sounding name, and the man who shot the
Quack had spoken, according to Foxy, with an American
accent. One could hardly suppose that a killer had been
smuggled in from U.S.A. just to rub out the Quack. There
must be bigger game in view. And the leading character of *A*

Gun for Sale was a man hired to assassinate a peace-making statesman. Furthermore, for what it was worth, Foxy had told Inspector Wright that the man whom Gray brought to the Durbars' party walked like a gunman on the flicks.

In high excitement, Nigel took up the telephone. At last a theory was forming which made sense of the disjointed, random occurrences of the past week. When Nigel got through, however, Inspector Wright was not available to receive the benefit of his theory.

The Inspector, at this moment, was engaged upon one of the trickiest jobs of his lifetime. Alec Gray's studied insolence was riling enough; but that was nothing to the difficulty of forming questions which should not betray the extent of the police's knowledge about Gray's activities or the nature of their suspicions.

"On the evening of the 6th, last Thursday," Wright was saying, "you went down to your cottage in Hampshire, returning by car the next morning?"

"So I said." Gray flicked cigarette ash onto the carpet. "But if your snoopers have discovered I wasn't there, I'll make it somewhere else."

"You wish to alter your first statement, sir?"

"I don't *wish* to. But I'm always ready to oblige."

"With the truth, this time?"

Alec Gray's small, congested eyes looked the Inspector up and down. "I don't recommend your taking that tone with me. It is rude, and it won't work."

"Your original statement, that you were in Hampshire that night, is not true?" said Wright equably.

"I was in London. In bed with a girl. I didn't want her brought into it."

"Her name and address, if you please, sir."

Gray scrawled them on the back of a visiting card, and flicked it at the Inspector.

"You wished to protect her honor?" said Wright, in his most neutral tone; a faint quiver of the mouth suggested his skepticism as to Gray's capacity for any such honorable motive, but the man was not so easily to be drawn.

"Does this young lady—" Wright tapped his nails on the visiting card—"own a sun-ray lamp?"

"I just couldn't tell you."

"I was wondering how you got the sunburn which you told Miss Massinger you got driving back from Hampshire."

"What a damned silly question!"

"You prefer not to answer it?"

"I never said so. I was sunbathing on my roof that afternoon."

Detective-Sergeant Allen, taking down shorthand notes at a desk in Gray's flat, gave his superior officer a fleeting glance. Wright's polite, interested expression had not altered.

"Coming to the next evening, Friday," he said, "you were at The High Dive from six-thirty to midnight?"

"We've had all this before."

"You don't wish to alter that statement too?"

"No. I'm quite happy about it. Aren't you?"

"I would be happier, sir, if any of the waiters or barmen had seen you there. No one seems to have noticed your presence till eleven P.M."

Gray stared superciliously at the Inspector, and swung his legs up on to the arm of the chair he was lounging in.

"Presumably the doorman saw me come in, and presumably your snooper didn't see me come out."

"What were you doing in the club between six-thirty and eleven P.M.?"

Gray sighed, as if in exasperation. "Having dinner, my good Inspector. With Sam Borch. In his private room. Antrobus, the manager, brought in the victuals. I've told you this before. No doubt Borch and Antrobus have corroborated it. I find you rather a bore."

"Yet the day before, Borch told me he was not on intimate terms with you."

"Do you have to be on intimate terms with everyone who gives you dinner? You must move in very peculiar social circles, Inspector. I put a bit of money into the club recently, and I suppose I'm entitled to discuss business matters with Borch and his manager?"

"Business matters. Ah yes." Wright was never one to signal his punches. "You know," he went on quietly, "that Sam Borch has been arrested?"

Gray's bullet head came slowly round. The public-school drawl was accentuated. "The devil he has! What have you pinned on the poor old sod?"

"He will be charged with receiving stolen property. An article belonging to Lady Durbar was actually found in his possession."

Alec Gray threw his cigarette in the fireplace, lit another, and expelled a jet of smoke toward Inspector Wright. "I *see*. So that's what you've been getting at. I'm supposed to be a cat burglar, or something, who passes on the takings to our Mr. Borch. That was the point of your heavy little act about the business matters he and I were discussing. Well, my God, what silly clots you policemen are!"

"Borch has not divulged the names of any of his associates. Not yet. Are you surprised to hear, sir, about these criminal activities of his?"

"I can't say I am. I'm prepared to believe anyone may be a crook, until it's proved to the contrary. But I should have thought women, or dirty post cards, were more his line. Not that he's ever actually whispered the address of some cozy little piece into my ear."

"No, I imagine that would not be necessary," remarked Wright, again in his most colorless tones. Unexpectedly, Gray took no offense at this; indeed, he almost smirked. Wright went on, as if talking to himself, "Egotism. Overconfidence. Conceit. They're the common factor in all criminals. You'd be surprised, sir. It's really pathetic—the way their conceit always betrays them, sooner or later. Just rank, infantile conceit."

"I got the idea first time."

"Sam Borch, for instance. Blind with vanity. Thought he could fiddle and diddle his way happily forever afterward. Now he'll fall to bits and spill the beans all round. He's just

like every other crook: take away his shell of conceit, and
there's nothing but a soft center inside—a miserable little
embryo of a human being.''

Sergeant Allen glanced up again from his shorthand notes.
He had not heard the Old Man in this vein before, and it was
highly instructive; moreover, he seemed at last to have got
under Alec Gray's skin. The man's smooth, pinkish face was
becoming suffused; the eyes showed more anger now than
arrogance. But Gray's self-control, when he cared to exercise
it, was remarkable; he made no other response to the Inspector's baiting.

"Take another instance, sir," the Inspector resumed.
"The fellow who kidnaped that boy, Bert Hale. I dare say
you've read about it in the papers. Dresses up as a policeman,
puts on a false mustache, and walks off with the lad. Overconfidence again. We've only got to paint in a similar mustache on the photographs of our suspects, and the boy's uncle
and aunt will pick out the right man at once.''

"Why don't you do it, then?" drawled Gray. "Or are you
still waiting for some suspects to turn up?''

"Because we want the boy more than we want the criminal. We believe he's got some information which would ena-
ble us to break open all these recent big—'' The Inspector
broke off, giving an admirable rendering of a police officer
who has fallen into a grave indiscretion. "Well, that is as
may be. My point is that arresting the kidnaper won't, at this
juncture, find the boy for us.''

"Too bad," remarked Gray coolly.

Sergeant Allen, wooden-faced at the desk, had got Inspector Wright's drift. It was the old, ever-new maneuver—the
same for the three-card operator as for the general about to
launch an offensive: trick your opponent into thinking you
intend to strike here, and then strike elsewhere. Wright had
been ever so subtly forcing Gray's attention toward the
burglaries, and holding it there—giving all the time the impression that the burglaries, and the kidnaping only in relation to them, were the center of police interest. This, no

doubt, was why Wright kept his strongest cards in his hand—the conversation, for instance, which Foxy had heard from the tree in the Durbars' garden. There was some bigger game afoot, and Gray was involved; all Wright's efforts were being directed toward inducing Gray to leave that flank unguarded.

"Got writer's cramp, Sergeant?" The Inspector's sharp voice recalled Allen to the fact the question and answer had begun again, unrecorded by his pencil. Flushing a little, admiringly thinking to himself that the old———didn't miss a ruddy trick, Allen resumed his shorthand.

An hour later, about six o'clock that Sunday evening, Foxy observed a policeman approaching the front door of his house. Foxy was what is called in the Notting Hill vernacular "an arab"; and now, like the Arabs, he struck his tent and departed—through the back door. The policeman had been instructed to fetch him for an interview with Nigel Strangeways. But Foxy was not to know this. He already regretted having been persuaded by Copper to tell the police all: they had not arrested him, or roughed him up; but the mere sight of a uniform now reminded him of the little jade idol and Gray's letter. The police must have somehow discovered that he had planted these on the men arrested in the Portobello Road, and they were going to take him up for it.

Foxy was indeed in deadly peril, though not from the quarter he expected. Alec Gray had, of course, heard about Borch's arrest before the Inspector informed him; he had also heard that a red-headed boy, whom he identified as that ubiquitous nuisance, Foxy, was mixed up in it. He did not know, however, that Foxy had already been interviewed by the police. After Inspector Wright and Sergeant Allen left, Gray acted quickly. He had never been sure how much, if any, Foxy had heard of the conversation in the Durbar's garden. If he had heard it, he'd presumably not passed it on to the police—otherwise they would certainly have arrested him, Gray, for complicity in the murder of Dai Williams.

But, now that Foxy was mixed up with the police over this other matter, there was a danger that he might come out with that incriminating piece of conversation. The boy must be questioned, and, if necessary, silenced. Nothing must get in the way of what was planned for next Thursday.

Gray had been touched on the raw by Inspector Wright, more than once, during their interview. His animosity now transferred itself to the brat who kept cropping up under his feet. He went downstairs—his own telephone, for all he knew, might be tapped by now—let himself into the flat of a neighbor, who was away on holiday, with a key he had found useful before, and picked up the telephone. . . .

Aimlessly walking the streets, Foxy found himself after twenty minutes in the vicinity of the house where the Quack had been shot. Since, when he'd gone out by the back door, he was on the lookout only for coppers, he had not observed the two youths who detached themselves from the wall of the pub opposite, nor did he notice that anyone was following him now. He was sick of being chivvied around by coppers, all because Lady Durbar had given him a present of a jade idol. It was bleeding unfair. Suddenly he snapped his fingers. Why hadn't he thought of it before? He'd go to Lady Durbar's house and get her to sign a paper saying the idol was a free gift from her. That'd fix the coppers all right, if they tried to pin anything on him.

The force of this simple idea turned Foxy on his heel, toward Notting Hill Gate again. As he reversed direction, he saw two youths, fifty yards away, on the opposite side of the road, stop dead in their tracks. His arab instinct warned him they meant trouble; his eyes, as he came nearer to them, confirmed it: he knew their sort all right. They began to cross the road toward him, and he darted left up a side street. This was a class neighborhood, and he didn't think the youths would start any trouble here, but for safety's sake he kept near a young man and girl in tennis clothes who were walking his way. He had only gone thirty paces when he saw a policeman turn into the street, ahead of him; at the same time he became aware of a bell tolling loud overhead and running footsteps behind. Caught between two converging forces, with a high blank wall on his left and a church on his right, Foxy, who had momentarily lost his head, sought sanctuary in a most appropriate place. He ran for the church.

A bleak-looking man in a sort of velvet gown gazed forbiddingly at him from the main door. The running footsteps caught up with him as he checked. It was a boy he knew at school. Foxy gripped his arm.

"Hello, Foxy," panted the boy. "Let go. I'm late."

But Foxy would not let go. "They're after me. Those two bastards. I've got to hide."

"Come on, then."

Foxy found himself towed through a side door of the church into a small room filled with men and boys in a garb which Foxy had only seen before on the films.

"Get a move on. You're late," said the senior choirman officiously.

Foxy's friend found him a cassock and surplice. The population of this particular choir was rather a floating one, particularly in the summer holidays. The choirmaster, who would have recognized Foxy as an interloper, was already at the organ. The clergyman, a *locum tenens,* did not know the personnel of the choir. The choirmen, gossiping among themselves with hearty voices and occasionally shushing the boys, assumed that Foxy was a temporary recruit. Only the choirboys, in the manner of their kind, regarded him with deep suspicion and hostility.

Outside the church, meanwhile, the two youths who had been sent to collect Foxy were at a loss. To them, a church was like a prison—a place you did not enter if you could possibly help it. But, as they lolled against the iron railings, the policeman whose appearance had deflected Foxy's course moved heavily upon them.

"Any business here, my lads? Move along, then."

"We're going to church. Any objection, copper?" said one of the youths.

"That's all right. Just remember, when they bring the plate

round, you put money into it—see?—you don't fill your pockets from it.''

Conscious of the policeman's eye upon them, the youths slouched into the west door. Congregations here being sparse, the verger had instructions to show strangers into the front pews. The youths, for all their brash swagger, were overawed by the atmosphere of the place, and followed him tamely right up the aisle.

Cursing under his breath, Foxy had at last done up the apparently infinite series of small buttons down the front of his cassock, and his friend popped the surplice over his head. The officious choirman, commenting unfavorably on the untidiness of Foxy's hair, thrust him beside another boy in the procession that was forming up. The five-minute bell stopped; the organ swelled; the clergyman said a prayer; and they sallied forth from the vestry at funeral-march pace.

"Keep in step, can't you, you silly clot," muttered the boy beside Foxy, hands piously folded on his stomach, eyes gazing angelically before him. Foxy was about to give the boy a hack on the ankle when he saw, in a pew far ahead, the two youths he had run away from. It would be unwise, he thought, to start a brawl just at present. Meekly, he fell into step, nearly tripping over the long cassock in the process.

Presently, without further mishap, they reached the choir stalls, and the parson gave out a hymn. Foxy, ever adaptable, following closely the movements of his companions, found the right book, held it high in front of him, and opened and shut his mouth soundlessly. At the second verse, he felt he had got the hang of it. So he gave tongue. A hoarse, tearing noise ensued, like the rending of calico, as Foxy slurred joyously from note to note. The choir wavered and almost broke down: the organist glanced over his shoulder. Foxy, made aware of a difference of timbre in his own vocalization, subdued himself to a rusty *piano*.

As they embarked on the third verse, he felt a smart jog in the side. The boy next him leaned his head nearer and piped, in seraphic tones:

> O Carrots, who the hell are you?
> What are you doing here?

To which Foxy cautiously sang antiphonal reply:

> You mind your business, chum, or else
> I'll do you after church.

A sharp tap on the shoulder from a choirman ended these exchanges, and worship proceeded normally for a while. When the parson moved to the lectern for the First Lesson, Foxy was startled by a sort of irregular, tiny fusillade behind him—a sound that might have been made by a file of unskillful trackers snapping twigs underfoot as they prowled through a forest. Turning his head, he observed that all the choirmen had broken off lengths of licorice or barley sugar, to refresh their larynxes against their further labors. Since this was the form, Foxy had no scruples about reaching under his cassock for a bag of toffee in his trouser packet, and openly offering it to his neighbor. An outraged choirman behind him at once knocked the bag from his hand: it fell, with a loud clack, on the marble floor of the chancel, and remained there—a spectacle totally demoralizing the choirboys during the rest of divine service. Foxy brooded on the injustice of life, which imposes one law for the young and another for the old.

He was thinking hard, too, as the parson read through the prayers, how he could evade those ill-favored youths in the front pew. They had already made covert signs to him, whose import was unmistakable. His only hope was to leave the church in a convoy of choirmen, but he had no idea what the proceedings would be when service was over. Perhaps he could slip out by some back door. But did churches have back doors? As it turned out, however, these speculations were wasted: for, in a few minutes, Foxy was to see the light. It began to dawn when the parson, having climbed into the pulpit, gave out his text.

13

No. 3 Berth

"From the Gospel of St. John; Chapter 15, Verse 13," announced the parson. " 'Greater love hath no man than this, that a man lay down his life for his friends.' "

It was not a very orthodox sermon. The parson, once a regular chaplain in the R.A.F., had been invalided out toward the end of the war. He had a small country living, which afforded him no money for holidays, and in lieu of them he took occasional *locum tenens* duty for a London friend. The Reverend James Roland's theology was shaky; his Christian zeal had been blunted by ten years of Church Parades and seven years of preaching to meager, lethargic congregations such as he faced this evening. As a parish visitor he was inclined to be lazy, while he treated his churchwardens with a certain officer-class brusqueness which did him no good in his own parish. It is doubtful whether he had converted a soul to his religion.

The Reverend Roland had, however, one sheet anchor and saving grace. He was a true hero-worshiper. Nothing would ever be so alive, so real for him as his friends in the R.A.F. who had ragged him, drunk with him, then gone up into the air to die. When he spoke of them, as he was speaking this evening—telling stories of self-sacrifice and courage—his mediocrity, his failure fell away from him, and he took on a little of the greatness which he was describing.

Foxy listened, enthralled. This was the goods. His cynical, perky, opportunist young mind, which up to the present had

fed on the doctrine of *sauve qui peut* and on the nasty little
crumbs that fall from Fleet Street and Hollywood tables,
responded to an appeal it had never before encountered. If the
Reverend Roland did not make a convert of Foxy, he at least
set him on a new course. Bert Hale was his friend, Foxy said
to himself. If he had gone to the police sooner, Bert would
never have been kidnaped. He and Copper had gone their
usual ways, since the kidnaping, with hardly a thought for
Bert; it wasn't good enough, reflected Foxy, listening to the
slangy, commonplace, heartfelt sermon. A God hanging on a
cross in Palestine to save the world meant nothing to him. A
pilot, whom the parson called by his Christian name, flying a
crippled bomber back over England, ordering his crew to bail
out, then turning out to sea again and going for a Burton so
that the 1000-pounder jammed in the bomb bay should not
endanger anyone on home soil—this was something Foxy
could take in and be exalted by.

The mood would not last long, perhaps. But so exalted was
Foxy at the moment that, if he could have saved Bert by
hurling himself on the razors of the two youths in the front
pew, he would have done it. Nothing so simple, however,
was called for. A much more cold-blooded courage would be
required to carry out the project forming in Foxy's mind. The
youths, he believed, must belong to the mob which had
snatched Bert. Why else should they be after him? And the
only way he could hope to rescue Bert was to let the mob take
him; then, keeping his ears open and his wits sharp, try to
find where they had put his friend and escape with the information.

When the service was over and the choir disrobing. Foxy
extricated himself from the awkward questions they were
beginning to ask him in the vestry, darted out of church, and
walked steadily over to the two youths who were waiting on
the other side of the road. The congregation had dispersed.
The rest of the choir had not yet emerged. No one saw Foxy
walk away with the youths; and it was the best part of forty-

eight hours before a description of them, gleaned from members of the choir, the verger, and the policeman who had spoken to them outside the church, could be circulated.

Nigel's first intimation that the boy he wanted to interview had disappeared came by telephone next morning, not long after a call from Sir Rudolf's secretary, inquiring on his employer's behalf about Nigel's progress.

"Please thank Sir Rudolf, will you? And tell him I'm getting on all right, but apparently they won't let me out for several days," Nigel had replied.

Clare, who was sitting with him, raised her eyebrows.

"I believe you positively enjoy being—what's the word?—hospitalized. You look perfectly healthy to me."

"What a suspicious-minded girl you are," said Nigel, reflecting that she had every reason to be in this case; for he intended to leave hospital secretly very much sooner, and future inquiries would be answered by the news that Mr. Strangeways had had a relapse. But this it was inadvisable for Clare to know. She had been given a part to play which she would play better if she believed in it.

"You're not nervous about tonight, are you, my dear?" asked Nigel.

"Not nervous, no. The prospect just fills me with repulsion, that's all."

The prospect Clare alluded to was a dinner-and-dance date with Alec Gray, which, on Nigel's instructions, she had successfully angled for the previous day.

"I wouldn't mind being used as a cross between a tethered goat and a call girl," she broke out, her dark eyes flashing, "if only I knew what it was all about."

Nigel took her hands. After a mutinous little struggle they remained in his. "You'll make a much better goat if you *don't* know."

"But what am I supposed to talk to him about?"

"Oh, the weather, the crops, the dance floor, Epstein—anything you like," Nigel offhandedly replied.

"Damn you, Nigel!" she exclaimed, snatching her hands from his. "Sometimes you're absolutely inhuman." She paced the room with that swift, swirling movement of hers which suggested flying draperies, silver-flashing limbs, arrows, Artemis.

"I'm sorry, darling," he said. "What I mean is, don't start up dangerous subjects like burglary, kidnaping, or N. Strangeways. He mustn't get the impression that you've been laid on to pump him. If *he* broaches them it's another matter. You listen, you encourage him, you know nothing about anything except that I was searching for Bert Hale and am now *hors de combat*."

"Oh well—"

"The one important thing is to keep him there as long as possible, and when he's leaving, go to the ladies' room and telephone this number." Nigel gave her a slip of paper, which she put away in her handbag.

"You *are* mysterious! What do I say?"

"Just say—let's think—say, 'Bobbles is on his way.'"

Clare gave her delicious giggle. Then her face clouded again. "Do I have to come back with him? In a taxi? I'm sorry, Nigel, but I don't like the idea. You know what he is."

"Certainly not. What do you take me for? I've ordered a hired car to bring you home. It will be waiting outside for you. The driver is a friend of mine, an ex-pugilist. If young Gray starts anything, just tap on the window and the pug will look after him."

Clare beautifully tilted her head, smiling a secret smile. "I take it all back," she said. "You're a wonder, and the joy of my life."

"Good Lord! You saved my life, didn't you? The least I can do is to preserve your honor. Have you got the key?"

"Here it is."

"Good girl," said Nigel, as Clare handed him the key of Alec Gray's flat which he had arranged with Lady Durbar to borrow.

"I suppose this is the key to some little love nest you and

Hess are setting up." Clare's voice did not sound quite as light as she meant it to.

Nigel's pale blue eyes regarded her steadily. "If ever I set up a love nest again, it won't be with her. And you know it."

When Clare Massinger had left, he turned over the key in his hand. It was the weakest point in this scheme. Hesione must know very well what he wanted it for, and he could not be certain that her past infatuation for Gray would not cause her to repent of thus betraying him. Well, the risk had to be taken. Someone must go through Gray's flat, and the police had good reasons for not doing it themselves as yet: a police search might spring the mine sooner than was advisable—Gray must not know just how close upon his heels they were; and secondly, Superintendent Blount had informed Nigel that very considerable influence was being brought to bear upon the Yard, from a quarter his Assistant Commissioner would not divulge, to lay off Alec Gray. The Yard, Nigel knew as well as Blount, was politically incorruptible. But it meant that any action taken against Gray must be backed by an absolutely watertight case, or else there would be a most unholy row and heads would roll.

That afternoon Nigel was smuggled out of the hospital and driven to a friend's house. A little before seven-thirty in the evening, the decorum of Radley Gardens was assailed by music from an ancient, wheezing gramophone. This instrument was being slowly pushed up the street in a pram, which had painted on its sides: *Old Clown. Out of work. Spare a tanner for Toto.* The individual pushing the pram would have wrung the heart of a Scrooge: tall, stooping, cadaverous; tattered plimsolls on his feet; in filthy, patched clothes, his wrinkled face almost invisible behind a jungle of hair, Toto tottered up Radley Gardens, radiating an aura of utter melancholy which the gramophone, tinnily screaming out *I Pagliacci,* did nothing to alleviate.

A taxi was waiting outside No. 34. As the old clown approached, his faded blue eyes were rejoiced by the sight of a beautiful dark girl, in a flame-colored evening dress, emerge from the house, followed by a pin-headed, slick-haired man. When she saw the dismal object wheeling the pram, she took a shilling from her bag. Averting those faded blue eyes, the clown held out a filthy claw, and in a husk of a voice said, "Thank you, lady. Gawd bless you."

Ah well, thought Nigel as the taxi moved off, if Clare could not recognize me, Alec Gray certainly did not. He wheeled his deplorable pram to the end of the street, collecting a few coppers thrown from windows en route; then, going down a deserted cul-de-sac on the far side of Campden Hill Road, he disposed of pram and gramophone among the debris of a bombed site, put on a long cloak and sombrero hat which had been concealed in the pram, and returned to Radley Gardens with a large, rolling gait, the image of a genuine, if disreputable, painter. He entered No. 34, went upstairs, let himself into Gray's flat, closed the door and put it on the chain, drew the curtains, and switched on the light.

His next step was to find an escape route, if there was such a thing. If Clare played her part correctly, and telephoned the number he had given her, he would not need it; but one couldn't be too careful. A little prospecting discovered the ladder which led up to the roof garden; and warily investigating this, Nigel found a fire escape leading down the back wall of the house. He returned to the sitting room. With his usual blatant disregard for his neighbors, Gray had left the radio playing at full blast. This was most convenient. It would cover any noise Nigel might make. Throwing off cloak and hat, putting on a pair of gloves, he looked round the room.

It was furnished and decorated with a good deal more taste than Nigel had expected. The radio and cocktail cabinet were vulgar enough; but over the mantelpiece, which was littered with invitation cards, there hung a tolerable Utrillo, and on the wall facing it a really fine Vuillard interior. A grand piano stood in one corner, a saxophone and a guitar leaned against another. There were two enormous armchairs, an expensive-looking divan, and a walnut escritoire. Nigel moved over to the latter. He had a jemmy in his pocket, and no scruples about breaking drawers open, for he intended the job to look like a straight burglary. In the present instance, however, no violence was needed. The drawers of the escritoire were not locked, and Nigel began methodically to go through the papers they contained. . . .

Clare Massinger was finding the evening less distasteful than she had anticipated. She had the pleasure of being the most attractive girl at the restaurant, and of being told so by her escort—not in a wolfish way, but boyishly, shyly almost. Alec Gray was doing his best to efface the impression of his first visit to her studio, she thought. He had undeniable charm, when he chose to exercise it. He possessed, too, the flair which every specialist in women cultivates—for intuitively choosing the right approach to the woman of the moment. With Clare it was gaiety, frankness, a faintly avuncular manner of teasing her, which altered from time to time into schoolboyishness. Gray seemed to be in the highest spirits: there was a sort of latent recklessness about his manner and conversation—Clare could imagine how stimulating, challenging it would be to a woman like Hesione. The cruder sexual weapons he was keeping in abeyance, though occasionally she was aware of his bold, confident gaze fixed upon her. He was solicitous about her dinner, suggested dishes not on the menu, kept the waiters on their toes, drank sparingly.

They talked a little about her work—Gray was no Philistine. He inquired after Nigel, hoped he would soon be out of hospital, apologized for the scene he had made in her studio.

"Afraid I was in a foul temper. That boy was an absolute pest. Damned cheek of his—running into your place."

Clare, who had been finding it more and more difficult to associate her companion with burglaries and kidnapings, or whatever Nigel suspected him of, saw the danger signal just in time.

"Oh, but I'd asked him to come and sit for me."

"Yes, of course, I remember. You told me. Have you finished the head?"

"He never came back again. You must have frightened him off."

"I'm sorry. He'd probably have pinched your jewelry, though. What charming topazes those are: just right for your coloring. Strangeways give them to you?"

It was the first flick of his impertinence. Clare ignored it.

"No. They're an heirloom."

"Does he make a living out of doing this detective stuff?"

"I've no idea. I didn't even know he did that sort of work, till a few days ago."

"There seem to be more hard knocks than halfpence in it this time," he said offhandedly.

Gray fell silent for a little. Clare reflected on her position. Why had he snapped the bait so readily when she angled for this invitation? She had assumed he would pump her hard about Nigel, but he seemed to take only the most perfunctory interest in that subject. On the other hand, if his womanizing urge was so strong as to have overcome the blows to his vanity which she had given him at their first meeting, it was odd that he should not now be following it up.

"D'you know Hess Durbar well?" he presently asked.

"Fairly. Better since she started sitting for me."

"Unfair advantage you have, studying people when they're trying to look interesting. I'd be terrified of you."

"I suppose people do find it alarming. But we're only interested in the surface, and the bone of course—not the nasty things crawling under their skin."

Alec Gray's eyes popped at her a little. He flicked cigar ash on the table. "I hear Hess has been visiting your—visiting Strangeways in hospital."

"Who told you?"

"Is it meant to be a secret?"

Clare laughed. "Good gracious, no!"

"Someone or other. I'm always hearing gossip. Comes of being an eligible young waster. I suppose Hess has told you I'm a bad hat?"

"Well, actually she's hardly mentioned you."

A slight frown appeared on his face, giving it a heavy look. Heavy and petulant. "I wonder why she chucked me," he said after a moment. "Frightened off, I suppose. You know, the police have got it into their heads that I'm a sort of master criminal."

He threw it off in his careless way—so carelessly that Clare was taken by surprise. He talked as if it was something they both knew about. There was a moment's pause before she expressed the proper astonishment and incredulity.

"You were a bit slow on that one, my dear," Gray said, grinning at her. "So Hess *has* been talking to you. Or was it Strangeways?"

Irritated with herself, Clare said at random, "Oh, I hear so much gossip. It was Sir Rudolf, I think."

"Now that is extremely unlikely." Gray's expression was amused.

"Why? He's got much more reason to dislike you than—"

"You're fighting out of your weight, my dear girl. During the war I did a spell of interrogating enemy prisoners. We weren't supposed to beat them up, so I got rather good at detecting lies by subtler methods."

His complacence had the effect of allaying Clare's exasperation. "You're just like a small boy boasting to his mother," she said smiling; then, seeing his expression, added hurriedly, "But I'm sure you were very good at it."

"Ah, ah! Pussy! Now let's stop bickering. Time to be moving on to the wild excesses of The High Dive, if you're ready. The proprietor, name of Samuel Borch, has just been taken up by the police. Sorry you won't be able to meet him. Fascinating type. He's one of my accomplices in crime, so they tell me. . . ."

Nigel had finished his investigation of the writing desk. The drawers had rewarded him with a few receipts, a head of unpaid bills, bundles of letters from women which would have made a fortune for certain Sunday newspapers, a social diary aggressively innocent in its entries, a stack of sheet music, eight packs of expensive playing cards, and among

the letters several photograph albums. Nigel inspected these
with considerable care. The first was absorbing as a pictorial
social register, but for no other reason. The second, devoted
to Gray's hobby of sailing, contained some excellent snap-
shots. In the third, a series of group photographs appeared—
school teams, OCTU and regimental groups. Nigel studied
each of them in turn. On the last page but one, there was a
picture of a Commando unit: sitting center was Alec Gray;
and in the back row another face appeared which Nigel could
recognize—the face of one of the two men whom Bert Hale
had pointed out to him in Kensington Gardens: the one, Bert
had said, with a knuckle duster.

Nigel removed the snapshot, put it in his pocket, and substituted for it a loose photograph which he found at the back
of the album. Then he flung all the objects from the escritoire
over the floor, kicking them about to suggest the debris left
by an impatient burglar, and went into the bedroom. Here
again he drew the curtain before turning on the light. To
reinforce the impression of a burglary, he fetched the cloak
and filled its pockets with a few articles from the dressing
table—silver-backed brushes, gold cuff links, a signet ring,
and so on. Then he started to go methodically through the
chest-of-drawers and the numerous suits which hung in the
wardrobe. As he set to work, the telephone rang.

It was not yet quite ten o'clock. Surely Gray could not be
on his way back already? Nigel lifted the receiver. "Yes?"
he said. A woman's voice replied.

"Alec, darling, I'm furious. I've been waiting hours for
you—"

Nigel replaced the receiver. It was a damned nuisance. If
the indignant female should upbraid Gray later, it would
come out that someone had answered the telephone from his
flat; and bona-fide burglars are not in the habit of answering
telephone calls while professionally occupied. . . .

As they entered The High Dive, the manager hurried ob-
sequiously forward, emitting a positive oil-slick of welcome.
"Hello, Antrobus," said Gray, in his most officer-class

manner. "This is my guest, Miss Massinger. I'll sign the book."

Making up in the ladies' room, Clare heard a few snatches of conversation from outside.

"So they've not arrested *you* yet?" Gray's hearty, clipped voice was answered by a smooth murmur which Clare could only just catch.

". . . police all over the place today, sir . . . said we could stay open for a while . . . all most unfortunate."

"If I know them, they spent half the time sampling the cellar, eh?"

A deferential laugh from the manager. "I don't think they found our Château d'Yquem, sir, anyway. Shall I bring you up a bottle?"

"Why not? We ought to celebrate."

The club was rather better than most of its kind, thought Clare, as they sat at their table. The usual Society riffraff were present, of course—angular girls with hideous, high-pitched voices and their escorts whose smooth, immature faces looked as if they had been fashioned, all from the same mold, out of the best butter. But the ventilation was good, the band clever, and the wine excellent. Indeed, Clare was feeling the first premonitions of tiddliness.

"I hope you like this stuff," said Gray, who had been nodding coolly to acquaintances in the room. "It's rather special."

"I do, thanks. And it's always nice not to have to drink champagne. Speaking for myself, it brings on the glooms. How unreal these places are. I hate harmless vice, don't you?"

"Good lord! Did you want to be taken to a thieves' kitchen?"

"Oh no, I'm quite happy here, really. Why 'kitchen,' I wonder?"

"Search me."

Clare pulled herself together. "We'd better dance. I'm starting to talk fatuous."

Gray was a superb dancer, and Clare began to enjoy herself thoroughly: she knew that many eyes were turned their way; and to be playing with fire was always exhilarating. But, as the night wore on, Clare became more and more puzzled. She had sensed some inner excitement at work in Alec Gray all the time, and assumed that she was the cause of it. Her relief, as time went by and he made no pass at her, was not unmixed with pique. Woman-like, she contrived somehow to blame Nigel for this: how dare he throw me into this man's arms? It would serve Nigel right if I did let myself go.

Clare pressed closer to Gray, feeling the man's strength and recklessness, and that strange, controlled excitement which communicated itself to her like the tingling of an electric current. An echo from far away, her voice came back, talking to Nigel in the studio—"That armor-plated type of cad does fascinate us girls. . . . We want to find the weak joint in his armor, or unbuckle it and see what's underneath." Suddenly Clare felt disgusted with herself.

"What bitches women are!"

She did not realize she had uttered her thought aloud, till he said, drawing one fingernail down the ridge of her back, "That's the way I like them."

His hot, hard voice completed her cure. She drew away from him, and when the dance ended, said she would sit down for a while. Gray did not pursue it. They talked, amicably enough, about her upbringing and art training, and his war experiences. It was really, she thought, the oddest evening. . . .

In the bedroom of Gray's flat, Nigel drew a deep breath. After going through every suit, every drawer, every conceivable hiding-place, he had drawn blank. Apart from the photograph in his pocket, there was nothing incriminating to be found. It was naïve, perhaps, to have expected it. Wastepaper baskets had been examined; blotters investigated; walls sounded. No doubt a police search would have ripped open the mattress and torn up the floor boards. But Nigel was too

exhausted to do more: his head throbbed again, and his heart
was sick. He set aside Gray's address book, for further
perusal, and stepped wearily into the bathroom.

An old coat was hanging up there, with a bathrobe.
Mechanically his fingers went through the coat pockets. Deep
down in the breast pocket, where his fingers only just touched
it, he felt something. A scrap of paper, crumpled up and
thrust there absentmindedly, no doubt, and forgotten. Nigel
unfolded it. A slip of paper, three inches by two, with a few
words typewritten on it.

No. 3 Berth all 12 sailing Harwich 13th

Nigel swayed, slumped down on a chair. Oh God, he
thought, thank God, we've done it! Here was the secret of
Dai Williams' message. Bert Hale had not made it up to
mystify his young friends. Somehow Dai Williams had come
into possession of this knowledge. Knowing his own extreme
danger that afternoon, he scribbled it on the margin of his
newspaper; then, dying, he had torn off that bit of paper and
given it to Bert. But he had torn off too little. His dying eyes
could not see that the scrap of paper he gave the boy did not
contain the whole message, only *Berth all 12*. Dai was an
uneducated man, in the extremity of fear. It was easy to see
how the rapidly scribbled words had become disjointed and
turned into *Bert Hale 12*.

Hurrying back into the bedroom, Nigel rang the Yard.
Blount was still there, catching up on his routine work. He
would stay, he promised, till Nigel arrived. All right, if it was
so urgent, he would have a police car waiting at the corner of
Radley Gardens and Church Street in fifteen minutes. Nigel
felt cool and capable again. He artistically increased the dis-
order he had made in Gray's bedroom; then, going out onto
the roof garden, ran down the fire escape noisily and climbed
up it again as silently as he could, for the subsequent police
investigation into the "burglary" must be allowed to find
footprints. Next, using his jemmy on the trapdoor, he did his
best to leave the impression that the burglar had broken in

from the roof garden. Finally, he rang up the friend who was to have relayed Clare's telephone message to him, when Gray left the club, and told him not to do so. He had thought of everything, surely.

Putting on the cloak and black sombrero, Nigel let himself out of the flat, and padded briskly toward Church Street. He had forgotten only one thing. In the heat of excitement, he had become quite oblivious of his disguise. As he went up to the waiting police car, the driver called out,

"Hey, grandfather, this ain't your Rolls Royce!"

Nigel put up his hand to his false beard, realized what he looked like, and laughed. "It's all right. I'm Strangeways behind all this hair. Superintendent Blount sent you for me."

In a moment, they were tearing east. When Nigel was shown into Blount's room at New Scotland Yard, the Superintendent quailed from the spectacle.

"My guid Lorrd! I naiver thocht ye'd come doun to this, Strangeways," he exclaimed, his native Doric returning under the stress of emotion. "Ye're looking poasitively verr-minous."

A few words from Nigel sobered him. He reached for the green telephone.

"This is something for the Top Brass, I doubt."

Ten minutes later, after a breakneck drive in the police car, they entered the study of a Very Important Personage. Nigel was conscious of a soldierly figure in pajamas and dressing gown, a pair of very keen gray eyes beneath bushy eyebrows, and a gentle, almost lisping voice, as their host greeted them.

"This is Mr. Strangeways, Sir Edward. I thought he'd better tell you his story himself."

"Ah yes. Quite right, Blount. Very nice of you to come, Strangeways. I knew your uncle, when he was Assistant Commissioner." The stern eyes twinkled. "He was fond of dressing up, too! I expect we could all do with a whisky—if Blount will let us drink, just for once, while on duty."

Nigel told his story. Once or twice Sir Edward lisped a searching question, and his eyes never left Nigel's face.

When Nigel came to the "burgling" of Gray's flat, he heard a subdued clucking from Blount, who always affected a horror for unorthodox procedure; but Sir Edward's expression never changed—he might have been listening to an account of some mild undergraduate escapade.

When he had finished, Nigel handed over the piece of typewritten paper. Sid Edward's bushy eyebrows were just perceptibly raised. After a long silence, he said, "Well, Blount, it looks as if our first idea about 'Bert Hale 12' was wrong."

Nigel felt a bit mystified by this. Had Blount been keeping something from him? Sir Edward turned to him, "You understand what this means, Strangeways?"

Nigel began to explain the Dai Williams reference, but his host raised a hand, saying gently, "Oh, I know all about that. No, my dear fellow, I meant the message itself. I—er, we must all be grateful to you." Sir Edward sipped his whisky. "You realize that the Soviet representatives leave this country on the 13th. It has been officially stated that they will go, as they came, by air. In point of fact, however, that statement was part of our security measures. The real arrangement is that they are to sail—it's a party of eleven, plus the Minister, as I expect you know—to sail from Harwich in a ship which will be docked at No. 3 berth. That, I should say, *was* the real arrangement. Thanks to you, my dear chap, we shall now alter it." Sir Edward's gentle voice grew gentler still. "What is, er, somewhat disconcerting—what we must all get down to, Superintendent—is this leakage of information. You see, Strangeways, there are only four people in the country—there *should* have been only four, I mean—who knew about No. 3 berth at Harwich."

14

Peace, Perfect Peace

Tuesday, for Nigel, got off to a quiet start. He slept late at his friend's house in Chelsea, had breakfast in bed, glanced idly through a magazine. His thoughts kept flitting back to Dai Williams' message. It was a pity that the newspaper from which the scrap of paper had been torn had never been found—blown into the Round Pond, perhaps, or picked up by a bystander, or removed by one of the men instrumental in Dai's murder. Dai must have overheard those words about No. 3 berth under suspicious circumstances; otherwise, he would hardly have made a note of them in his last moments, for they could not themselves have held any sinister significance to an informer engaged upon ferreting out information about robbery and receiving. Nigel was in no doubt that they now had the correct substance of the message; but he would have liked to know if Dai had also jotted down, on the margin of the lost newspaper, any note as to how he had come into possession of it.

No. 3 Berth all 12 sailing Harwich 13th. Two men had been killed, two boys kidnaped, to keep the secret of that message; the enemy had removed Foxy, so Nigel imagined, partly to obviate the danger of his identifying for the police the unknown man to whom Gray had talked in the Durbars' garden. It was amazing that a message upon which so much depended should be left lying in the breast pocket of an old coat. Amazing, but not at all impossible. Little, flagrant carelessnesses were always tripping up criminals; they made the most elaborate, tortuous plans, then ruined them by a neglect of the obvious. And it was in Gray's reckless character to stuff such a piece of dynamite into his pocket, and forget it was there.

Alec Gray. Nigel's hand went to the telephone, and he rang Clare's number. She was evidently startled to hear his voice.

"But they told me you'd had a relapse, when I rang the hospital just now."

"Oh, they've given me up as a hopeless case and pushed me out to expire off the premises. Last night go all right?"

"Yes. I think so. He behaved very correctly."

"Bad luck."

"But I still don't understand why—"

"Come along here this afternoon." Nigel gave her the address. "And don't tell anyone, repeat *anyone,* that I'm out of hospital."

"You sound awfully mysterious and cheerful, darling."

"It's just the effect of delirium. I'm longing to see you. Good-by till then."

An hour later, Inspector Wright looked in, a picture of cheerfulness. He announced that they had got Sam Borch cold at last. The police search of the High Dive on the previous day had been more successful than Mr. Antrobus realized. They discovered the previous wine bin that swung back on a hinge, and the secret passage. On Wright's advice, the Divisional Inspector in charge of the search agreed to play ignorant about it. After the surfaces had been fingerprinted, and the direction of the passage explored, they left everything as they had found it, even sifting a little dust artisically over the bin. Mr. Antrobus was informed that everything seemed in order down in the cellars.

A few minutes' work on a sketch map indicated the point which the secret passage must lead to. The police entered the second-hand clothes shop from the alley, took the woman in charge, and began a rigorous search. In one of the rooms above the shop a very cleverly concealed safe was at last discovered, and in the safe some of the proceeds of the recent robberies. Confronted by them, the woman broke down. She turned out to be a Pole, a cousin of Mr. Borch, who had been doing slave labor for the Germans during the war, and then come to Britain. Borch had set her up in the clothes shop. For a year or so, her business had been a perfectly honest one. But then Borch compelled her into less reputable activities. If she did not comply, and keep her mouth shut, Borch would have the authorities informed of her being in England with a forged passport, and the result would be deportation.

The woman's new duties were not very onerous. If anyone came to the shop with some old clothes, and said that "Stanley had recommended it," she was to take the clothes, tell the person she would pay him in a week's time, and lock them up among a selection of garments in an upstairs room. Mr. Borch paid frequent visits to this room, transferred the valuables from the pockets or linings of the clothes into his safe, and gave the woman an appropriate sum, in pound notes, to hand the customer on his next visit.

It was all remarkably simple and innocent-looking. Indeed, the procedure had worked so well in the past that the police decided to continue it for a while. A policewoman was substituted for the Polish tenant, and a discreet watch kept on the shop. But Borch's arrest had shaken the criminal grapevine too violently, and only one fly was to walk into the parlor—a cracksman who had been rusticating and was not *au fait* with recent happenings in the underworld.

The only setback Wright could announce was that both Borch and the commercial traveler, Chalmers, would not give tongue. They were, quite evidently, frightened men. Borch, of course, had to confess to receiving, when he heard the evidence against him; but under no inducement would he admit to any criminal association with Alec Gray. The man Chalmers, taxed with his attempt to kidnap Bert Hale, remained obstinately silent. He would not say where his orders came from, or who were his accomplices; and he persisted in denying all knowledge of the letter which had been found in his pocket.

"So there we are," Inspector Wright summed it up. "The set-up is obvious now, though we're almost as far as ever from proving it. Gray could get all the necessary information about these big houses that have been burgled. He passes it on to Borch, who distributes it among the professionals. And it'd be through Borch that Gray contacted the thugs he needed for the other job.''

"Gray's got at least one ex-Commando on tap, too.''

"Yes. Superintendent Blount's told me about that photograph you found. We've got a net out for the chap.''

"Has Gray reported a burglary yet?''

"Some people have a nerve," said Wright, rather ambiguously, his nostrils twitching with amusement. "He rang us up at midnight. Created like hell. What does the taxpayer support the ruddy police for, etc., etc.? Young Allen went along. Had a great time, by all accounts. Seems he forgot to mention to Mr. Gray that the trapdoor to the roof had been broken open from *inside*.' ''

"How very odd,'' remarked Nigel equably. "Well, now you've found a secret passage at The High Dive, bang goes Gray's alibi for the night Bert Hale was kidnaped. I hope to God that boy's all right. . . .''

Bert was, in fact, engaged upon writing his autobiography—or rather, plunging *in medias res,* a detailed account of his adventures during the past ten days. It would be of interest to the police, if not to posterity, should he ever get out of his bizarre prison. An only child who, until he went to school, had had to provide his own amusements, he was less afflicted by captivity than most boys would have been. Also, he was buoyed up by the hope that his message would at any moment pass, via the dustman, into official hands, and that rescue was imminent.

In this, alas, Bert was doomed to disappointment. The shell-covered box had indeed been discovered, but only after the contents of the bins were tipped onto the Urban District Council rubbish heap. The box attracted a dustman's attention: he took it home and gave it to his wife, who has it still on her mantelpiece. But, when it was tipped out into the dump, its lid flew open, and the message it contained fell out and disappeared from view.

Bert had not been allowed outside the house again. But yesterday, and again this morning, in response to his wily argument that boys need a great deal of exercise, the old woman took him for a walk through the huge house. Her nephew insisted on accompanying them—no risk of Bert's bolting was to be taken: but the boy quite enjoyed these perambulations through the tall, empty rooms, which Nanny garrulously peopled with the house-parties and junketings of former days, when the old master and mistress were in residence. Not only did these conducted tours help to pass the time; Bert was memorizing the layout of the mansion, and he believed that, after a couple more of them, he would be able to draw an accurate diagram of the rooms and passages on each floor.

Meanwhile, whenever he heard a sound outside, he rushed from his memoirs to the window, expecting it to be the harbinger of rescue. A distant tractor was the engine of a police car approaching; a blackbird fluting or an owl calling was a signal to the police cordon closing in. Even after hope began to fade and Bert to admit that he was kidding himself, he kept up the fantasy. It was consoling.

"Now, let's take things one by one. Elmer J. Steig first."

Superintendent Blount, embattled behind the desk at New Scotland Yard, raised an index finger. "The American authorities have no record of such a man."

Nigel's face fell. He had hoped for results from what Hesione Durbar had told him.

"But," continued Blount, in his deliberate, Scots manner, "they offer us a gentleman by name of Jameson Elmer. A former Federal agent, got the rap for corruption two-three years ago, took to crime, from the—e'eh—the nonprevention end. He was always a crack shot; and the G-man training stood him in good stead, no doubt, when he became—"

"I'm sorry, Blount, but what's this to do with our man?"

"Jameson Elmer, it seems, has an ungovernable passion for sucking violet cachous."

"Ah. That's better."

"He disappeared from view about three weeks ago. The U.S.A. authorities have radioed a photograph to us, and they're flying a selection of photographs over. The radio one isn't much help. It might be you or me. You, anyway. A villainous-looking smudge."

"Thanks very much. So this Elmer could be the 'gun for sale.' Height, walk, etc., correspond more or less with Foxy's description of the man Gray brought to the Durbars' party?"

"They are not—e'eh—inconsistent with it," replied Blount cautiously.

"Presumably Dai Williams, while he was tailing his 'toff,' Gray, stumbled across Elmer—overheard some conversation between him and Gray, maybe. But that's by the way. The important point is, why should Gray bring this gunman to the Durbars' party? And lock him in the study? The thing's crazy, unless it was for a rendezvous between Elmer and Sir Rudolf himself."

"Oh, well now, Strangeways, you know that's a vairy wild sort of conjecture, and—"

"I know Sir Rudolf is God Almighty, and his name mustn't be taken in vain. All right. We pass on to the Quack. The Quack was shot by a man with an American accent. Elmer being encouraged to keep his hand in. The next morning, Gray returns from a long drive. He is freshly sunburned. And the sunburn markings suggested the direction he'd come from. It's a reasonable inference that he drove Elmer northeast that night—to catch a boat at Harwich, we conjectured at first. And we weren't so far out, either. I bet you Elmer's holed up in Harwich, or somewhere near it, waiting for the boat the Russians are supposed to be sailing on."

"We've just had a report from Harwich. A man answering to Gray's description turned up for breakfast at the Alexandra Hotel early on the Friday morning. He was alone, though. We're following it up."

"Good. That's that, then."

"Sir Edward takes a very grave view of it," said Blount. "The American angle, I mean. If the Soviet Minister was assassinated by an ex-Federal agent, on British soil, you can imagine what the anti-West clique in Russia would make of it. It'd be the end of any hope of a rapproachement for ten years: the cold war would continue, or be hotted up. It's just the pretext the isolationist element in the Kremlin will be praying for."

The police were going to turn Harwich and its environs inside out, said Blount. This screening would convince the enemy that there was no alteration in the secret plan for the Russians to sail from this port; and it might catch the elusive Elmer. But their best chance of catching him was through Alec Gray, the gunman's only known contact in this country. Gray must be left at liberty for a while yet, lulled somehow into a sense of security, and every movement of his watched. Blount had already put a team of picked men onto this job. For it was not enough to change the plan for the Soviet delegation's departure; there might be another leakage of information, and as long as the gunman was at liberty, the Soviet Minister's peril would be acute.

"The only way to stop the leak," said Nigel, "is to put Sir Rudolf in the cooler for the next few days."

Superintendent Blount raised his eyes to heaven. "When will you get that bee out of your bonnet? Mind you, the Security people are investigating this last leakage—Sir Edward is chasing them all right; and if anything is turned up which points to Sir Rudolf—"

"By that time, it'll be too late."

"I see I'll have to take you in hand, Strangeways. You'd better come to the Kingsway Hall meeting with me tonight. Perhaps that'll cure you of these hallucinations."

"I don't see—"

"You will, my lad, you will."

Soon after Nigel got back to Cheyne Walk, Clare arrived. With her hands on his cheeks, she gave him a long scrutiny, then turned abruptly, her black hair swirling, and sat down.

"Couldn't you have trusted me?" she said.

"About what, Clare?"

"How long have you been out of hospital? I—it was cruel, letting me think you'd had a relapse. Don't you care about my feelings at all?"

"You know I do. And about your safety even more."

"Yet you order me to spend the evening with that brute, just so that you can—" Clare broke off.

"So that I can what?" asked Nigel gently.

"Was it you who burgled his flat?"

"It was a poor old superannuated clown called Toto."

"A poor old cl—?" Clare's angry expression changed into an April radiance, and she began to laugh. "Oh, Nigel, d'you mean to say that filthy old man was you? And I never recognized you!"

Nigel made her tell him all about the evening with Gray. There were certain points at which she did not meet his eyes, and Nigel guessed that she was feeling a little guilty about something: perhaps she had come for a moment under Gray's spell, was ashamed of it now, and being a woman, had taken it out on Nigel instead. Unaware of the ease with which her mind was being read, Clare chattered on about the dinner party. Nigel always wanted to know exactly what everyone had said, and she enjoyed telling him.

"So he seemed excited about something, all the way through?"

"Yes, I assumed he was working up to make a pass at me. But the pass never really materialized. Most humiliating. It was—I dunno—as if he was just passing the time."

"That's very interesting," said Nigel. "Passing the time till something happened?"

"Yes." Clare looked puzzled; then her face lit up. "I couldn't think what it reminded me of. Now I've got it. You know those anglers you see on piers. Smoking and gossiping away to one another. Not even holding their rods, sometimes—just leaving them propped up against the railings. Do you see what I mean?"

"I suppose so. But I've never felt a strong inward excitement radiating from those old geezers."

"Oh Nigel, you're so literal. What I mean is, it was as though he knew he could haul me in at any time, but it was so enjoyable on the pier, with the sun and the wind and the gossip, that he wouldn't bother yet. Of course, he's madly conceited. He'd assume I was on the hook. You know, I believe he'd enjoy hauling one in and then just throwing one back into the water."

Clare had spoken rapidly, almost breathlessly. Nigel gave her a quizzical glance.

"So you had no trouble in the car?"

"No. He was rather distraught, coming back. Didn't even try to kiss me good night. Just jumped out and scampered away upstairs. Perhaps he was expecting to find some other girl lusciously disposed on his bed. Why are you looking at me like that?"

"I was looking at your funny little word-pictures. You're an illuminating creature. And very disturbing." Nigel blinked, shaking his head, as if to clear it. " 'Lusciously disposed on his bed,' indeed!"

In a cellar near the Shadwell docks, Foxy lay nursing his bruises, twisting on the filthy paillasse and heap of rags. Four men were playing cards, with a packing case for table, and the air was foul. It seemed far longer than two days since he had given himself up to his pursuers. The youths had hurried him along to a backyard near Notting Hill Gate. Then he was pushed into a small van and driven off. On arrival at their destination, the man traveling in the back of the van had stunned Foxy with a vicious blow to the temple: when he recovered consciousness, he was in this cellar. The men soon got to work on him. They gagged him first, then knocked him about for a bit—"just to loosen up his tongue." His chief tormentor, a hulking Clydeside Irishman, invited him to talk first, if he didn't want to be bashed properly next time. An evil-faced man called Fred drew a knuckle-duster from his pocket, and gave Foxy a light, agonizing rap across the cheekbone, after removing the gag.

"Don't be a little berk," he said, as Foxy showed signs of recalcitrance. "We've got all night to educate you."

Foxy pretended to turn milky. It wasn't difficult. He answered the men's questions, till they began asking him if he'd gone to the police with his story. He denied it violently at first. But then they worked on him again. After that, writhing with pain and utterly cowed, he could resist no longer. He admitted the police had taken him up after the Portobello Road affray; he said they had forced him to tell them what he knew about Dai Williams' message and the man he had seen accompanying Gray to the Durbars' party. Something warned Foxy that it would be fatal for him now if he had also passed on to the police certain words he had heard at this party. So he declared he'd been unable, from his hiding place in the tree, to catch the conversation between Gray and the unknown man: the noise of the band, he convincingly protested, had drowned their voices.

"O.K. Anything else, now you've got your memory back?" said the Clydesider. Foxy shook his head vigorously. This was not quite true: Foxy had omitted the episode in the derelict house, which had for the time being slipped his mind.

Fred had already left the cellar, with instructions to "pass it on to the Big Boy."

"We'd have a right to molder this little bleeder."

"Chuck him in the river, Mac."

"Time enough, time enough."

The mood of exaltation which had brought Foxy here was quite evaporated now. Instead of it, he nursed a boy's bitter resentment and a determination to get his own back. Hour after hour, while the men played their interminable game of cards, he lay on the paillasse. He was given bread and marge, and cups of strong tea. From time to time one or two of the men, but never all four together, would be away on mysterious assignments, or in response to a slatternly woman who appeared at the stairhead, go up to answer the telephone. So, for two days, Foxy was buried alive. . . .

At seven forty-five that Tuesday night Nigel met Superintendent Blount outside the Kingsway Hall. Since he was supposed to be still in hospital, and would be in the company of a distinguished C.I.D. officer, Nigel had, with the aid of a macintosh, a felt hat, a pair of boots and a mustache, disguished himself impenetrably as a plain-clothes policeman. Blount instantly picked him out in the stream of people approaching the hall.

"So there you are."

"Ordered to report to you here, sir," said Nigel smartly, standing to attention.

"Well, I doubt it's more sanitary than that fearful beard you favored last time," murmured Blount as they entered the hall.

"Disguise, not hygiene, was my intention," Nigel whispered back.

"Oh, I get it. You're dressed up as a sanitary inspector? But where's the wee black bag with the spanners and washers?"

"My assistant will be bringing it," replied Nigel austerely. "Now where's the bad smell—I mean, the offensive odor—you complained about?"

"The whole place hums, if you ask me. Strong smell of red herrings."

At the door there had been young women, with spectacles and severe expressions, selling the *Daily Worker* and *Peace News*. The stewards wore red rosettes. Up and down the gangways passed men soliciting signatures to a petition for the reprieve of the latest "victims of American tyranny." The platform was draped with the Union Jack and the Hammer and Sickle. The meeting had been called by various professional organizations concerned in the cause of peace, to support the present negotiations by what Nigel's *Daily*

Worker called' "a monster demonstration of progressive in-
tellectuals." Looking round the audience, he reflected that
the *D.W.* did sometimes hit upon the *mot juste*. It was
disheartening—the way good causes stirred up this scurry of
freaks, neurotics, careerists, hairy men and ill-dressed yearn-
ers. Then he rebuked himself; for these types, though they
caught the eye, were seen on closer inspection to be only a
minority among a mass of decent, normal, intelligent-looking
men and women, who had come here because they believed it
was worth taking some trouble about peace, and were determined not to leave the world's future to the tender mercy of
professional politicians.

Nigel had no more time for audience research. The speakers were filing onto the platform, led by an elderly clergyman. They took their seats; and Nigel was amazed to behold,
sitting next to the chairman, no less a person than Sir Rudolf
Durbar. Blount dug him in the ribs, muttering, "What about
that bee in your bonnet, now?"

"It's whizzing around still, with a high-pitched and suspicious buzz. Could I interest you in a bottle of our best
eyewash?"'

The chairman rose. He was not, he declared, the Red
Dean, only a Pink Canon. After several more clerical jokes, he
gave out the names and qualifications of tonight's speakers,
none of whom, he hastened to add, needed any introduction.
He introduced them, however, first en masse, and then at
even greater length before each rose to speak. Judging by the
wincing and muttering among these distinguished people, as
he misquoted their degrees, honors, and attainments, an
elementary introduction to them was just what he needed
himself.

When the chairman finally resumed his chair, the speakers
in turn mounted their several hobbyhorses and galloped
vigorously off. An eminent scientist gabbled his way through
several sheets of typescript, inaudible even to the party on the
platform. An eminent doctor revealed the glories of Chinese
medicine and the horrors of Glasgow slums: his colleagues,

he declared, were reactionaries to a man, hiding their heads
in the sand, etc., etc. An eminent novelist unleashed a flight
of paradoxes, whose direction was uncertain though their
style was impeccable: he then unbuttoned his Savile-Row
jacket and spoke with feeling about the effect of international
tension upon authors' royalties. An aged composer told a
number of aged anecdotes. A Civil Servant and a Quaker
schoolteacher followed. Then a young painter, glowering at
the audience, assured them that only by close co-operation
with Russia and the infusion of new blood would English art
be rescued from subjectivism and total decadence; as an
example of what could be achieved he called attention to four
gigantic and insipid figures on the wall behind the platform,
symbolic of Peace, Democracy, the Workers, and the Arts,
which Nigel supposed had been run up by a gang of mentally
arrested children, but which turned out to be the communal
work of a number of members of the Painters-for-World-
Peace Movement.

So far, everything had followed the usual pattern of such
occasions. Some of the speakers had been sincere; others,
who found peace a convenient whetstone to grind their own
private or political axes on, had struck a few sparks from the
subject. The audience applauded each—dutifully, impar-
tially, but without great enthusiasm. One felt that they had
hoped for a clarion call, and were politely disappointed to
have heard only a set of variations on the penny whistle.

"You know, Strangeways," said Blount behind his hand,
"I don't care for politicans, but at least they make their
platitudes sound convincing. Those wee fellows up there
have a lot to learn: they're terrible amateurs at the job."

"You should be thankful you're an English copper. Anywhere else they'd be tossing bombs about, not woolly balls."

The chairman was on his feet. They had come now to what
he ventured to call, with due deference to their other brilliant
and distinguished speakers, the *bonne bouche* of the evening.
They had on the platform a dangerous man, a real live
capitalist (a mild stir of interest went through the audience,

and the chairman smirked); nay, a captain of industry and a king of finance. Sir Rufus Dunbar, er—that is to say—Durban, he went on, peering at the sheet of paper before him, needed no introduction to the audience: he was a household name wherever his products and, ah, his philanthropies were, hum, known. A historical personage known as Jesus, whom he, the chairman, believed to be the Son of God—but of course every man was entitled to his own opinion about that—had said that it was more difficult for a camel to go through the eye of a needle than for a rich man to enter the Kingdom of heaven. Jesus Christ was speaking figuratively, of course. But He had also said, "Blessed are the peace-makers." So there was hope for Sir Reuben yet. And in short, the chairman concluded, wobbling to a stop like a mechanical toy running down, they were all eager to hear with Sir Rufus Drummond had to say on the vital issues which they had assembled this evening to er, hum, ha.

In the brief silence that followed before Sir Rudolf got up, Nigel heard a *New Statesman* type, sitting in front of him, say to his companion; "Fancy *him* in this gallery. Met him once or twice. Used to have a stately home near us, when I was married to Emmeline. Stourford Hall."

Sir Rudolf was on his feet. "I may be a rich man," he began, "but I am not a camel. I only wish I was. Camels can go for a long time without a drink." Sir Rudolf glanced briskly at his wristwatch, then proceeded to hold the audience in the palm of his hand for the exact ten minutes alloted him. Speaking wihout notes or pomposity, he gave an object lesson in the workings of personal magnetism; the audience, at first suspicious and skeptical, were intrigued, then amused, then interested, and before long convinced of his sincerity. The gist of his speech was that, although he had no love for the Communist way of life and no belief in their economic system, as a practical businessman he could see no dividends in East and West cutting each other's throats. Sir Rudolf did not attempt to go out of character and present himself as an idealist: he was forceful, witty, a little cynical, down to earth—all of which, after the wafflings of the other speeches, the audience found immensely bracing. He sat down to a storm of applause.

The chairman rose, to put the resolution. At the same moment, a fog-horn voice came from the body of the hall: "I want to ask the last speaker a question."

"I'm afraid we have not time for questions," bleated the chairman.

"Is this a free country?" the fog horn inquired.

Other voices, from different parts of the hall, bellowed righteous indignation, to an indignant shushing from the assembled intelligentsia. A scuffle began in one of the aisles, as stewards tried to prevent two malcontents approaching the platform. A smoke bomb was lobbed at the chairman who, like a Homeric warrior under the protection of a deity, disappeared from mortal view in a cloud. Fighting had broken out here and there. The counter-demonstration was obviously an organized one. Policemen poured through the doors. The peace meeting was warming up nicely.

"Come on," said Blount. "Unless you want another knock on the head."

"Just a minute." Nigel caught the *New Statesman* type, who was ducking out of the affray, by the sleeve. "Excuse me, sir, I heard you mention Stourford Hall," he said, when they had got outside the main door.

"Scandalous! An absolute disgrace! We pay the police for protection and—"

"Stourford. That sounds like Suffolk."

"What's that? Oh, the place Durbar owned? Yes, it's in Suffolk all right. A deliberate attempt by reactionary elements to block the resolution!"

15

The Weak Joint

"But he doesn't own it any longer," Blount was saying the next morning.

"Who does then? Who lives there?"

"It's empty. A caretaker. Durbar sold it several months ago, but he hadn't lived there for some time before that."

"Who did he sell it to?"

"The solicitors say they are not at liberty to divulge the name of the purchaser. They're a sticky lot."

"Sold it to himself, under another name. Or to some figure of straw."

"Och now, Strangeways—"

"A big empty house, standing by itself in a park, in the southeast corner of Suffolk, under twenty miles from Harwich—my dear Blount, surely you must see that's the ideal place for this gunman to be holing up in."

The Superintendent's face took on its most patient expression. "The decision that the Russian party should sail from Harwich was only made a few weeks ago. Durbar sold Stourford Hall in May. Even if it was a phony sale, the thing just doesn't connect. He couldn't have known, in May, that it would be a convenient jumping-off place for—"

"The Russian visit was fixed up in April. Durbar could have planned then for Elmer to hide up in the house until the moment came to strike."

"You've got Durbar on the brain."

Nigel had lain awake for an hour, the previous night, trying to recapture an elusive memory. At last he got it. Hesione

Durbar, when she visited him in hospital, had unconsciously given him the clue. "Do you know the Stour Valley?" she had said; and then something about its being "maternal." It was after he had asked her if she knew of any hideout Alec Gray might have in East Anglia. Then, by an association of thought, she had switched to her husband's maternal streak—how, when she was expecting the child who had been stillborn, "Rudie spent hours studying catalogues of baby apparatus." It must have been at Stourford Hall that she had awaited the baby. But the heir never survived, poor kid.

Poor kid! Nigel started up in bed. "Poor little boy," Hesione had said, more than once, when she heard about the kidnaping of Bert Hale. And what an ideal place Stourford Hall would be in which to hide, not only a gunman, but a small boy!

"Blount, you know my hunches have sometimes been right," he said urgently now. "I beg of you to have that house investigated."

The Superintendent's face was bland. "The Suffolk police," he said, glancing at his wristwatch, "are visiting it just about this very moment. We're like the politicians, you know—we never leave a stone unturned."

Nigel gave him a long look. "Sometimes, Blount, I wonder why I don't murder you with my bare hands."

"You should always use gloves. I'd have thought even your limited experience of crime would have taught you that."

Bert Hale had carefully planned out what he would do if rescue loomed near. But when he heard at last, this morning, the distant approach of a car, he had no time to put his plan into operation; for the taciturn caretaker was in the room the next moment, slapped some adhesive plaster over Bert's mouth, blindfolded him, and carried him through the door. Bert's memorizing of the house came in useful here. In his mind's eye, he traced their passage, down a flight of stairs, twenty paces on, turn left, then right—into a room: it was the oldest part of the house, and this room had not been visited during their tours. Bert guessed why. From one of its windows the mysterious guest had shot at the target on the lawn. Bert heard a click, and at the same time a bell ringing far away in the house below him. He began to struggle; but he was thrust into what he thought must be a closet. There was a second click, and the hole he had come through became a wall behind him. The closet had a strange smell which Bert could not immediately identify. Also, it was pitch dark. No, it was this blasted thing round his eyes, of course. Bert raised his hands to tear it off, a sudden appalling conviction in his mind that he'd been put into a gas chamber. A voice that instant said, "Keep still, bub! Don't move, take it easy, and maybe you'll have a long life."

The voice whipped coldly, like a snake's tail. Bert had heard it before. It was the voice of the man who had shot the Quack—the American gunman who, Foxy once told him, smelled as if he sucked violet sweets: this was the strange smell he had noticed in the closet. But it couldn't be a closet. The voice had come from too far away for that. It took Bert only a few seconds to realize he must be in a secret room— perhaps one of those priest's holes he'd read about—cooped up with a killer.

It was this knowledge that prevented him drumming with his feet, beating his fists against the wall, when hours later, as it seemed, he heard movements in the adjoining room. He knew that his companion was a killer, and the hands round his throat would tighten if he made a sound. The air was close; Bert became aware that the gunman was sweating. Surely he could not have been living in this hole for the last few days? And if not, the police would find signs of the next room being occupied. But presently the sounds ceased. The police, if it was they, were presumably satisfied.

Bert felt in his pocket the journal he had been writing. He had always kept the notebook there, for fear of his captors' finding it. If only he had left it in the nursery, for the police to find! As it was, there would be no clue: the caretaker, Tom, had put Bert's spectacles in his own pocket before bandaging his eyes; the old woman always tidied the nursery first thing in the morning—not that Bert had any possessions or spare clothes for the police to discover there. Wait a minute! The bed. Although it had been made, the sheets and pillows would not be clean.

The gunman was talking. Bert could not understand half what he said: but, in the close, sweltering little room, the voice went on and on, crackling like a transmitter, reminding Bert of another room, another man who had talked interminably. This man was not mad, like the Quack. He was, though Bert did not realize it, lonely and bored; he had had no company for days but the taciturn Tom and Tom's imbecile old aunt.

"Hey, son, are you dumb?... Oh, sure, that tape. Don't raise your voice, I've got my gun here."

Bert felt the muzzle of a revolver against his neck, then a flash of pain as the adhesive tape was ripped away from his mouth. Tears came to his eyes. When he could speak, he said, "Can't I take this bandage off?"

"No. Take a candy."

A sweet was put in his hand—a violet cachou. He sucked it, rubbing his sore mouth. The killer was not going to kill him; but Bert felt like a blinded mouse lying between a cat's paws.

"Why can't we go out?" he said.

"They've got to let us out. There's no spring this side."

Bert digested this. "Then, if the police have arrested them, we'll never—"

"Don't be so dumb. I could shoot a hole through the panel. Say, kid, you go to the movies?"

They began to compare notes. For Bert, it was like that stage in a dream where you know it is a dream and accept it as such, submitting to its weird sequences. At any moment the bare boards beneath him might dissolve into a cloud, or the wall at his back turn into the padded seat of a racing car. Meanwhile, he talked enthusiastically about the latest spaceship film he had seen.

"Visitors from Mars—guys with legs like the Eiffel Tower

and whiskers growing out of their craniums—it's crazy! I like Westerns, gangsters. The G-man always wins. Like hell, he does! Say, did you see—?''

There was movement in the adjoining room: the sound of a panel sliding back.

"O.K. The cops have beat it," came Tom's voice.

Bert was pulled through. Deliberately, he stumbled and fell. Lying on the floor, he dragged the bandage down, for an instant, from one eye. The room was absolutely empty, unfurnished—what Bert could see of it. And Tom was pressing an acorn on the molding of the mantelpiece. As he did so, the panel to the right of the fireplace closed.

"A washout," said Superintendent Blount. He had received a report from the Suffolk police, and was summarizing it for Nigel's benefit. An Inspector and Sergeant from Ipswich, with the village constable, had gone to Stourford Hall, on the pretext of looking for an escaped convict last seen in these parts. They rang the bell several times before gaining admission. They went through every room in the house, and then examined the outbuildings. It was unoccupied, except for the servants' quarters—a kitchen, a sitting room, two bedrooms, where the caretaker and his aunt lived—and a nursery, at the top of the house, above them.

"A nursery?" Nigel pricked up his ears.

"Yes. It was a bit eerie, the Inspector told me. A nursery, all fitted out with tiny garments, books, toys, and the like, all brand new. It gave him quite a turn."

"All fitted out for the heir to the Durbar millions."

"Just so. There's a cot in it, and a wee bed. The Inspector thought he was onto something there, for the bedclothes were not clean. But Tom Ryle—that's the caretaker—explained it. His aunt is soft in the head. She used to be Durbars' nursemaid, and would have been nurse to his child, if it had lived. He pensioned her off—made her nephew caretaker and lets her live there with him. She's quite harmless; but she's got delusions that she has a baby in her charge—Durbar himself, or the baby that died—God knows which. So, when the delusions come on, she sleeps in the bed in the nursery, looking after a ghost child.''

A sentimental expression came over the Superintendent's face, normally as bland and noncommittal as a bank manager's, and he sighed heavily.

''Aye. It's vairy pathetic. That accounted for the picture book, too.''

''The picture book?''

''Aye. They found a picture book which had been colored, and a box of paints recently used. It was the auld Nanny again, amusing her nonexistent bairn.''

''You make me weep,'' said Nigel rudely. ''Did the auld Nanny corroborate this touching story?''

Blount looked rather shocked. ''Och, she's a havering auld body—they couldn't get much sense out of her. But she did tell them she had a wee baby boy in the nursery.''

''A wee baby boy of twelve, with spectacles?''

''Och now, Strangeways—''

''You and your dream children! From Blount and James Barrie, good Lord deliver us!''

''I'm telling you, Bert Hale is not there. He may have been there, but he's not there now. Nor this Elmer. They searched every cranny of the house and grounds.''

Nigel was looking profoundly dissatisfied. ''If Durbar doesn't own the place any longer, why is it stuffed with old Nannies and nursery furniture?''

''No doubt he made some arrangement with the purchaser to keep them on till he took up residence.''

''Ah. That mythical purchaser. Another of your bonny dream children.''

''Well, why not ask Durbar yourself?'' said Blount, exasperated.

''That's just what I will do. I suppose your Ipswich colleagues wouldn't think to inquire of the local shops whether extra food has been sent to the house recently?''

''That's all being done. Don't fuss. They're keeping an

eye on the place, and interviewing people right and left in the locality. But it's a vairy—e'eh—secluded place. It might take days, or weeks, to find witnesses of goings-on there, if there *were* any goings-on.''

And we haven't got days, let alone weeks, thought Nigel as he returned to Chelsea—not with a gunman at large, and two boys kidnaped. Sir Edward was moving heaven and earth to trace the leakage of information: but, until it had been traced, there was no certainty that the change of plan for the Russian Minister's departure would not come into the hands of the enemy.

Worse still, ever since his conversation with Clare yesterday, Nigel had been growing more and more uneasy about the value of his discovery at Gray's flat. Clare had touched it off with her account of Gray's peculiar state of mind on the previous night. The inner excitement; the impression of one just passing the time till something happened; and then Clare's odd simile of the anglers on a pier, ''not even holding their rods—just leaving them propped up against the railing.'' It could be a detestably illuminating analogy. Gray leaving the bait in his flat and going off for a jolly evening; giving his opponents plenty of time to search the flat; making the crucial object extraordinarily difficult, but not impossible, to find.

Why had Gray agreed to take Clare out for the evening at all, after she had made her dislike of him so plain, if not because he realized it was a ruse to get him out of the flat—a ruse he could turn to his own ends? And why leave so incriminating a document in his pocket, unless he wanted it to be found? Of course, criminals do slip up and make these elementary errors; but it is never wise to take such an apparent error at its face value.

Suppose Gray had planted the Harwich message as bait, what did this imply?—that he had extracted from Bert the words written by Dai Williams on the newspaper margin, and from Foxy the information that the police now knew what these words were. Then why leave in his pocket, for the police to find, a full, unabbreviated text of Dai Williams' message? Obviously, to mislead. "Bert Hale 12," luckily for the conspirators, could be made to expand into a sentence derived from their illicit knowledge of the plans for the Russians' departure. But, if their blow was really to be struck at Harwich, the last thing they would do would be to let the police know about it. Therefore the blow was not to be struck at Harwich; and the piece of paper Nigel had found was a brilliantly ingenious device for directing the authorities' attention exclusively upon Harwich, while the stroke was planned for elsewhere. And perhaps for an earlier date. At any moment now the finger might squeeze the trigger.

With consternation, Nigel realized that he was back where he had started. All along, both the police and Bert's own friends had suspected that "Bert Hale 12" might be a fabrication of the boy's, not the original message at all. Gray's men had presumably got it out of Foxy, when he was kidnaped last Sunday, that he had told the police about this "message." So Gray could have been stringing the police along, fixing their attention upon "Bert Hale 12," when Dai Williams' real message had been quite a different one. More than ever now, it was imperative to find Bert Hale and get the truth from him.

Nigel had rung up Hesione Durbar, to make an appointment. She had to be out till six P.M., but would be glad to see him then. She was alone in the drawing room when Nigel was announced. After warm inquiries about his health—she was surprised and pleased to find him out of hospital so soon—Hesione poured drinks for them both. Her husband, she said, would be back soon; he'd been a bit poorly last night—the effects of a smoke bomb at a political meeting.

"Political meeting? I didn't think he—"

"Oh well, it was a peace meeting. Rudie was asked to speak, at the last minute. He's getting quite public-spirited in his dotage," she said gaily.

Nigel remembered how, last time he had been in this

house, she had expressed such astonishment at her husband's accepting an invitation to a reception for the Soviet Minister. He said,

"What an indefatigable man he is! Doesn't he ever take a holiday?"

"We go abroad a good deal. And occasional week-ends in the country."

"At Stourford, I suppose?"

"Oh no. We don't go there any more. Rudie's sold it."

"What a pity! It's a beautiful house, I'm told."

Hesione grimaced. "I suppose so. But talk about the back of beyond! Nothing to do all day but feed the ducks and listen to the damned peacocks screaming. Give me the bright lights! Besides, we haven't happy memories of the place."

Then the story came out. The child who had died at birth, Sir Rudolf's bitter disappointment, the nursery, preserved as a sort of shrine to his dead hopes.

"I think he minded much more than I did," she said, brooding. "Funny, I'd never have thought he had a soft streak in him like that."

Nigel asked more questions about the house. Hesione routed out a photograph album, and sat down with him on the sofa to show pictures of it, her shoulder rubbing against his, her deep blue eyes glancing at him with a look half provocative, half almost childishly innocent. She retained the actress's gift for using her physical charms without inhibitions and yet without committing herself.

"This is the oldest part of the house," she said, turning a page. "It originally belonged to one of the old Catholic families. Rudie's father bought it from them."

Nigel felt a wild excitement welling up in him. "Catholic families? Did you have a priest's hole?"

"Oh yes. All the proper accessories. There's even a room which used to be their private chapel." She turned over some more pages. "You see that sprig of oak leaves and acorns on the mantelpiece? You push one of the acorns and that panel there slides back. I found it, quite by accident, one rainy Sunday. Life was one long rainy Sunday down there.''

It was as simple as that. Or was it?

"By accident, you say? How thrilling! You didn't know about it before?"

"No. There must have been a tradition in the family not to mention it, even after they'd stopped persecuting the Catholics. The guide books don't say anything about it.''

So that was why the police had overlooked it during their search. Nigel knew he must get away quickly and communicate with Superintendent Blount; but, if he left too abruptly, it would seem odd to Hesione, and her husband would her about it.

"Well, Nigel, you didn't come to discuss stately homes, I'm sure.''

A few minutes were wasted, while Nigel made a pretext for his visit. He was just rising to go, when the door opened and Sir Rudolf entered.

"Ah, Strangeways, very glad to see you up and about again.'' He shook hands vigorously. The dark, lively eyes held Nigel for a moment, then turned to Hesione on the sofa, with the album still open beside her. "Well, my dear,'' he said, and bent down to kiss her. Then, to Nigel, "Will you excuse me a moment while I wash my hands?''

"Actually, I was just going.''

"You must stay a little longer. Hess, you persuade him.''

"Please, Nigel. You haven't even finished your drink.''

"Well, a few minutes more,'' he said, thinking that it would put sir Rudolf on his guard if he rushed out straight away. His host had already left the room. The invitation to stay on had been thrown out so lightly, it was absurd to imagine—yet there was the open album, and the dark eye which missed so little.

Sir Rudolf was back in a couple of minutes. As he poured himself a drink, Nigel noticed that a small ink stain, which had been on his index finger, was gone. Sir Rudolf *had* washed his hands then. No time for that, and a trunk call; of course, there was always that discreet, anonymous-looking secretary.

"I see you've been looking at photographs of Stourford Hall," said his host pleasantly.

There was nothing for it now, thought Nigel, but to set an attacking field and try a few bumpers.

"Yes. We're interested in the place just now."

"We? The police?"

Nigel nodded. Hesione's eyes opened wide.

"Oh, Nigel," she said reproachfully.

"Yes. I'm sorry. I *was* pumping you a bit! I've got a secretive mind—it loses me all my friends, sooner or later."

"But what's the mystery about?" she asked. "We don't own the house now."

"That's the trouble. We can't find out who does."

Sir Rudolf broke in, at his most incisive. "Let's get this straight. Why are you interested in the place?"

"Because," said Nigel, unleashing his first bumper, "there's a good deal of evidence been accumulating that the kidnaped boy, Bert Hale, was taken there."

Hesione gave a little gasp. Her husband, putting down his drink, asked, "Surely the police have investigated the possibility, then?"

"Oh yes. They went all over the place this morning. Found nothing. But of course they didn't know about the priest's hole."

"Well, my dear chap," said Sir Rudolf, "hadn't you better ring Scotland Yard straight away? If there's the remotest chance that the boy's been hidden there? Use my telephone."

Nigel experienced the sensation of a fast bowler whose most intimidating delivery has been hooked off the batsman's eyebrows to the boundary. Almost, at this moment, he believed that his suspicions of Sir Rudolf must be delusions. But he remembered what had happened to him last time he let down his hair in this house. It was too risky for the only person who knew about the priest's hole at Stourford Hall to go to the telephone: he might never reach it.

"Time enough for that," he said, wondering the next instant if he had seen, or only imagined, a faint relaxation in Sir Rudolf's pose. "Do you know the present owner personally?"

"No. It was all done through agents and solicitors."

"Rudie just wanted to get rid of the place," said Hesione.

"The solicitors are apparently being rather sticky. You know what these needle-noses are like. Of course, the police can compel them to divulge the purchaser's name, if they prove good reason. But—"

"My dear fellow, I'd tell you like a shot, if I knew it. But I was interested in his money, not his name. A fair price was offered, and I was advised to accept it. Look here, do have a drink, your glass is empty."

Nigel accepted, rose with alacrity to help himself. There were about fifteen bottles on the tray, and they couldn't all be drugged. But Sir Rudolf had made no attempt to rise; he remained in his habitual posture, sprawling back against one end of the settee, his hands clasped high on his chest. Nigel through wryly—he's got me on the jump: ridiculous; Durbar would no more pour out a drugged drink than he'd personally conduct the negotiations for selling a house. He's the Big Boy, the Disposer Supreme, the Prime Mover.

"Did Alec Gray ever stay with you up there?"

"Did he, Hess? We had so many visitors. But it was before his time, I should say."

There was the barest perceptible unsheathing of a claw in the last phrase. Hesione looked quickly at her husband, and away, flushing, as she answered, "No. He never came there. But, Nigel, surely you're not suggesting—?"

"Did either of you ever tell him about the secret room there?"

"No," said Hesione without hesitation. "Rudie had a fancy for keeping it a secret."

"What about the caretakers? your old nurse, and her nephew? Are they reliable?"

Hands locked behind his head, Sir Rudolf lay back on the settee, utterly relaxed. "As far as I now. Old Eva is a bit potty, but I don't see her kidnaping anyone. And the nephew had good references, I believe. I made an arrangement through the soliciters that she should stay on; and I understand the new owner may keep the nephew on as house man when he moves in. No, I honestly don't see how either of them could be mixed up in this affair."

There was no getting at this man, enthroned on his own superb self-confidence, cushioned by his army of underlings, secretaries, agents, contact men. Nigel found himself succumbing to the hypnotic normality of it all—Hesione's beauty and forthright manner, the exquisite yet homely room where they were talking, Sir Rudolf's friendly, resonant voice. One seemed to be insulated here from the ruder shocks of life—from kidnapings, violence, treason, all the raw realities.

"Poor old Nanny," Hesione was saying. "She always treated you as if you were still in the nursery."

"Yes. They get that way. Bossy. Proprietorial. Can't afford to let anyone grow up—not with the stake they've put into childhood. Permanently unfulfilled mothers, I suppose."

Hesione winced a little, but her husband went on ruminatively, not noticing. "Of course, Eva always was a bit potty about some things. Full of old wives' tales and superstitions. She wouldn't kill a spider. She thought a crack in the ceiling meant the Devil was trying to get in. Never put butter on her bread, only jam. I've seen her push buttered bread aside, and she refused to brush her hair when it rained because of lightning, and she'd never touch a box of paints because her little sister had poisoned herself with paints thirty years ago or some such."

16

The Battle of Stourford Hall

"What'll we do with the nipper?" said the third man.

"Tie a stone round his effing neck and sling the effer in the effing Thames," suggested Fred.

"Eff that!" the hulking Clydesider roared. "Big Boy's orders—got to take him with us. Where's me glim?"

"In yer sky, yer silly berk.''

"What I say, I don't like it.''

"You got a touch of the seconds? The Big Boy'll steer us. And two grand to carve when the job's done. It's all sewn up."

"I still don't like it. How d'ya know eh's not leaving us in the middle?"

"You turn Charlie and we'll do ya. Look at da kid. He's not milky, are ya, Foxy-Poxy?"

It was six-thirty P.M. on Wednesday, and in the Shadwell cellar Foxy's captors had sprung into activity like a gun's crew. A trapdoor had been raised; from a cavity beneath, the three men were transferring Sten guns and ammunition to a big laundry basket. The fourth man, who had just returned, was at a grating in the cellar wall, looking out and up. Foxy himself, stupefied by three days of captivity, bad air, meager food, was almost beyond fear now. He knew they were taking him somewhere else; he thought they were not going to knock him off, in spite of Fred's menaces. Mac, the Clydesider, seemed to have taken a fancy to him; and what Mac said went, though the others might grumble or snarl. Foxy didn't care what happened, as long as he got out of this cellar. He'd even stopped thinking what he'd to to Fred if ever he had the chance.

The men gagged and bound him, dumped him on top of the weapons in the laundry basket, padlocked the lid. The basket smelled of oil. The guns and ammunition clips ground painfully into his thin body. He felt the basket being carried up the cellar steps, put down, a long pause, then jogging movement, another violent jolt, the sound of an engine starting, a jerk, swaying, rattling motion, the swish of traffic. Foxy felt sick and suffocating. He kicked out at the wicker walls in a frenzy of panic—went on kicking till the lid was lifted. In the gloom of the van's interior Mac was looking down at him, curiously, fixedly, without compunction, as a child might gaze at a beetle it has shut up in a match box. Presently Mac lifted him out, untied his arms, and propped him against the wall of the van.

Nigel had taken the precaution of hiring the car with the ex-pugilist driver to convey him to the Durbars'. He was surprised to be walking out of the house unhindered, and glad to see the tough driver waiting for him; his knowledge, he felt, must have been written on his face; but no, Sir Rudolf had said good-by most affably, made no attempt to detain him longer. Wherever Bert Hale was now, he had been taken to Stourford Hall first. The Ipswich Inspector had found a recently used paintbox; but old Nanny had a phobia about paints, wouldn't touch them. And there was the priest's hole. If the boy had been taken there, it was two to one the gunman, Elmer, had been hidden there too. And, with a nation-wide search for those two—with every policeman in Britain on the lookout for them, it was unlikely they have been moved. But they'd have to be moved now, the secret of the priest's hole being out.

Nigel ordered the driver to go straight to Scotland Yard. Public call boxes were too vulnerable. Besides, if there was going to be an exodus from Stourford Hall, it would hardly take place before dark, since the house was under police observation: that would give Blount the best part of two hours to get Ipswich onto the job. They'd need a fair-sized cordon, and an armed one; for, if Elmer was there, he'd certainly try to shoot his way out.

At this critical moment, things began to go wrong. For once, Blount was not at H.Q. when Nigel arrived: he was in conference with Sir Edward, and on no account to be interrupted. Furthermore, Blount's second-in-command had suddenly gone sick, and the officer doing duty for him was not *au fait* with the situation. Red tape began to rear its ugly head; the officer was maddeningly deliberate and inclined to be skeptical about Nigel's standing. At last, however, he consented to pass Nigel's information to the Ipswich police. But it was already seven-thirty P.M.

Not till eight-thirty did Blount return. But now, after Nigel said a few words to him, things began to hum. Blount rang Ipswich; and while the call was coming through, blew his overcautious subordinate out of the water with a few well-chosen phrases. A police car was ordered to be in readiness; large-scale maps were fetched; sandwiches and a thermos flask arrived from the canteen.

"... The village constable is at the lodge?... Aye, just so. But this man, Elmer, is a killer: it'll take more than a village constable to stop him, if he tries to break through. ... You're putting road blocks out? Good, good. Watch the Harwich side particularly.... And the railway stations: good.... We'll be with you at ten-thirty—a little before, maybe.... No, if I may suggest it, don't start the search till we arrive; I'm bringing a gentleman who knows how to get into this secret room."

The lasso was being flung all right; but it would take time to tighten, Nigel reflected, and they might be too late. For that matter, the whole thing might be a gigantic mare's nest; in which event, the thought of Blount's reactions would not bear contemplation....

At nine-twenty Police-Constable Hogg was keeping an eye on the window and discussing the culture of chrysanthemums with the Stourford Hall gardener, who lived at the gate lodge. A car engine was heard approaching. Hogg went out, to see a plain van drawing up to the gate. He was not a quick-thinking man; and besides, his orders were to report by telephone if anyone *left* the Hall—he had no instructions what to do about arrivals. He had hardly opened his mouth in measured, official inquiry before two men leaped from the back of the van, coshed him, trussed him up, and lifted him over the tailboard. A third man ran into the lodge, and holding up the gardener with a revolver, tore out the telephone wire. The gate was opened (its opening automatically rang a bell at the Hall, which explained how Tom was warned of the police car's approach this morning), and the van bumped along the quarter-mile drive to the house.

As they stopped in the back courtyard, Foxy—bound and gagged again—heard rapid talk between the driver and a man who had come out of the house.

"Where's the Yank? We've come for him."

"Gone. He took a powder."

There was a flood of profanity from the driver. It emerged, after a good deal of this, that the Yank had left the house about three hours ago. Telephone instructions had come from the Big Boy, and the Yank had set off on Tom's bicycle. There was a rough track leading westerly across the park, in the opposite direction to the drive. By this track, it later turned out, Bert Hale had been conveyed up to the house, thus avoiding the notice of the gardener at the gate lodge away on the park's eastern side.

The four men were all in the courtyard now, arguing furiously.

"Where the hell do we go from here?"

"We've been stood up. What did I tell you?"

"Let's scarper."

"Whadda we do with the effing bogey?"

Tom's voice broke in. "Boss's orders—you've gotta get the kid away, and dump him—"

"Another bleeding kid? Gawd's truth, does he think we're effing scoutmasters?"

"It's Bert Hale."

Foxy just caught the low mutter. His heart leaped up. So good old Bert was here, and alive. At that moment a voice came from beside him in the van: Police-Constable Hogg had recovered consciousness.

"You can't get away with this, my lads. There are police blocks going up on all the roads hereabouts. You've had it, mates, see?"

"Bastard's bluffing. Let's load the nipper on and mosey."

"Take it easy," came Mac's voice, a rasp of command in it. There was a hurried colloquy between him and Tom, which Foxy could not catch; then a long pause. Tom had taken Mac up onto the roof. From that vantage point, they saw car headlights approaching to the east along the main road, stopping—two cars; the same westward, where the track debouched into a lane. The bogey had not been bluffing.

"Into the house! Make it fast!" ordered Mac on his return. The other men grumbled; but they were out of their depth now, they obeyed. As Foxy was unlashed and hustled toward the back door by Tom, he saw them lifting the laundry basket and the policeman out of the van. Tom hurried him upstairs—three flights—pushed him into a room, locked the door on him. It was a brightly painted room, such as Foxy had never seen, full of kid's toys and such, with a wall paper on which romped a pattern of Noah's arks and animals. Sitting up in the bed was Bert Hale. The stared at each other for a moment.

"Hello, Bert."

"Hello, Foxy."

"Doing yourself well here, aren't you?"

"You been kidnaped too, Foxy?"

"Yeh. *And* beaten up," said Foxy, not without pride. "Take a dekko at my bruises."

Downstairs in the servants' hall, while the old Nanny stared at them wild-eyed, the men held a rapid consultation with her nephew. There were four courses open to them. They could hide the arms here, and drive out of the park to be picked up by the police, relatively un-redhanded. They could drive away armed and try to shoot their way past the road block. They could scatter, each man attempting to escape across the fields by himself. Or they could stay put and shoot it out. Two of the men were in favor of the first or third course. But Mac and Fred had too much to lose if they fell into the hands of the law—Fred as an accomplice in the murder of Dai Williams, and Mac for a robbery with violence, whose victim had died of it. Besides, there was the Bert Hale factor. The Boss had sent word on the telephone, said Tom, that at all costs the boy must be kept from the police for another twenty-four hours; after that, it wouldn't matter; if they brought it off, the Boss would stake them another grand apiece. This inducement, plus the more forceful personalities of Mac and Fred, won the day. They had plenty of ammunition; and if they couldn't fight off the bogeys for twenty-four hours, they'd deserve to be topped, was Mac's view. They'd stay here and shoot it out till the next night, then attempt a getaway, each man for himself, under cover of darkness.

"Why don't we just croak the little bleeder?" asked Fred. "That'd stop him gaffing to the flatties—for more than twenty-four hours."

"Nark it," said Mac. "The Big Boy wouldn't like that sort of talk."

"Who the hell is he, anyway?" Fred snarled.

"Don't ask tactless questions, Cuthbert. We don't know who he is. We do not know, we cannot tell. He's where the dough comes from. Isn't that good enough for you?"

"I still say, croak the—nah, croak 'em both."

"You make me tired. And if you lift a finger at my Foxy-Poxy, you horrible little runt—"

Fred's hand flashed to his pocket and came out with a razor in it. But Mac had drawn his revolver still faster. The two glared at each other—the reptilian-eyed Fred and the huge Clydesider, dangerous as a rhinoceros. Tom broke the tension.

"For crying aloud! Can't you see we got a couple of aces

in them kids? Hostages. We tell the bogeys if they try to rush us, we'll hand the kids over—the quickest way—drop 'em off the roof.''

"You've got something there,'' said Fred. "Sort of stalemate. You want the kid. We got him. O.K., you can have him dead, or we keep him, alive. It's a sweet thought.''

"You keep your sweet effing thoughts to kiss yourself good-by with,'' growled Mac. "The discussion group will now dismiss. What's the layout of this joint?''

Tom gave him a rapid survey. All the ground-floor windows of Stourford Hall were heavily shuttered. It should be easy enough, from first-floor windows, to pick off any policemen before they could force their way through. The same applied to the main door, in the east face. The back door could be heavily barricaded against an attack from across the courtyard. That left the south and west approaches. Both these sides of the house had French windows, which were shuttered. The eastern end commanded the main drive, the western the only other route by which vehicles could drive up to the house.

Mac and Fred had had experience of house-to-house fighting during the war. They knew that, resolutely defended, a building can be held for a period out of proportion to the size of its garrison, except against tanks. On the other hand, Stourford Hall gave them an uncomfortably broad front to defend, and they had no sandbags to fill up the windows from which they would be firing. What Mac banked on was the difficulty of a night attack for men untrained in such operations; some of the police might be old soldiers; but it was unlikely that any concerted attack would be launched till daylight, particularly if the police—always cautious movers, in Mac's experience—were given the impression at the outset that the defenses were heavily manned.

Mac's final dispositions were as follows: one man to cover each side of the house from a first-floor window, while Tom would keep on the move from room to room, to make it appear that the defenders were a numerous body, and also act as a runner for Mac. Mac himself had the advantage of a turret room, at the southeast corner of the house, whose two windows gave him a 90° arc of fire. The van was moved a little to the left of the archway which led out of the courtyard, and placed so that its headlights shone diagonally through it onto the spot where the main drive branched, but would be partly protected by the courtyard wall. Tom's motorcycle was placed on the southern terrace for its headlight to point southwest. Finally, the unfortunate P.C. Hogg was dumped in a cellar, while the old woman was locked into the nursery with the two boys.

At ten-twenty-five Blount's car drew up by the police barrier on the main road. It was a dark night, with the suffocating stillness of August. Blount and Nigel were directed to the gate lodge, where the Ipswich Superintendet awaited them. Here they learned that, an hour before, a number of men in a van had driven through to the house after capturing the constable on duty and disconnecting the telephone. The gardener swore that no one had passed out onto the main road between then and the arrival of police reinforcements. Nigel was, on the whole, relieved to hear this; it meant that his hunch had been correct—the enemy had sent an armed party to Stourford Hall, presumably to bring Bert and Elmer away; and they had only missed the trick by a matter of ten minutes or so.

The Ipswich Superintendent, Hallam, had wireless communication between his own car and the two police cars which blocked the other exit from the park, to the west: no one had attempted to get past that way. There remained the north and south. Hallam pointed out on his large-scale ordnance map how the land lay. A hundred yards from the south front of the house, between its lawn and the park proper, he said, there was a ha-ha. Into this he was filtering half a dozen armed policemen. To the north of the house lay a group of outbuildings, with the river running half a mile beyond them. He had sent four men to patrol the stretch of land between outbuildings and river; but he did not think there would be a breakout in that direction, unless the fugitives were prepared to swim.

Hallam then showed them, on a smaller scale map, the railway stations and road junctions which were now being watched. There were some familiar names on this map—Dedham, Flatford.

"I see we're in the Constable country," remarked Nigel.

"I could do with fifty more, sir, at this moment," said Superintendent Hallam. "Well, we'd best be getting along. See if they mean business."

It was soon evident that they did. As the two police cars, moved up the drive, headlight beams bouncing and sliding off the trees that lined it, Nigel saw the roof of Stourford Hall traced dimly against the dark sky, but the lower stories were hidden behind a strong beam of light which struck diagonally across their path.

"By God, they're going to make a break for it," said Hallam. "Stop!"

But the beam did not move. It made a pool of light, stationary and sinister, where the drive forked—a pool of light, a moth trap, thought Nigel, as the car crawled ahead once more, almost up to its brink, then stopped. Nigel realized that the police drivers had switched off their own lights.

"'Is there anybody there, said the Traveler,'" he murmured to Blount, on the back seat beside him. The voice of Superintendent Hallam, calling through the loud-speaker, came as an echo.

"Is there anyone there? We are the police. We are armed. I have a warrant for the arrest of Jameson Elmer. Come out, all of you."

"Come and get us, flatties!"

The shout was followed instantly by a lucky burst of fire, which knocked an armed policeman from the running board of the first car and shattered the windshield of the second. The police were firing now, from the cover of the two cars; but the diagonal beam obscured their target as effectually as a smoke screen.

"Shoot out those bloody headlights!" shouted Hallam.

So well placed, however, was the van in the courtyard, that it was difficult to get at them without coming into their beam. Another policeman was wounded, attempting to do so; and Hallam, after picking up the casualties, order a retreat.

Up in the nursery, Bert jumped as he heard the burst of fire. He was engaged in drawing accurate maps of the several floors of the house; it was quicker than trying to explain them to Foxy by word of mouth. Foxy was reclining on the bed, ravenously eating chocolate Nanny had brought for Bert. The old woman had, as Foxy put it, fallen apart: she crouched in the rocking chair, plucking her fingers, muttering that she'd never heard of such goings-on, and what was the world coming to, and when would that man give her back her uniform. This last remark the boys interpreted to mean that the gunman had borrowed the old nurse's clothes as a disguise to help him escape. Between them, they had arrived at a pretty correct picture of the state of affairs; they also guessed its urgency; for Bert told Foxy how he had discovered the meaning of Dai Williams' message, and tomorrow would be the 12th.

The blatter of the automatic weapon they now heard could only mean that the house was being attacked. Turning to each other, the boys stuck up their thumbs in signal. It was time to put their plan into operation. Bert had written several copies of a statement, giving all the information they had at their disposal. These were to be put inside the paint box, the Noah's ark and a Chinese puzzle egg, which would be thrown out of the window as soon as the police approached. But, peering downward through the bars, they could see no police—only the night, and the swathe of light which the headlamp of Tom's motorcycle cut through the darkness. They turned away, disconsolate, unaware that their faces, outlined in the lighted window, had been spotted by one of the policemen entrenched in the ha-ha.

Word presently came to Blount and Hallam that two boys had been seen in a top-floor window on the south side of the house. Blount silently patted Nigel on the back: the hunch was vindicated. The two officers, after a short conference, agreed that no second attack should be made tonight. They had not enough men at their disposal to risk rushing the house, and the men were unfamiliar with the terrain.

"Thank God this isn't London," Blount remarked, "or we should have to be using three-quarters of them to hold back the sight-seers."

The wounded men were returned to Ipswich by ambulance, and reinforcements sent for. Hallam ordered sniping from each side of the house (it was safe enough, now they knew which room the boys were in), to draw the gangsters' fire and get some idea of their strength. The reply suggested to him that there were about half a dozen men in the house, all equipped with automatic weapons. He ordered cease-fire, and began redistributing his meager force so as to tighten the cordon. Apart from the foot patrols, one police car blocked the main drive, another the western exit, while two more crusied about the park to north and south, their headlights feeling this way and that like antennae, startling the owls and ruining the night's sleep of a herd of deer.

At dawn, after they had had a cup of tea in the lodge, Nigel and Blount went on a reconnaissance. It was a bizzarre sight—the beautiful house taking shape out of the darkness and early morning mists. No sound, no smoke from the chimneys, no life at the shuttered windows. It seemed quite dead; or like a Sleeping Beauty's palace, unreal, lapped in a cataleptic trance. But it was not dead, only deadly dangerous. A bullet clipped the trunk of an oak from behind which Blount was peering. The van had been moved, so that it blocked the entrance to the courtyard now; if the house was to be attacked from this quarter, either the van must be shifted or the police must scale the courtyard wall; either way, it would be suicide. Yet this north side was the only one which gave cover, in the wall and outbuildings, for the first stage of an assault. To east, south, and west the ground sloped gently away from the house, so that even the police in the ha-ha were pinned down. Even if they could rush the hundred yards between it and the south terrace, they would still be faced with the task of breaking through the shuttered windows, under fire.

Hallam wisely decided that the job was too big for him. He had only rifles and carbines, against automatic weapons. His men could probably rush the house, if they attacked from all sides, but at the cost of casualties he was not prepared to risk. Valuing his men's lives higher than his pride, he drove off to get in touch with the military authorities. Events soon proved how right he was.

At seven-thirty Tom fetched his aunt to make breakfast for the defenders. In her absence, Bert and Foxy tried to break open the locked door; but it was stoutly built, and all they broke was the chair with which they battered it. They then went to the window, and yelled out to the police in the ha-ha. When they had attracted attention, Bert dropped the Noah's ark with the message through the bars; it burst on the terrace below, and the paper fluttered through the stone balusters onto the lawn. A young policeman began scrambling out of the ha-ha to fetch it; he held an iron shield before him, which was some protection against Fred, shooting at him from the room above the French windows. But Mac, enfilading from the southern window of the turret, cut the policeman down as he started to make a dash for it. He writhed for a little, then lay still.

The gangsters were now committed. They had killed a man, and could expect no mercy. Bert, ashen-faced, lay sobbing on the bed; he felt it was he who had killed the man, and he almost welcomed the blows which Tom presently gave him and Foxy for trying to communicate with the rescuers. The boys were taken down to the cellars at pistol point, bound, and left there for what seemed hours.

And indeed, it was hours before the military machine could be set in motion. Hallam had to unwind a certain amount of red tape: the nearest army detachment could not be made available, and troops had to be sent from a distance of fifty miles. By the time they had been equipped and got under way, it was midday. The vehicles, carrying a company of

infantry and headed by an armored car, rolled through the
park gates a little before two P.M. There was then another
delay, while the military commander conferred with the
police officers. It was decided to engage three sides of the
house with a platoon each, while the police withdrew to form
an outer cordon; then the armored car would shoot a way for
the remaining platoon to enter the main door at the east.

Mac, from his turret window, could see the armored car
between the trees lining the drive. The military dispositions
elsewhere were reported to him by Tom. Well, they'd had it
now. There was little hope of holding out for the remaining
six and a half hours till darkness fell. But Mac was fighting
mad; he would not take any soft options now—not that they'd
be offered. Would the others cave in, though? Even Fred?
The only thing to do now was to play his last card, in the hope
of gaining time. He dispatched Tom to fetch the hostages.

The loud-speaker on a police car crackled and uttered:
"We give you two minutes to surrender. Two minutes to
surrender. Walk out of the east door, with your hands up."

Bert and Foxy heard it faintly, as they were hustled upstairs, into an attic. Tom went ahead, climbed a ladder,
opened a skylight.

"Up you go, sonnies," said Mac, behind them with a
revolver.

They emerged onto a flat roof—quite a big expanse of it.
The men drove them to the far end, thirty yards away, where
there was a two-foot coping.

Bert shrank back with a moan. Foxy's teeth were set in his
sharp, white face. At the coping, the roof stopped, a pre-
cipice of gray stone, tree tops level with them; and far, far
down, faces like white disks began to turn up toward them.

"Just sit down there, sonnies," said Mac, "till I talk to the
army of liberation."

They sat down on the coping, with their feet supported by a
ledge above vacancy. Mac was on his stomach behind them
now, invisible to the soldiers and police. Nigel heard a fog-
horn voice.

"Can you hear me, blue bottles and brown jobs? . . . If you

start anything, we'll shoot these two nippers off the edge of the roof. So b—— off home now with that little toy on wheels!''

Nigel, craning upward, saw one of the two tiny figures on the skyline—the red-haired one—put his arm round the other. Tears pricked his eyes, blurring those figures on the coping. The whole thing had been so fantastic: the steel-helmeted soldiers behind their Brens, the armored car throbbing amid the trees, the loud-speaker crackling—all in the summer afternoon, the gracious, derelict park. But now that voice from the rooftop had shattered the fantasy. And time was passing.

''Well, what's the form now? Bit of an impasse, isn't it?'' The captain in command of the soldiers was talking to Blount and Hallam, behind his armored car. I suppose all warfare is like this, thought Nigel—brief oases of action in deserts of inactivity, of waiting, of conferences and post-mortems: but time is passing: how much more have we? a day? six hours? an hour?

His reverie was broken by the loud-speaker. ''Surrender Jameson Elmer! Hand over Jameson Elmer to the police, my lads, and you may do yourselves a bit of good. You haven't a hope otherwise. Surrender Jameson Elmer!''

''Surrender my Aunt Fanny!'' boomed back the voice from the roof. And it's just as well Jameson bleeding Elmer isn't here, thought Mac, or the boys might begin to weaken.

''All right,'' said the loud-speaker. ''We can wait.''

But they couldn't. Nigel knew that, and Blount knew it. The tiny figure up there, the boy huddled on the coping, possessed information which might affect the peace of the whole world. If they attacked, he would be shot; if they waited till the gangsters caved in, it would be too late, and this weird little action in a Suffolk park might beget, as its final issue, a world war. A third time, the loud-speaker blared.

''Calling Bert Hale. Calling Bert Hale. Keep your chins up, Bert and Foxy. You'll be all right. You're doing fine, both of you. Got a view up there? Grandstand seat?''

It was Blount hailing them. Nigel felt a surge of affection for his friend; there were not many men who, under these desperate circumstances, would think about reassuring the terrified boys.

"Call out to us, Bert. We'll hear you. What was written on the paper Dai Williams gave you?"

Bert opened his mouth. A voice from behind him said, "Shut your trap, kid. One sound from you, and I'll shoot."

In the police car, Blount mopped his brow. Well, that was that. Nigel saw a rook, unsettled by the loud-speaker's brayings, come gliding down again into a tree top. The next minute he was talking urgently to Hallam and the Company Commander.

"I should think we can lay it on, old boy," said the latter, "if the Brylcreem boys will play."

Soon a message was being tapped out from the radio truck which stood further back in the drive. Half an hour passed. Three quarters. The radio set crackled again. A runner came to the Company Commander.

"At sixteen hours, sir."

"We'll get cracking at fifteen-fifty-eight," said the Captain to Blount and Hallam. "This is going to be a shaky do."

"It's that, or nothing. We've just got to take the risk."

"Poor little blighters. Hope someone gives them a medal."

From the turret window, ten minutes later, Mac saw the movement starting. He had come down again, leaving Tom on the roof with orders to shoot Bert Hale if anything went wrong. Foxy could be spared—for the present, at any rate. Foxy had guts. Mac could do with people who had guts. Now, looking out, Mac saw the armored car turning, maneuvering off the drive, passing along the south side of the house and disappearing. What the hell were the bastards up to now? The droops were on the move, too, filing this way and that at the double, and the line of carriers had started up their engines. Could it be a withdrawal?

Tom, still covering the boys with his revolver, crawled to

the southern edge of the roof and cautiously peered over. The armored car was approaching from the west, roaring along the lawn between terrace and ha-ha. Beyond the ha-ha, two police cars were bumping over the grass of the park land, their loud-speakers bellowing orders.

There was a great revving-up of engines, a tramping of feet, a shouting of commands; and in the midst of this pandemonium, it's approach downed by the din, a helicopter came floating like thistledown from the east, almost brushing the tallest tree tops.

Foxy and Bert saw it at the same moment. Foxy gripped his friend's wrist, muttering fiercely. "Ssh! Keep still!" Bert flinched away a little, almost fell back off the coping, for it looked as if the helicopter's wheels were going to part his hair for him. But, like thistledown in an eddy of air, it lifted at that very instant, its vertical screw turning fast. And at that instant Tom heard its engine, looked up, saw the aircraft looming monstrously above him. He was just about to withdraw his eyes from it and take aim at Bert Hale's back when the objects began falling from the helicopter toward him. Jesus! they were bombing. Tom lost his nerve, and with a yell of panic dashed for the skylight. The objects burst on the roof, one behind him and one in front, and Tom was caught between two rising walls of blinding, suffocating smoke.

The falling of the smoke bombs was the signal for a general assault. The Bren-gunners poured in their fire at the first-floor windows, concentrating particularly on those which covered the main drive. The armored car, which had now reached the point where the drive forked, made a sudden sweeping U-turn over turf borders and flower beds, accelerated hard, drove forward, bucking up the broad, shallow flight of steps which led to the great east door, and rammed it at an angle, then backed to allow the infantry file, following close behind, to enter. It had been beautifully synchronized—the whole operation. But what was happening up there amid the coiling smoke on the rooftop, Nigel wondered. Already the helicopter was making another approach;

this time it would land on the flat roof, and its occupants leap out to occupy that strong point in case the gangsters should attempt to make a last stand there.

As the smoke bombs burst, Bert and Foxy had thrown themselves flat on the roof behind the coping. Foxy was up in a moment, dragging Bert by the hand, running full tilt for the cover of the smoke. They could hear Tom, coughing and gasping. They made a detour, eyes shut, holding their breath, and by great good luck stumbled upon the skylight. There was no time to fasten it behind them. They had only one thought—to get away from Tom and his revolver. Down the ladder they tumbled, into the attic, through the door, along a passage, down a flight of stairs. They heard Tom cursing as he blundered along, somewhere behind them. They heard the crash and rattle of firing; paused for a moment, uncertain what to do, at the foot of the stairs.

There was a shattering above them, a groan, and a body came bumping down the stairs at them—Tom, shot dead by a random bullet which had entered the landing window. The boys tore down the next flight, as though the body were still pursuing them. On the next landing they checked again. They could distantly hear the troops breaking through into the other side of the house, and were about to move in that direction when at the far end of the corridor a door cautiously opened, the muzzle of a weapon protruded, then a face; it was the face Bert most feared in the world—that of the man who had threatened him with a knuckle-duster in Kensington Gardens. Bert plunged through a door behind him, dragging Foxy. They locked it, and fled into the adjoining room.

"Quick, I know where to hide," Bert gasped. His memories of the house served him well now. They darted in and out of rooms and corridors. Once a burst from Fred's gun brought the plaster showering in their tracks. But soon they had reached the room Bert was making for; he pushed the acorns on the mantelpiece; the panel of the priest's hole slid open, and Bert shoved Foxy in. He could just reach the secret spring from inside. He pressed it again, and the panel closed as he hastily withdrew his arm. There was a thudding explosion outside—Fred shooting out the lock of the door; a curse, as he found the room empty.

"They'll never find us here," said Bert exultantly. "Smashing hiding place, isn't it, Foxy?"

He remembered, the next moment, that the panel could not be opened from inside, and that the only person who knew its secret had just been killed. Well, it didn't matter. The police would search for them, and they could bang at the panel. But quarter of an hour passed, no searchers had come, and the boys began to notice a faint, frightening smell—the smell of smoke, of a house on fire.

17

The Object of the Exercise

Nigel and Blount had gone in shortly after the first wave of
the assault, but there was nothing much they could do till the
gangsters were mopped up. Two surrendered at once. Fred
was shot down by a party he ran into while still hunting for
the boys. But Mac, in his turret room, firing round the door
which commanded a passage, proved difficult to dislodge.
The passage was too long for him to be rushed, as the attackers discovered at the cost of several casualties. Finally one
of them—a National Service man who played cricket for a
first-class county—fast-bowled a hand grenade down the corridor first bounce into the turret room, and Mac was mortally
wounded.

Meanwhile troops were scouring the rest of the house.
They discovered P.C. Hogg and the old nurse locked in a
cellar. Then they moved up to the ground floor, hurrying
from room to room, calling out. The three men who had
disembarked from the helicopter found no one on the roof:
the boys had evidently got clear away, and must be in the
house somewhere. One of the surrendered mobsters told
Superintendent Blount that Jameson Elmer had left the house
the previous evening. It was a bitter blow, and made it all the
more urgent to find Bert Hale. Moreover, during the fighting,
the oldest part of the house had caught fire, and its paneled
room walls were beginning to blaze dangerously before the
fire was noticed.

"Where the devil have those boys got to?" said Blount.

Nigel set off for the room Hesione had told him about. From her description, he knew it was on the first floor, in the original part of the house. There was just a chance that the gangsters might have caught the boys escaping from the roof, and locked them in the priest's hole. Soldiers were running upstairs with buckets of water, looking vainly for fire extinguishers on the stripped walls. Smoke was seeping and creeping along the passage, as Nigel flung open door after door, looking for the room whose photograph Hesione had shown him. The fourth door he opened showed him,' through the smoke, what he wanted: the noble proportions, the exquisite molding, the mantelpiece with its carved bosses and medallions; and fire was climbing its panels in angry waves and darts. From behind one panel came shouting, banging. Nigel hurled himself through the smoke, pressed the acorn clump.

Bert and Foxy scrambled out. Nigel led them through the door, one last tentacle of smoke coiling round their ankles and falling away. Blount hailed them from the end of the corridor.

"Well done, my lads. Vairy nice, vairy nice." He clapped the two bedraggled figures on the shoulders. "We're proud of you. Damn this smoke—it's got in *my* eyes now."

Blount produced an enormous bandanna, and mopped vigorously at the tears which might or might not have been caused by smoke.

Two minutes later, out on the lawn in the sweet air, Bert was saying, "When I was kidnaped the man asked me to write down the message—the one I found in my boat—he was dressed as a policeman, so I thought it was all right. So I wrote down 'Bert Hale 12'; and just as I was writing—it was in the car—my hand jogged, and it became 'Bert Hall 12,' and I remembered the bit of paper had been torn off very close to the B—it might have been a capital letter or an ordinary one, you see, because it was scrawly writing—and I saw what the whole message was—I mean, what it could have been. Albert Hall 12. Then I thought, perhaps 12 was a time, or a date. Today's the 12th. Is anything happening at the Albert Hall today?"

Superintendent Blount removed his spectacles, breathed over them, rubbed them, and put them on again.

"A concert," he said gently. "A very grand concert, old son." Then to Nigel and Hallam, "In honor of the Soviet Foreign Minister. Starting at eight P.M."

Nigel looked at his watch. It was now four-fifty-two.

"I say, sir. Do you think the American gunman is going to shoot the Russian Minister? He was practicing shots with a rifle out of that window—at a target on the lawn."

"Deflection shots," said Blount. "That's a help. I dare say you're right, son." He beamed at the boy. "You're not— e'eh—wanting a job in the C.I.D.? Looks as if I should be retiring and handing over to you."

"Hadn't you better get cracking, mister?" Foxy had re-covered his perkiness. "What are we waiting for? Tell you something else. The gunman escaped in that old woman's uniform—nurse's uniform. Disguise, see?"

"Come along, sons. Ever seen a wireless truck?"

The boys stared their fill, as Blount transmitted a string of instructions through the signalman at the radio. Then he drew the Company Commander aside, and there was a muttered conversation. The officer presently climbed into the truck, pressed down a switch, and said,

"Army calling R.A.F. Can you hear me? Over."

"Receiving you loud and clear. What can I do for you, General? Haven't you won your battle yet? Over."

"If you can get that god-awful contraption off the roof, you intrepid birdman, I have another job for you. Over."

"Always happy to oblige. I shall be with you in a moment, dear. Over."

"It would be well to move fast. The house is on fire under-neath you; repeat, the house is on fire underneath you. Your comments will be welcomed. Over."

"Ha, ha, ha . . . By God, so it is! I can't wait to be with you. Shall we meet on that sweet little lawn your horrid vehicles have been cutting up? Over."

"Rendezvous approved. Mind the flower beds. Out."

Looking up, the boys saw the helicopter raise itself off the roof, sidle away, tilt, begin to drift gently down. As they reached the lawn, the pilot leaned out and made a rude sign at the army captain, who called up to him, "I've got a couple of V.I.P.'s for you. They want to go to London. Can you find London?"

"I *might*. Of course I'm only a beginner. These gentlemen?" said the pilot, looking at Blount and Nigel.

"Oh well, they might go too. But I meant these chaps." The captain indicated Bert and Foxy.

"Us?" Foxy exclaimed hoarsely. "Go in *that?* Gawd blow me down! Didya hear, Bert?"

"Oh boy," Bert solemnly ejaculated. "Oh *boy*, oh boy!"

Blount turned away, and blew his nose on his bandanna—a sound like the Last Trump.

"Steady, sir," called out the pilot. "Mind my machine."

The boys eyed each other, giggled, broke into convulsions. As the aircraft moved, the Company Commander stood to attention and snapped off a smart salute. Foxy acknowledged it with a grin and a royal gesture of the hand. Bert did not even see it; he was gazing, with the rapture of a faithful Mohammedan first viewing Paradise and its houris, at the helicopter's instrument panel.

Ten minutes later, while Bert and the pilot were engaged in a highly technical discussion on the subject of aerodynamics, Nigel turned to Blount on the back seat beside him.

"I must say you're taking all this very calmly—this Albert Hall lark."

"Oh well now, oh well now." Blount vigorously slapped his bald dome. "We've not picked up this Elmer laddie yet; but he hasn't an airthly chance of bringing it off."

"That's not quite what I meant. You're being evasive. *Was* Bert's information really a surprise to you?"

Blount looked a trifle guilty. "I'll not say it hadn't occurred to us that 'Albert Hall on the 12th' mighn't be the meaning. But I'll admit we were properly foxed for a wee while by the Harwich notion."

"And I never saw it."

"Och now, you'd had a sore clout on the head."

"So my wits were addled? But why didn't you tell me?"

"There were reasons, Strangeways," said Blount uncomfortably.

"Ah. I see. Not just the old man being secretive?"

"You were seeing quite a lot of Durbar and his lady. It was just possible Durbar was mixed up in this business. If he was, it wouldn't have done for him to discover we'd guessed about the Albert Hall. And if *you'd* known it, he might have got it out of you, one way or another."

"So I've just been a pawn in your large, red hands?"

"Hoots-toots."

The pilot turned to Bert, huddled up with Foxy on the seat at his side.

"You care to take over, old man? Wheel in front of you. Fly her on the artificial horizon. Nothing in it."

Bert blushed crimson, swallowed twice, bit his lip, gave one side glance at the pilot—for whom that moment he would willingly have died—then, with a look of religious awe and professional concentration, laid hands on the wheel.

Sir Rudolf Durbar was dressing for the concert. An extremely knowledgeable amateur of music, he looked forward to it with mixed feelings. And it was a tribute to his amazing faculty for—dissociation, should one call it? or concentration?—that these mixed feelings sprang entirely from the nature of the official program, and not from any unofficial contribution to the night's proceedings of which he might have cognizance. The program would be composed of British and Russian music only. The Vaughan Williams *Sixth* and Walton's *Belshazzar's Feast* were unexceptionable; but the Soviet half of the program, chosen by the organizers after considerable research into the question of which Russian composers were at the moment deemed correct in official circles, looked less desirable. The Soviet Foreign Minister was also an ardent devotee of music; perhaps he should have been asked to choose his own program, Sir Rudolf reflected—on the principle of the condemned man who is allowed to order whatever he fancies for his last breakfast.

As a person inured to the taking of tremendous risks with his own money, Sir Rudolf had no qualms at all about taking risks with other people's lives. Not that he wanted war, which he well knew would be almost as disastrous for himself as for the world in general. What he wanted was a continuance of the *status quo:* disarmament, which the success of the present negotiations had turned from a dream to a possibility, would be quite unthinkably inconvenient for him—he had too many eggs in the other basket. Of course, America might not play. But, after last year's announcement that Russia possessed the hydrogen bomb, even the most chauvinist circles in the U.S.A. had been drawing in their horns. There was no certainty now that the present negotiations would not lead to a world conference on disarmament; already the markets were pointing that way.

While the valet tied his tie, Sir Rudolf switched his mind from music to murder. He did not, of course, think of it in such terms. Nor, on the other hand, did he indulge in any idealistic self-deception about the necessity or virtue of political assassination. Like his financial campaigns, this was a remote-control enterprise: he pressed certain buttons, and through an intricate chain of reactions, a desired effect was produced at the other end. In the present instance, the reasoning had operated like this: if the Soviet Foreign Minister were assassinated, it would protract the East-West impasse for, say, another ten years, and rearmament would continue; if the assassin proved to be an ex-Federal agent, Russian suspiciousness would jump to the conclusion that it had been done with the connivance, at least, of influential circles in the U.S.A.; therefore, the assassin himself must be exposed. If the man, Elmer, were to be killed after shooting the Minister, his identity would be discovered; and also, since dead men cannot talk, any faint chance of his connection with Sir Rudolf being traced would disappear. And this was where young Gray came in. . . .

Alec Gray was dressing for the concert. He had never needed Benzedrine before a raid: the prospect of action, excitement, working upon his own hard, reckless nature, produced all the stimulant he required. He reviewed the plan for tonight—or rather, the two plans; for things were not going to follow quite the pattern which had been laid down when Jameson Elmer was briefed. The Yank would be occupying, alone, a box on the second tier which had been procured for him, giving an excellent view of the Russian party; the provenance of this box could not be traced to Gray or Sir Rudolf. Gray would sit, with some friends, in the next box but two. The Yank was not to shoot till the very end of the concert, when the Soviet Minister rose to acknowledge the applause of the audience; at that moment every eye in the hall would be upon the Russian party, and Elmer, concealed behind the curtain of his box, could take aim and fire without apprehension of interference. He could then dart out and mingle with the stream of people leaving early, as some always did, to catch the last buses or trains to the suburbs. Gray would be at hand to convoy him from the hall, drive him away to the secret rendezvous where an airplane was awaiting, and pay him off.

Those, at least, were the arrangements agreed upon with the Yank. The thing would not, however, go according to plan—not for Jameson Elmer. Gray had no intention of helping the gunman to escape. On the contrary, he would start a hue and cry after him. Elmer would be intercepted at one of the exits, try to shoot his way out—and that would be the end of him. With so dangerous a man as Elmer, the police would certainly shoot to kill; and, if they did only wing him, the Yank was the type who'd turn his revolver on himself rather than fall into the hands of the Law.

The Yank himself would not have talked; and Gray had dropped him half a mile from Stourford Hall on the night the Quack was shot, so nobody there had seen the two together. Dai Williams had been silenced in time. There only remained the information which that wretched brat, Foxy, had given the police—about the man whom he saw Gray bring to the Durbars' party. Alec had a story ready to account for that, and a stooge to corroborate it; if Inspector Wright assumed that the man was a burglar, whom Gray had introduced into the Durbars' house, good luck to him. How fortunate it was that Foxy had not caught the conversation between Durbar and himself in the garden, thought Gray; it'd have been a job to explain this away; but Mac was certain Foxy had not heard it, and Mac would be keeping Foxy out of harm's way till Gray left the country.

His escape route had been carefully planned. No doubt, what with the kidnaping of Bert Hale, the burglaries, and the message found in his flat, the police were apoplectic with suspicion of him by now. And the only possible reason they had not pulled him in was that they wanted Jameson Elmer even more, and hoped Gray might lead them to Elmer if they gave him enough rope. Well, by God, he'd lead them to Elmer tonight. He would have to undergo a severe grilling, no doubt; but, without more evidence, the police could not hold him—not with Sir Rudolf's influence at work behind the scenes. And then he only had to slip his shadowers, and there was the airplane ready, and South America at journey's end, where Durbar's agents would look after him. He and Durbar knew too much about each other for there to be any danger of betrayal. Gray's mind went back to that day, some months ago, when Durbar had confronted him with the knowledge of his liaison with Hesione and his activities as inside man for Sam Borch. It gave Durbar a stranglehold over him; but what he had done for Durbar since then leveled the balance. Between them, they had planned the wave of robberies to coincide with the Soviet deputation's visit, the political incidents, the Yank's *modus operandi*. Durbar had the ideas—including the idea of his own house being burgled as a blind—Gray the contacts. It was a fruitful partnership, giving satisfaction on both sides. . . .

When Blount and Nigel arrived at the Albert Hall, crowds were already gathered outside. Ticket holders had been requested to take their places a quarter of an hour before the concert began, but sight-seers had turned up in hundreds to watch the arrival of the Soviet Minister and other celebrities. A cordon of police kept them at a distance from the approaches to the hall. The park railings opposite were lined with spectators. At every door there was a group of policemen, and just inside the doors stood plain-clothes men, each of whom had a copy of Jameson Elmer's photograph.

"We're taking every precaution, you see," said the Superintendent.

"I'd feel happier if you'd got him in the cooler."

Jameson Elmer had been traced to a railway station five miles from Stourford Hall, where he—or at any rate a person in nurse's uniform—had caught a train the previous evening. It was a stopping train, the coaches without corridors, and the person could have changed clothes in any empty compartment before reaching the junction. Here the trail had petered out. The local train caught a London express: but, so far, inquiries at the junction and Liverpool Street had failed to identify Jameson Elmer as having traveled by it.

On arrival in London, after arranging for Bert and Foxy to be restored to their parents, Blount had taken Nigel with him to Sir Edward, and made a report. The great man was seriously concerned. It would be possible, of course, to advise the Soviet Foreign Minister not to attend the concert; but he was an obstinate man, who loved music no less than he disliked losing face; nor would it increase the prestige of his protectors if they told him he was in danger for a solitary gunman whom the whole police force of Britain had failed to catch. Moreover, considerations of high policy were involved. The Minister's presence at this concert would set a public seal on the negotiations of the last ten days, and symbolize the hope of better international relations arising from them. After a brief telephone conversation with Number 10, Downing Street, Sir Edward decided that the show must go on. The measures already taken for protecting the Minister were to be most stringently enforced, and additional precautions taken.

Alec Gray was made aware of this the moment he entered

the Albert Hall. Two large men politely asked him to step this way; he was rapidly and thoroughly searched for weapons, before they let him rejoin his party. Not even Sir Rudolf, though he was one of the organizers of the concert, could pass unchallenged; his tickets were carefully examined, and two plain-clothes men took up their positions in the corridor outside his box. The Special Branch had found, only this morning, a loose end in his closely woven fabric of respectability, and it was only a matter of time before the whole thing was unraveled.

"Elmer hasn't an airthly chance of getting in," Blount was saying now to his companion. "And I don't see how he could do anything outside. Just take a look." He pointed to a knot of policemen on the Albert Memorial; others were scanning trees in the park and windows along the route—any vantage point conceivably within range of the Soviet Minister's arrival: Blount had been impressed by Bert Hale's information that the gunman had practiced deflection shots at Stourford Hall.

"He could have got in during the day, couldn't he?"

"He might," said Blount grimly. "But, as soon as they got my message from Stourford, they searched the hall— every damned square yard of it. Do you know, it has nearly forty rooms, under the auditorium and behind the platform— absolute rabbit warren. He's not there. I'd stake my pension on it."

Blount would have lost his stake. Five minutes ago a smallish man with a drooping mustache, a loose black coat over his evening clothes, had entered the hall. He entered it, carrying a violin case, in company with several members of the orchestra, by the artists' entrance; at least, the police on guard assumed him to be in their company, and any doubts they might have had were set at rest by the card which he produced—all members of the orchestra and choir had been required, as an additional precaution, to show a pass officially supplied to them. But Jameson Elmer was a master of disguise; if he had to look like a musician, he could be relied on to disappear behind the role.

He went downstairs. Presently, emerging from a lavatory, he entered the band room, where he stood the violin case against a wall, then, slipping out again, made his way through the subterranean labyrinth upstairs toward the boxes. He had a map of the place in his head, supplied by the same thoughtful provider as the evening clothes, the mustache, the pass, and certain other articles which he had found awaiting him, on his return to London, at the rendezvous. Mingling now with the stream of concert-goers, buying his program, having the box unlocked for him by an attendant—one of the Corps of Honorary Stewards—who took his ticket, he had somehow changed character again: though his face and dress were the same, he looked like a music-lover, not a professional musician. He walked differently, even—with a slight stiffness, not quite a limp, in one leg. Inside the covered part of the box, he took out from a deep inside pocket of his overcoat the stock of a Winchester rifle, from his trouser leg its barrel—he had transferred them there from the violin case during his brief visit to the lavatory—and rapidly put them together; then laid the rifle along the side wall, drew back a chair over it, well away from the open front of the box, and peered through the curtains. It was in the bag, so far. Without exposing himself at all, he commanded an excellent view of the ceremonial box on the Grand Tier, below him to the right.

In the vast auditorium a stir of excitement manifested itself, as if telepathically communicated by the cheering, inaudible here, of the crowds outside the building: heads turned; the hum of talk kept dying away, then starting again—wafts and flaws of sound, of movement, under the cavernous dome, like the restiveness of the air before a thunderstorm—the storm of applause which broke when the Prime Minister entered the ceremonial box with his distinguished guest, and, leading him forward into full view of the audience, stepped back. The Soviet Minister stood there a moment, stocky and impassive; then, as if thawed by the warmth of his welcome, the granite face relaxed into a smile; he waved, and drew the Prime Minister to his side. The audience were on their feet, the orchestra rose; the conductor held supreme silence poised for a moment on the tip of his uplifted baton. There was a distant, muttering, growing thunder of drums, and the National Anthem began.

As the concert proceeded, Superintendent Blount, from the southwest side of the auditorium, raked the upper tier with his opera glasses. White shirt fronts, white shoulders, orders, jewels, tiaras—it blazed like a July flower bed, bringing back memories of a richer, statelier age. They were certainly doing the Russkis proud. He could see Alec Gray leaning forward, apparently absorbed in the music; the last chance that young thug will have to enjoy himself, thought Blount grimly. There were one or two empty boxes up there, he noticed, feeling vaguely disquieted. Well, God Almighty, they'd been searched, hadn't they? And every box-renter had had to show his card. I've just got an attack of the bogeymen.

At the interval, Blount and Nigel went out for a breath of fresh air. They walked round the building toward its southeast corner, Blount checking the vigilance of the police at each entrance; even at this stage there must be no relaxing.

"Well," he said presently, "I think we've made it. D.V. But I hope I'll never—"

"Blount! What's this?" Nigel's voice was shaky. He was stooping down over the pavement. He straightened up, holding out on the palm of his hand a thin, faintly violet-colored disk. Blount grabbed it, smelled it.

"Threw it away as he came in. The artists's entrance," said Nigel.

"Is he the only man in the world who sucks these things?" demanded Blount angrily over his shoulder. But he was already on his way in. The policemen at the door swore that no unauthorized person had entered, nor anyone who answered to the description of Jameson Elmer.

"A faked pass," muttered Blount, brushing past them. "You could carry an arsenal in some of those damned instrument cases."

He found an attendant, demanded to be taken instantly to the conductor.

"But Sir Malcolm is changing," expostulated the man, deeply shocked. "It's quite out of the question to—"

"I don't care if Sir Malcolm is doing handstands in his birthday suit. I'm seeing him, this instant. Superintendent Blount, of the C.I.D. Get cracking, blast you!"

The attendant scattered like chaff before Blount's explosive violence. Nigel followed them into the conductor's room. Blount introduced himself, gave a rapid explanation of the trouble.

"Afraid I may have to ask for the second half of the concert to be delayed, Sir Malcolm. I've got to make inquiries among the orchestra."

"I quite understand," said the conductor with a courtly gesture of the hand. "There's the choir too, my dear fellow: hundreds and hundreds of them. I'll just come with you, and explain, shall I? Then I must be getting back. The P.M. is bringing round some of our Russian friends to see me in a minute."

In the band room, the members of the orchestra were engaged, after the manner of their kind, in ferocious games of poker and even more ferocious gossip. Sir Malcolm found the leader, entrusted Blount to his hands, and withdrew. Here, and later in the six dressing rooms which accommodated the choir, Blount asked if anyone had seen a man, or a woman— for the gunman had already disguised himself once that way—who was not one of their members, coming in at the artists' entrance before the concert; if so, he would like a description.

Highly disciplined in the performance of their art, orchestral players are apt to be tough, skeptical, contumacious individuals outside it. Dozens of pairs of eyes were fastened upon Blount, with the same unencouraging expression as they were wont to turn upon a nervous young guest conductor. Nigel could almost see these instrumentalist calculating how much overtime pay they should get for answering questions during their sacrosanct interval. Blount, too, was aware of a certain lack of co-operativeness.

"I've greatly enjoyed your performance, gentlemen," he briskly remarked, "and I'm looking forward to the second half. But I'm afraid we shan't be able to start till I've found out this fellow who's been masquerading as a musician."

The orchestra recognized that note of authority. There was also the unthinkable possibility of having to catch a later-than-usual train home.

"It's not on, chum," volunteered an intellectual-looking trombone. "Somebody'd have noticed any stranger coming in at our entrance. We all know one another.

"Too bloody well," remarked a viola, who had just been fleeced at poker by the last speaker. . . .

The conductor was deep in musical discussion with the Soviet Foreign Minister. Sir Rudolf and Lady Durbar were there, among the organizers of the concert. The Prime Minister was chatting to Sir Edward. An attendant whispered in the latter's ear—Superintendent Blount would like a word; he made his apologies and went out.

"I have greatly enjoyed our conversation," said the Russian Minister presently. "You must bring your orchestra to my country one day. They are good, very good. A little roughness in the second violins, perhaps. But there is nothing perfect—" his quick smile flashed out—"not even in Soviet Russia."

"It's been a privilege to play for you. I believe you will find the Walton interesting. And it's an excellent choir, though we could do with some of your Russian basses."

"Now, Sir Malcolm, I expect you want to get rid of us."

"Not a bit, sir. In fact, we may be a little delayed." The conductor lowered his voice. "It seems there is a possibility that some unauthorized person got into the hall. And the police—"

"Ah, the police! They do fuss, don't they?" The Minister laughed heartily, his eye lighting upon three stocky compatriots who stood by the door. "It will give my bodyguard something to do. They are so bored, poor fellows. I'm afraid they do not care greatly for music."

Sir Rudolf, who had been within earshot of this conversation, politely took his leave, Hesione with him.

Two minutes later Jameson Elmer, who had not left his box during the interval, heard the deep, resonant voice of his employer talking to someone outside the door.

"Yes, we're a bit late starting. The police have apparently discovered that some unauthorized person got into the hall.... Well, they may start searching the place again, I suppose. Damned nuisance.... No point waiting. If I were him, I'd disregard the police and fire away at once."

A nod was as good as a wink to Jameson Elmer.

Sir Rudolf's acquaintances outside understood the last remark to refer to the conductor. Elmer knew better. A lot of dames in white dresses, like Aimee Semple McPherson's "angels," were climbing onto the tiers behind the orechestra. The killer's cold excitement welled up in him. He was not doing this for a cause, for a belief; the international repercussions of the act meant nothing to him; even the big money he would get for it weighed little with him now. His mind's eye was pinpointed upon the spot he would aim at, just below the grizzled hair on the left temple—aim at, and hit—he hadn't the slightest doubt about that. Then a quick getaway. The guy Gray knew the timing had been changed, he presumed. Well, with Gray or without him he'd make it. Have to move fast; but he reckoned he could get to the nearest exit before news of the assassination reached it. Might have to shoot his way out. So what? These Keystone cops in Britain weren't even armed. Elmer reached down for his rifle: a small, deadly, high-velocity job, one expanding bullet, curtains.

Superintendent Blount was at a loss. If Jameson Elmer had entered the hall, no member of the orchestra or choir had noticed him. Worse still, one of the latter admitted to a penchant for violet cachous; she did not think she had—hem—discarded a a cachou at the artists' entrance, but she could not be absolutely sure. It was all so maddeningly, frighteningly vague: a ridiculous mare's nest, or a deadly menace. Sir Edward, appealed to, decided that they could not hold things up any longer. He would advise the Soviet Minister to sit well back in the box, out of sight of the audience, during the rest of the concert, and to have his bodyguard packed round him when he moved forward to acknowledge the applause at the end of it. Afterward, they would clear the passage and the approaches to the hall before the official party left.

So the choir and orchestra filed back onto the platform. The sounds of tuning up could be distantly heard. Blount and Nigel were ascending the stairs from the artists' rooms when they heard footsteps hurrying behind them. They turned. It was the leader of the orchestra, and with him a nervous, white-faced man. The latter had felt ill at the start of the interval, gone to the bar for a brandy, and then walked about outside to get some fresh air; so he had not been present when Blount interviewed the orchestra. Yes, he had seen a man whom he did not recognize as a member of it, coming in just before him—a smallish man with a drooping moustache and a violin case. He had not noticed him particularly, or thought any more about him; he was percussion himself, and he knew the strings were being augmented for tonight's concert.

Blount waited to hear no more. The Soviet Minister should be safe enough for the present, if he stayed within the covered lobby of the ceremonial box. The danger would come later, when he would have to show himself to the audience. In the meantime, the police must check once again those danger spots from which a marksman could enfilade. They knew what to look for now, at any rate—unless some other disguise had been substituted for the drooping mustache.

As they went to find Blount's second-in-command, they heard the applause greeting the conductor's entry, and the first notes of *Belshazzar's Feast*. Blount and the Inspector held a rapid conference, to alter the disposition of their forces. The handful of police who were armed had to be collected, and four of them picked out for the search party. Blount was taking no risks with a gunman of Elmer's reputation. . . .

Jameson Elmer arranged the curtain at the right-hand side of his box, so that he could peer through the chink; the muzzle of his rifle, steadied against the wall, would be invisible. Everything was set. Everything except the target. The god-damn Russki—where had he got to? Those guys in tuxedos, those crummy babes in white were bawling their heads off; the band was playing fit to burst. In all this shenanigan the whip-crack of a small, high-velocity rifle would never be heard. He could pick off every stuffed shirt in that box, and no one know but they'd fallen dead with heart attacks.

The Soviet Minister's frosty eyes sparkled. This was music. The barbaric exhilaration, the clash and bray and blare, the riptide rhythms thrusting, conflicting,. throwing up great shimmering sprays of notes—this was after his heart. He was a man who reveled in combat no less than in fine music: a fighter. Lost to everything but the glorious ferocity of the Walton, he edged forward to the front of his box. He liked to see an orchestra at work, the bows and slides and fingers sleekly or strenuously moving, like the components of some immensely elaborate machine, manufacturing sound. A hand was laid on his sleeve, but impatiently he shook it off.

Blount and his armed party were moving along the corridor behind the uppermost tier of boxes, with an attendant to open them, scrutinizing the occupants of each in turn. Glancing into one box, Blount noticed Alec Gray, with his party, leaning forward on the ledge; Gray did not even look round; he knew nothing of what had happened in the interval—Durbar had not thought it advisable to communicate with him, for there would be plain-clothes men about. Gray would hear the shot, or at least see its result, and that would be a signal for him to take the requisite action in respect of Jameson Elmer.

Releasing a hiss of breath, Elmer raised his rifle, cuddled the butt to his cheek, and peered over its sights, through the gap between wall and curtain, downward to his right, where the target had at last gone up. A tiny circle of skin and gray hair. The Russki had liquidated plenty; now it was his turn. Allow for deflection. Wait for the band to go into its next paroxysm, drowning the shot. Only one shot—he'd never needed more. Then a deep breath, another deep breath, a gentle loving squeeze of the trigger.

Taking the key from the attendant, Blount quietly unlocked the door of a box. A wild burst of music flooded through. His back to Blount, only a few feet away from him in the little lobby, a man was standing.

The solid fifteen stone, which had so often butted its way through enemy packs at Murrayfield, launched itself, and Blount's lowered head came like a cannon ball at the chest of the man within, who that instant, hearing the door open, had dropped his rifle, whipped round, and was just reaching inside his jacket. The impact sent Elmer staggering back against the wall of the lobby. He seemed to writhe, then rear up, like a striking snake. He was fast all right, very fast indeed. But, as the hand flicked out with a revolver, Blount gave the man a bear-like clout under the right ear which dropped him senseless. There were scandalized mutters and shushings from the two adjacent boxes, as Blount looked out toward the ceremonial box. The Soviet Foreign Minister was there, in full view, leaning forward; his fingers were tapping to the music's rhythms on the plush-covered ledge. Blount heaved a great sigh. They had been just in time.

"Get that man!" came Nigel's voice from outside. There was a scuffle, a groan of pain. Alec Gray had emerged from his box, to investigate the sound he had heard from Elmer's. He saw the back of a policeman, standing at the door, and Strangeways in the corridor beyond him. He turned on his heel, kicked atrociously in the groin the plain-clothes man who tried to intercept him, and ran for it. At the end of the corridor, he saw police mounting the stairs below him. He swung round and raced upstairs instead, with a vague idea of getting into the gallery and losing himself, if only for a breathing space, among the audience there. But the doors at many stairheads in the Albert Hall are locked during performances, to prevent dishonest members of the audience slipping down and occupying better seats than they have paid for. Gray had got into one of these dead-end stairways. On each landing he found a locked door, and the police were hard at his heels.

They got him right at the top of the building. He was battering with his fists at a door which, had he known it, gave onto the balcony running round the outside of the building. They pounced on him and handcuffed him. He looked like a surly, spiteful boy, the degenerate he was. One policeman, who had seen what Gray did to the plain-clothes man below, raised a large hand, contemptuously ruffled Gray's smarmed, flaxen hair, and said, "Quite a pretty little gentlemen, isn't he? I could fancy him for my butterfly collection."

When *Belshazzer's Feast* had ended, Sir Edward put in his head at the Durbars' box and lisped a gentle request for a few words with Sir Rudolf. The latter had seen nothing of the incidents on the upper tier; he assumed the gunman had failed to understand his message, or had lost his nerve and made good his escape from the building. It was vexatious; but surely not catastrophic. He would have to make other arrangements. Already his powerful, unbalanced mind was dissociating itself from the whole abstract pattern in which Jameson Elmer and Alec Gray had so darkly figured.

"Just a bit of trouble," Sir Edward was saying, apologetically. "I thought, as an organizer of this—er—show tonight, you should be consulted." His voice tailed away. He led Sir Rudolf to a dressing room under the platform, opened the door, and stood aside for him to enter. Gray and Elmer were sitting close together on hard chairs, handcuffed to each other, police on guard over them with revolvers.

"God bless my soul! Alec? What are *you* doing here? And who's this fellow?" said Sir Rudolf.

Jameson Elmer's cold, obsidian eyes dwelt upon Sir Rudolf. After what seemed a long, long pause, he said, "No, bud. You're not getting away with that."

"I fancy Durbar will not be getting away with anything, ever again," came Sir Edward's voice. "Superintendent Blount, charge this man, if you please, and remove him with the other prisoners."

Sir Rudolf knew at last that from this bad dream there would be no waking.